Killer Twist

C. A. LARMER

Copyright © 2011 2018 2019 Larmer Media

ISBN: 978-0-9871872-3-9

To Christian,
for showing me the way

Also by C.A. Larmer

An Island Lost

The Posthumous Mysteries:
Do Not Go Gentle

Do Not Go Alone

The Agatha Christie Book Club:
The Agatha Christie Book Club

Murder on the Orient (SS)

Evil Under the Stars

The Ghostwriter Mysteries:
A Plot to Die For (Book 2)

Last Writes (Book 3)

Dying Words (Book 4)

Words Can Kill (Book 5)

A Note Before Dying (Book 6)

CONTENTS

ACKNOWLEDGEMENTS

Sincere thanks to all my family for their patience and support, especially Christian, Nimo and Felix for letting me get lost in storyland, my siblings and their partners for being my cheer squad, and my parents for always ensuring there are plenty of great books in my life.

Thanks also to Sophie Hamley. Your belief, advice and enthusiasm gave me courage, determination and success.

PROLOGUE

Her eyes were wide with frenzy and despair, her lips icy blue as she stretched them into a scream that was lost into the night. All around her, ragged gray strands of hair clung like seaweed to the surface, now broken with one more push, one final grab at life as she thrust her mangled hand out before sinking from sight.

1 A CLOSE SHAVE

A cool breeze slithered in through the open window and Roxy Parker stifled a smile as she slipped a deep blue, velvet jacket over her T-shirt and jeans and pushed her legs into long, black boots. She pinned a small diamante broach onto the jacket and slipped some dangly earrings on. She adored autumn and winter: the clothes, the crispness, the chance to stay snugly indoors with little more than a good book and a decent bottle of red to keep her company. No need to hover over the answering machine, listening with guilt; in cold weather you were *allowed* to stay home. Not that she was doing so today. Her agent had called her in and she was running late.

The silver clock on the mantelpiece read 9.25am and Roxy scowled at it as she scooped up her keys and smartphone, dropping them into her oversized leather handbag, and pushed her glasses into position on the diving board to her nose. A long, thin scarf had been left drooping over a chair and she retrieved it, wrapping it around her neck and losing her shiny black bob in the process. As she glanced around, ready to depart, she spotted the newspaper, discarded on the coffee table.

'Oh, that's right,' she said, grabbing it and studying the small headline that had caught her eye earlier. '*One-handed corpse washes up in Rushcutters Bay.*'

Practically her own neighborhood, she thought, before ripping out the page and darting into her office to wedge it into a well-thumbed manila folder. Back in the lounge room, she quickly checked her reflection in the hall mirror (straightening the glasses, retrieving the hair) and then slammed the front door solidly behind her.

'Urgh, fug orf!' growled a foul smelling mass of brown rags on the pavement downstairs and the young woman diverted her eyes and breathed in through her mouth as she stepped around him and away. Checking that her bag was securely zipped, she dug her hands deep into her pockets and strode swiftly through Elizabeth Bay. If she picked up her pace she might just make it in time. Roxy took a hard right at the old police station, cutting past the fountain, through to Macleay Street and towards Kings Cross station. The city-bound train was late as usual and by the time Roxy reached Martin Place she was racing, up the grimy escalators, past the sullen stream of commuters and out onto Macquarie Street. Then across to Elizabeth Street, a quick glance around, a light change and a moment of calm before everything turned to pot.

In retrospect, Roxy would remember a definite hand print on the small of her back just moments before the bus tore past, but for now she was simply flying, her chin propelled forward, her arms flailing about as she tried to regain control. Somewhere along the way her glasses—her beautiful tortoiseshell glasses—also took off, rendering her blind. Somehow, miraculously, Roxy managed to break her fall, and landed in a huddle in the gutter, her face pressed hard against the cold cement, one arm twisted up beneath her. She moved the arm carefully, checking it wasn't broken, and then struggled to her feet just as a large, grayish blob swooped down towards her.

'You okay, love?' the blob asked, helping her up. 'That was bloody close, you nearly caught the bus to Bondi!'

Roxy nodded unconvincingly in his direction and made her way through the crowd to what she hoped was a wall. Ah yes, a low brick one. She leant against it, her cheek throbbing a little, and scrounged through her handbag for her emergency spectacles while the world whirled on around her. The glasses were an old set, gold and garish, but they would do. Pushing them onto her nose, she straightened her fringe down, dusted off her jeans and looked around again. Her tortoiseshell glasses were nowhere to be seen and the gray-suited man was walking slowly away, glancing back occasionally, wondering if his job was done. She waved him away and turned back in the direction from which she'd come, eager to find the stranger she'd glanced at a split second before she went flying. There was something suspicious about his eyes, the way they darted sideways the moment she looked at him. She suspected premeditation. Within minutes Roxy acknowledged defeat and turned back.

'Damn it!' she hissed beneath her breath, and made her way down a few more blocks to the next corner, then looked around before dashing along an alleyway and up to an unmarked door. She quickly stabbed in a code and watched as the door swung open, then entered, making sure it shut firmly behind her before ascending the stairwell two steps at a time until she reached an office marked *Horowitz Media Management*. Panting heavily, she let herself in.

'Jesus, Roxy, you look like shit,' Oliver Horowitz announced as she strode past reception and straight into his office.

'Hello to you, too, Olie. Can I use your mirror?'

'Yeah, go for it.' He pointed one pudgy thumb towards the small bathroom in the corner of his office. She went in and surveyed the damage relieved to see just a small graze where her skin had made contact with the pavement. She splashed her unsettled expression away with some cold water and returned to the outer office where Oliver tossed her a towel. It had the word *Nike* printed across it.

'So,' she said, wiping her face before tossing it back and then dropping down into a scratchy sofa in front of his desk, 'what's up?'

'Huh?'

'Earth to Olie. You left a text message for me to get in here at 10. Pronto.'

'I did?' Roxy narrowed her eyes and waited for him to click. 'I didn't leave any message, Roxy. What is it with those glasses? Bit retro for you, eh?'

'The chic ones died a death this morning. What do you mean you didn't leave me a message?'

Oliver surrendered some papers to his desk and sat upright in his overstuffed, leather chair. 'What's going on?' he asked.

'Not sure yet.' She dug about in her handbag for some lipstick. 'Well, I'm here now, got anything for me?'

'No I don't. You in trouble, Roxy? Again?'

'I'm never in trouble, you know that.' Roxy brushed the lipstick across her bottom lip, painting it a matt red hue, and then flung it back into her bag as she rolled her lips together, spreading the color evenly. 'Come on, Olie, darling,' she continued, sea green eyes sparkling through provocatively wide eyelashes, 'you have to have something for me. I can't wear these dowdy specs for much longer.'

'Oh, I dunno, they're kinda growin' on you.'

'Olie.'

'How's the Musgrave biography going? Is everything okay?'

'Fine, fine.' Her eyes glazed over. 'It's not exactly riveting stuff.'

'No? You don't find church fundraisers intriguing?'

Roxy smirked back at him. Sydney socialite Beatrice Musgrave wanted her life story told and had approached the Horowitz Agency for a ghostwriter, someone with a gift for words who could help her construct her story into a half-decent 'autobiography'. The deal with all of these jobs was simple: while Roxy never got any credit for the book (ghostwriters remain just that—a ghostly presence behind the scenes), she did get compensated sufficiently to squirrel some away and pay off the much-abused Visa card. And that's the only kind of credit she cared about, at least while she had a mortgage to contend with.

Oliver had wasted no time calling his favorite ghostwriter, Roxy Parker, who'd been on his books now for many years. While the money was substantial—double what Roxy had ever been paid for ghostwriting before—the job, so far, was extraordinarily dull. She would have exchanged the cash for a little conspiracy in a heartbeat.

'Not every story has to be about mystery and intrigue,' he reminded her, doodling on some paper with a biro. 'Anyway, I was thinking maybe I should just pass it on to Klaus.'

'Ha! Don't make me laugh!'

'Don't knock Klaus, he's a good writer.'

'Yeah, if you like your stories like his hair: thin on top.'

'Well at least he doesn't bring headaches into it.'

'What headaches?'

Oliver stood up, his beer belly peeking through where several buttons on his '50s-style bowling shirt were undone, and shuffled over to the office door.

'Shazza! Where the hell are you?'

'Awww, I'm here, boss, fixin' the photocopier!' came a hoarse smoker's voice from the next room.

'Good, get us a coupla coffees will ya!'

'Milk and two sugars for me, thanks!' Roxy called out and watched her agent as he wedged himself back into his chair. She wondered if he had once been a good looking man before a steady diet of doner kebabs and cold beer ruined him. Her agent was in his late 40s, single, a hard worker with a lopsided grin and a kind of roguish charm that forgave his sloppy looks and smart-ass ways. Roxy liked him. He called a spade a spade and that was a prerequisite in this business.

'What headaches?' she repeated, smiling innocently.

'Oh, let me think, Roxy, sweetheart, what headaches? Oh maybe the time I sent you out to interview a band grieving their departed drummer and you came back with some cock 'n' bull story about the ex-girlfriend and how she might've done him in.'

'It was a possibility.'

'It was a self-administered drug overdose. He was a friggin' junky. Full stop.'

'Well, in any case, it made good reading for the *Tele* and you got your 15 percent. Anyway, that was ages ago. I've been good lately.'

'That's what I'm worried about.' He eyed her for a moment and then asked, 'Still keeping *The Book of Death*?'

Roxy shifted uneasily in her seat. 'It's not a book of death!' She scoffed. 'It's a crime catalogue.'

'Same difference.'

'Hardly. Besides, it has a purpose.'

'Yeah, right.'

'What's the big deal, Oliver? All good writers file clippings away. You never know when you might need them.'

'Do all writers focus only on crime articles? I swear, Roxy, it's like you're planning the perfect murder.'

She shrugged wishing the subject away and was saved by Oliver's secretary who appeared at her side, two *Horowitz Management* mugs in her hands and a half-finished cigarette dangling from her mouth. Sharon was a middle-aged woman with short, spiky red hair and a penchant for extremely tight, brightly colored spandex that only worked to accentuate her scrawny, stick-thin form. But perhaps that was the idea.

'Oh Sharon sweetheart,' Oliver gushed as she thumped the mugs down. 'What ever would I do without you?'

'Hmph!' she snorted back, offering Roxy a cheeky wink before moping out again, the fag still firmly in place.

'Thanks, Sharon,' Roxy sang after her. They eyed their coffees for a while and then Oliver stood up again and shuffled over to the door to close it. Roxy rolled her eyes in response.

'Come on, I know something's up.'

'Like what?'

'Like, you get a strange message from me that I never left, then you get beat up—'

'Hang on a minute—'

'I can see the scratch, Roxy.' She reached one hand up to her cheek instinctively, running her forefinger across the web-like mark.

'Oh the cat did that.'

'You don't have a cat.'

'And now you can see why.'

They sat back and sipped their drinks, Oliver shaking his head reprovingly, Roxy ignoring him as she glanced around the room. She wondered, as she always did, how he could get it so dusty. They were three floors up. Tatty posters of sci-fi films had been sticky-taped to the walls, and every possible bench was cluttered with assorted memorabilia from past events and publicity gimmicks. There was a teddy bear draped in an oversized T-shirt that read, 'Mardi-grass 2001, Nimbin', a mug shaped like the Opera House and a pair of 3D glasses with one lens missing. She connected eyes with a giant cardboard cut-out of a buxom blonde in a stretchy red dress with the words 'Tina Passion—Writing passion into your life!' scrawled across the bottom, and wondered as she often did, how she could possibly share an agent with one of the country's corniest romance writers. Romance was always the last thing on her mind.

'Okay, then,' he relented. 'I'll see what else I can find for you. If I do find something, will you swap the Musgrave biography for it?'

'Um, no, you don't seem to get it. I want *more* work not less. Can't stand it when I'm not busy, you know that. Besides, I'm a third of the way through the bio, why on earth would I stop now?'

'Just a thought. Look, Roxy, be careful, alright? Enjoy the down time. Take a trip somewhere. *Relax*. Here,' he fetched his iPhone and held it out to her. 'Look it up on my dictionary app, it's a useful word.'

She dismissed him with a wave, got to her feet and was halfway out the door when he called her back.

'Why don't you call one of your old contacts, that sexy Greek chick from *Glossy* for instance?'

'Oh, you mean the one who never comes through? Pah!'

As it turns out, Maria Constantinople, the editor of one of the country's top-selling women's lifestyle magazines, had come through the day before, offering Roxy 'a big one, baby, a big one!' She was on her way to the *Glossy* offices now, she just didn't believe it would amount to much. Roxy wrote a lot for Maria, mostly mundane articles about women's health, relationships, money, anything Maria wanted, really. They were always fairly safe subjects, the kind of stories she'd written a hundred times before and would write a hundred times again. The only challenge was changing the heading, introduction and content sufficiently enough to confuse the readers into believing they hadn't read the exact same thing just 12 months before. Pure trickery, of course, and not something she was particularly proud of, but, hey, it paid the bills. Well, it almost did. The worst part of the whole deal was that these articles were never very long, 1200 words at best. At 70c a word, it didn't amount to much. She wasn't about to go renovating the kitchen, let's put it that way. Roxy longed to sink her teeth into something wordy, something original, something *she* wanted to read.

Yeah right, she thought, *like that's ever gonna happen*. This was a briefing session with *Glossy* magazine, after all, not *The New Yorker*.

This time, however, Roxy couldn't have been more wrong.

'Sorry to keep you waiting, gorgeous,' Maria boomed when, after 30 minutes chewing her lips in the lobby, Roxy was ushered through to the editor's spacious corner office by her new assistant, Trevor.

'Bit of a hunk, eh?' the editor whispered, eyeing the young man up and down as he closed the glass doors behind them.

'Yeah, I guess, if you're a bloke.'

Maria's thickly penciled eyebrows shot skyward. 'Oh shite, you don't reckon he's gay do you?'

'We're in Sydney. He's got the body of Adonis. I rest my case. So what have you got for me?'

Roxy was not a big fan of Maria Constantinople, and not just because of her lack of originality and depth. The woman was loud and brash, and prone to stomping her five-foot frame around like a rugby player, tossing expletives about as though they were superlatives and playing God over her quivering staff. But even that Roxy could have forgiven— Olie was hardly the Prime Minister of office politics, let's face it—yet there was something else, something she couldn't quite put her finger on. Perhaps it was the feeling that this editor would sell her out for a headline in a heartbeat.

Well into her 50s, Maria wore her thick, dyed auburn hair in long, wild curls, and plastered her face with a gelatinous coat of foundation, the type that implores you to play naughts and crosses with your nails.

'Oh, I got a treat for you, Roxy,' she said, clasping her bejeweled hands together, prayer-like in front, 'and I need it done fast.'

'No problem.'

'Coffee?'

'No thanks.'

'Well then, let's get straight to it.' She reached for a file marked 'Heather Jackson, Artist' and flung it across her sparkly glass desk towards Roxy. 'You've no doubt heard of this one. One of Australia's top modern artists. She's super private and, as far as the rumors go, a complete freakin' cow. But I've scored an interview and I want you to do it.'

Roxy flipped through the file. A selection of old press clippings had been placed inside, along with a black and white print, autographed, and a tattered leaflet which read, 'Sydney Art Gazette Annual Competition, 1989'.

'Why me?' Roxy asked, surprised.

'Why not?'

'Well, for starters, I know very little about art.'

'So improvise.'

'Why not use your art writer?'

Maria sighed heavily. 'Because I'm giving you a bloody break. Do you want the job or not?'

'Of course I do.' Deep down, though, Roxy wondered what the woman was up to. She wasn't in the habit of doing Roxy any favors. Besides, it wasn't her style to commission the good stories out, especially when she had one of the best editorial teams in the country assembled right under her oily brown nose. Roxy smelt a rat, but didn't push the matter further. Ten years as a freelance writer had taught her that. You just take the job and run.

'That's the spirit!' Maria said as she adjusted a collection of gold chains that had lost themselves in her cleavage. 'All the info you need's in the folder. Thursday seems to work well for Heather. You give me a time and a place and I'll set it all up. Too bloody easy if you ask me.'

They chatted for a bit longer before Maria started playing with her watch and, getting the hint, Roxy closed the folder and got to her feet. 'I'll give you a call this arvo to talk time and money.'

Maria pushed her eyebrows together. 'What? You want some freakin' dosh for this?'

Roxy just laughed as she saw herself out.

2 A THREATENING NOTE

'**Hey**, Parker is that you?'

'No Max, it's your Fairy Godmother. *You* called me, remember?'

'Oh cut the sarcasm,' came a deep, raspy voice on the other end, 'I'm still trying to work my remote dial on my new smartphone. Smart my ass. So, what you up to?'

'Just been running some errands.' Roxy plucked her own phone from its perch by the gearbox and placed it to her ear. 'How was your date?'

Max Farrell groaned loudly and Roxy couldn't help a chuckle. She had little sympathy for the guy, he brought it upon himself. 'Too gorgeous for his own good,' she'd heard both men and women say of him and, reluctantly, agreed. While not exactly handsome, Max had that relaxed, couldn't-care-less look that lured women in droves: thick, tousled hair, baggy, surf-style clothes, and a smile that came easily, creasing up his entire face, so that it seemed he'd never heard anything so hilarious in his life. And that, coupled with his decidedly fashionable occupation (photographer) made him quite a favorite with the hip, inner-city crowd.

In fact, it was while working at a celebrity press conference two years earlier that the two first met. The conference had been a bit of a scrum, photographers and journalists vying for the limited attention of some visiting Hollywood starlet. Amidst the frenzy, Roxy had remained up the back, disinterested in the whole affair, and Max admired her indifference and the fact that she didn't try to win him over as most women did, and so they became instant friends.

'I gather she left empty-handed, so to speak,' Roxy baited.

'Quite the contrary, she borrowed my jacket and I forgot to get it back.'

'So now you've got to see her again.'

'Arrrgggh.'

Clutching the phone to her shoulder with one ear, she maneuvered the gears and steering wheel of her navy blue VW Golf around a tight bend, then grabbed it back up and let out another chuckle.

'That's called karma, Max.'

'No, Parker, it's called manipulation, she did it on purpose.'

'Desperate to see you again?'

'Naturally.'

'Oh give me a break. Just call her up and ask her to send it back.'

'It's a leather jacket, not a letter.'

'Okay, then get her to drop it in to your agency and make damn sure you're not there when she does.'

'Oh, yeah, good idea! You're a bloody genius, I knew there was a reason I adored you.'

Roxy pulled her car into an empty spot in the curb outside her apartment block in the inner eastern suburb of Elizabeth Bay and cut the engine. 'That and the fact that we've never bonked so you don't have to try to avoid me. Anyway, I'm home now, gotta go.'

'We're still on for Thursday?'

'We're always on for Thursday, you know that. Oh, by the way…'

'Yep?'

'You haven't sent me any stupid messages lately have you?'

'Huh?'

'Oh never mind, bloody junk mail, you know how it is. Alright, Maxy, I'll see you later.'

She hung up and slipped the phone into her handbag, unlocked the car door, got out and then quickly relocked it. With her keys still firmly in hand, she marched across the pavement to an old brick building that had been painted white too many seasons ago. She looked around swiftly then let herself in. At the mailbox for apartment 8A she tapped on the door several times and, determining that it was hollow, turned away and scurried up four flights of stairs.

Inside the apartment Roxy deadbolted the door, placed her keys and phone on the mantelpiece and then headed straight for the fridge. She was famished. Unfortunately (typically!), she was also out of food. She reached for a bottle of water and swigged several mouthfuls, then returned to the living room and dialed Wanton Thai Takeaway.

'Timmy? Hi it's Roxy Parker…Yeah, *very* hungry!…Yep, yep, the usual. Oh and tofu, not chicken, I'm trying to have at least one meat-free day a week…Okay, then. Thanks, Tim…Huh?…Oh, 20 minutes is fine. Bye.' She hung up.

The mantelpiece clock said it was just past 2pm and Roxy moved towards the large glass window that faced the bay beyond to drink in a view that never ceased to satiate. She noted that a few sailboarders were out braving the cold and shivered on their behalf, then strolled into the sunroom.

Roxy adored her small apartment despite its size and mostly because she had it all to herself. The walls were whitewashed and chipping in places but she liked the chips, they gave it character and spoke of a life lived within. It was just one bedroom, but the living area was spacious enough and opened out onto a sundrenched deck that had been glassed in on three sides so that you could enjoy it all year round. In this room she had placed an old rustic red cedar table that served as her desk and, upon it, rested a small laptop, printer and files. There was also a thick glass vase brimming with wilting tulips and she scooped it up, returning to the kitchen to extract the dead stems and replenish the water before depositing it back on the office desk. After that she watered her ferns, checked her voice mail and logged online.

As Roxy waited for the computer to whir into action, she pulled off her long boots, jeans and jacket, and changed into an old blue sweater, gray tracksuit and woolly socks. Winter was still officially a month away, but the chill had set up camp early and Roxy couldn't have been happier. Summer was fine for those who liked to spread themselves like barbequed chooks on a beach somewhere. For Roxy, with her fair complexion and inability to sit still (let alone lie somewhere half-naked), it was all SPF 30, over-sized hats and waiting anxiously for sundown.

A faint 'doodle-oo' announced the arrival of some emails and Roxy slipped back into the office, piling her long legs up beneath her on the chair and clicked on 'Open'. There was a note marked 'Only Your Mother' and she shook her head irritably before opening it.

'Hello, darling. Remember me? Please call, want to catch up. Mum.'

She trashed it. Mum would have to wait, she had bigger fish to fry. She scrolled down the inbox, past a stream of junk mail which would eventually need erasing, until she got to a letter marked 'Warning!'. She felt her mouth go dry and double clicked.

'Attention Roxy Parker,' it began. 'Have a nice trip? Today was just a warning. Give up the story – ITS (sic) NOT WORTH IT!!!'

The message had arrived two hours earlier and was unsigned, the return address marked to a Hotmail account with the initials AIL. She wondered if it was traceable, and wished she knew what the hell it was referring to. It was the second threat in two days and she recalled smirking at the first, assuming the sender was Max. Now she was almost certain it was not.

Retrieving the original message for another look, she read it aloud: *'This is a warning. Don't do the story and live to tell the tail (sic).'* She recalled the morning's push and a bright pink blush swept across her face. Who was doing this to her? What did they want? And, more importantly, which story could they possibly be referring to?

Roxy chewed her lower lip for a few minutes and then moved her cursor to the 'Reply' symbol, clicked, then typed the words, 'What is this about?' She double clicked and waited for the email to disappear from her screen, her heart now somewhere near her feet. Then she had a thought. She counted to five, drew in a deep breath and clicked on the 'Send/Receive' button. Within seconds, there it was, a message from the Mail Delivery Subsystem marked, 'Returned Mail: See transcript for details'. She exhaled. *Damn it.* Her message had not got through. Either AIL at the hotmail address no longer existed or it had some kind of Smart Screen software attached. This was one of those fancy new technologies that enabled you to screen your emails and disallow any 'foreign' messages. Well, she figured, it was to be expected. But she did have one more option.

Roxy picked up her phone and located the morning's text: 'Be at my office by 10am. No later. VERY important. Oliver Horowitz'. She emitted a loud groan. It wasn't Oliver's style, why hadn't she spotted that? He wouldn't have bothered spelling out all the words—'B at office' and '18r' were more his style—nor would he have signed his full name. There was one other glaring clue. The text originated from a number she didn't recognize, certainly not one of Oliver's. She shook her head at herself. *Clumsy!*

Not yet defeated, the writer's thumb went to work on her own smartphone, locating the foreign number and pressing the 'Call' button. After many rings it answered, sending a shot of adrenaline through her body, but it was just one of those recorded messages alerting her to the fact that the number was no longer connected. *How surprising.* She relaxed again and made a note of the message in a file marked 'Viruses', adding the two email messages by cutting and pasting them onto the page.

Roxy sat back in her chair for a few minutes trying to think. Who ever had sent those messages was no fool. They had managed to erase their tracks. But then, Roxy was no fool, either. Nor was she completely empty handed. She glared at the Hotmail email address again: AIL. She assumed they were someone's initials, but perhaps they were a business name? Feeling increasingly exasperated, Roxy logged off and began scrolling through a folder marked 'Ongoing Stories' to see if anything leapt out at her. There was a feature she'd just completed for *Cosmo* on the joys of being single but wondered who, short of a marriage celebrant, could take offense with that? Then there was the biography she was writing for Mrs Musgrave but so far the well-known socialite's life has been as riveting as a game of her treasured Mahjong. The only other alternative was the story Maria had handed her that morning, the interview with an artist not accustomed to giving interviews. Surely that was little more than harmless PR?

'Besides, I haven't even started that yet!' Roxy moaned, leaning back in her chair and staring with glazed eyes out at the ferns. Eventually, she conceded that the likeliest option was the Musgrave biography. Perhaps old Beattie did have a few skeletons amongst the twin sets in her wardrobe. She made a note to look into it and then, in the 'Viruses' folder jotted down a quick description of the man she thought had pushed her that morning while it was still fresh in her mind: *'Fattish, hairy (greasy ponytail?), dark clothes. Shorter than me. Unfamiliar. Determined.'* The doorbell buzzed and she clicked the file shut before dashing to the speaker. 'Who is it?'

'Wanton Thai,' came a voice at the other end.

'I'll be right down!' She slipped black sandshoes over her socks and fetched some notes from her wallet. Through the smudged glass door of the lobby, Roxy could just make out a small, black-headed figure holding something white, and she opened the door swiftly.

'Ahhh hello Missis Roxy.' A young Thai boy beamed as he thrust a bag of food towards her.

'Hi Lee,' she replied, handing him the cash. 'Busy day?'

'Oh not so busy todaaay,' he sang. She thanked him and locked herself back in.

Back upstairs, Roxy placed the takeaway on the coffee table and fetched a bowl, some chopsticks and the file Maria had given her. She replenished her water glass, scooped some rice into her mouth and began to read. The *Glossy* job seemed straight-forward enough. A simple celebrity interview with a diva of the Australian art world. Questions: probing and insightful. Duration: One hour max. Copy: upbeat with a fresh angle and just a hint of attitude. Result: *Glossy* sells more magazines, Heather Jackson sells more artwork, Roxy gets paid. And that was her only interest in the matter.

Until she started reading from the file.

Like most Australians, what Roxy knew about the interviewee wouldn't fill more than a paragraph. The *Sydney Art Gazette*, one of the city's longest-running and most credible street rags, had sponsored an Emerging Artists award some 20 years back and the winner, an unknown 30-year-old called Heather Jackson, not only scooped the coveted first prize but had gone on to become one of Australia's most famous living artists whose controversial portraits—brightly painted and slightly abstract—earned her notoriety in art circles around the world, from Paris to New York. Even more notorious was her disdain for the press, she hadn't done an interview in five years.

'So tread carefully with her,' Maria had warned. 'One wrong question and she's out the door.'

'What's a wrong question?' Roxy asked. 'She's just an artist. She's not a politician for God's sake.'

'Yes but she's a *private* artist and a very freakin' famous one at that. It's a bloody miracle she even wanted to do the interview.'

'That's my next question,' Roxy said. 'Why do an interview at all? It's not like she needs to.'

'Everybody needs to, eventually.'

'But why *Glossy*?'

Maria stared at the writer, hard. 'Because *Glossy* is the Mecca of magazines. Of course! Look, the point is I need you to be polite, tactful and keep her on side. I just want a lovely, "Look Who We Got" story and nothing more.'

'I'm all manners,' Roxy promised, but looking through the file now, she was not sure she wanted to be. While Heather shunned official media interviews, she lived the celebrity life to the hilt: the file was brimming with paparazzi pictures of the artist, arriving, head down, blinged fingers up to shield her face as she entered or exited one cocaine-fuelled, A-list party after another. There were blurry pictures of her cavorting with near-naked men on exotic beaches and all kinds of salacious rumors, as well as a few disgruntled lovers who had threatened to 'reveal all'. But as far as Roxy could tell, none had ever made good on their threats. She wondered why.

All of this was of little consequence to the writer, except that it was in such stark contrast to the woman she was now reading about in the form marked 'Entry Forms: Emerging Artists/Sydney Art Gazette'. Heather Jackson's original application letter for the art competition that made her a household name had been copied onto the form, her flowery handwriting as surprising as the words themselves: *I want to portray real people. Not film stars and fluff. I want to document the people that matter.'*

A color snapshot of her entry portrait was also attached and, while the photo was not great, it was clear the painting was. Done in bold, bright strokes with proportions askew, it showed a young, physically disabled woman flinging her hands about with the words, *'Not Drowning, Waving'* written in the same black scroll below it.

It was a startling picture and Roxy could barely tear her eyes from it as her food grew cold before her. It was the perfect career launcher, imploring you to seek out more, to discover what sort of person could capture such an image so sublimely. Roxy wondered where the original was and, placing it to one side, made a note to ask Heather during the interview. She also decided to look up Heather's other works. She didn't remember them being quite so beautiful.

But first she had a small personal matter to contend with. Picking up the phone again, Roxy wandered to the hallway mirror to stare somberly at her reflection.

'Mr Hamilton, hello, it's Roxy Parker here...Yes, thanks, I'm great. I'd like you to order me in another pair of the Prada glasses...Yep, that's right, same style, same prescription...Oh you do? Fantastic, thanks, I'll be down there tomorrow.' And then she hung up with a smile.

Stifling a yawn, Roxy went into her office, opened a folder and retrieved the news piece she'd been reading earlier that day. Taking a pair of scissors, she sliced around the article and then reached for a giant scrapbook and some glue. As she pasted the page securely into place she reread the sub-heading and felt her interest grow: 'Mutilated Corpse Baffles Police'.

***

The woman reread the newspaper report about a Joan Doe discovered mutilated at Rushcutters Bay. It made her stomach shudder and she hid it, quickly, out of sight. She knew she should not be reading it.

Breathing deeply, she leant forward in her chair and applied strong brush strokes, slowly, surely, across the clean white canvas. She didn't like the man before her but she didn't have a choice. The green would make good skin coloring she thought, wickedly, and began mixing the palate, relishing the sensuality of the paint as yellow merged with blue to form a glowing green hue. It reminded her of Limrock Lane and the old days, before. Things weren't so good now but at least she had her paints. It was really all she needed.

3 CATCHING UP

The frothy white foam was missing its chocolate sprinkles and Lorraine Jones was about to complain when she noticed Roxy's scowl and shut her lips. Her daughter had no patience for her, she knew that, and she knew why. They were like chalk and cheese, it had to be said, there was no helping that. But she really wished her daughter would try slightly harder to be a little more, well, *accommodating.*

'I don't know why you like this place,' she said, unable to help herself as Roxy stared into her latté.

'It's full of...' she lowered her voice a little, 'gays.'

'So?'

'So. So you'll never meet a husband in here.'

'Who says I want to meet a husband?'

'Well you have to meet one to marry one, dear,' her mother scolded, missing the point. Or at least pretending to.

Roxy stared past her to the bustling room beyond. They were in inner-city Surry Hills in a small cafe called Lockies, with cozy lounge chairs to snuggle into and a fireplace that roared in winter. The walls were cluttered with amateur works of art, mostly by the owner, a gangly Scottish guy called Loghlen, and Roxy wondered now if he knew anything about Heather Jackson.

'So what happened to your face?' her mother was asking and Roxy reached her hand up to stroke the fine scratches still left along one cheek.

'Fell over myself yesterday.'

'So that explains the glasses.'

'Yes, I know. Hideous.'

'They're fine dear, better than the other ones, they made you look like Nana Mouskouri, or whatever her name is. Easy with the sugar dear.'

Roxy continued pouring the sugar dispenser into her coffee. 'So how's Charlie?'

'Fine dear.'

'Shot any living creatures lately?'

Lorraine glared at her daughter, weighing up her sarcasm and then said, 'Nothing wrong with hunting, dear. Man has been doing it since the Stone Age.'

'Yeah and you would have thought we'd progressed a little since then.'

'We have,' she said. 'We use rifles now not spears—a far more accurate kill.'

Roxy couldn't help a smile and Lorraine winked back. 'Roxanne you really shouldn't take life so seriously.'

'Hmf!' she snorted but let the subject drop. She wasn't in the mood for politics, certainly not that of Lorraine and her stepfather Charlie. They were old-school conservatives, and the antithesis of Roxy. As the older woman scooped up her froth, Roxy wondered how they could be so different. Lorraine was almost 60 but a smattering of freckles on her nose leant a certain girlishness to her face which she played upon when she could. Her hair was dyed ivory blond and cut into a bob above her neck, and she was wearing a velvet headband, like snooty English schoolgirls were prone to do. Her jumper was camel-colored with a thin gold necklace popping out deliberately over the collar, and her nails looked like they'd been manicured only that morning, the clear nail varnish gleaming as she twiddled her spoon. She dressed and acted like an aristocrat, Roxy thought, without the fortune to go with it. A regular two-bob snob.

'Charlie wants to have you over for tea next Monday night,' Lorraine was saying, 'You available?'

Like her own mother couldn't invite her. 'What's he got planned?' she said instead.

'Oh, I don't know, a nice home cooked meal.'

'No, *planned*. What's up his sleeve?'

Lorraine placed her cup down noisily. 'Really Roxanne you are the most ungrateful—'

'Who's coming over, Mum? Who's he setting me up with this time?'

Lorraine shook her blond head angrily and turned her attention to her nails, holding both hands out before her as she scrutinized them. 'I believe he's a very nice chap.'

'Muuum!'

'Now listen, Roxanne, he's a charming young man called Mason Gower, a lawyer for Featherby & Phillips I believe. You'd really get along.'

'No, actually, we wouldn't.' But there was something about his name that rang a bell.

'Well how do you know unless you give it a go?'

'Mum, I'm 30. I know.'

Lorraine pushed her empty cup aside and searched through her brown, imitation Gucci handbag for a handkerchief. When she located one, she dabbed at her lips, removing traces of coffee that weren't actually there. Roxy glanced about the cafe at the growing clientele. Like-minded people enjoying each other's company. She felt oddly melancholy.

'How are you ever going to meet anyone if you don't accept our help?'

'Mum!'

'No, Roxanne, I'm serious. Marriage may not be one big bowl of roses but it's better than hanging in...' she lowered her voice, '*queer* cafes and living all alone like a nun for goodness sake. Better to be with a man than miserable.'

'Who says the two are mutually exclusive? Besides you make marriage sound so unromantic. And you wonder why I'm avoiding it.'

'I *know* why you're avoiding it.'

'Because nobody's asked?'

'Nobody's had the guts to! Your problem Roxanne is that you're too independent for your own good, always pretending you don't need anyone but yourself.'

'It's worked well enough for 20 years.' She regretted the words instantly, not interested in arguments today. But her mother had already taken the bait.

'Your father deserts me and I'm supposed to struggle to bring you up and be the perfect mother at the same time?!'

'No but just being a mother some of the time would have helped, and he didn't desert you. He died, remember? He *couldn't help it*. Look, Mum, I don't want to get into all of this. You called me, you wanted to catch up. Was it to fight or did you have something to say?'

Lorraine placed her coffee cup aside and pouted her penciled lips.

'I'll consider dinner,' Roxy said, trying to cheer up but her mother was still pouting and she felt her own anger rising. *Why did Lorraine insist on doing this, every time they met?* Roxy drained her cup dry.

'Look, I've really got to go. Oliver's given me a big biography to write. Better get on with it.'

'You're still working for that slimeball?'

She took a deep breath. 'That slimeball pays half my mortgage. And besides, he's not really a slimeball—'

'Looks like one.'

'Hmmm…Come on, let's pay.' Roxy scooped up the bill and dashed towards the till.

At the door, mother and daughter exchanged quick, conciliatory kisses and strode off in separate directions. At the corner, Roxy hesitated and, turning around, watched her mother disappear across the street and out of view. She retraced her steps and slipped back into the cafe.

'Forget something, Roxy?' the young waitress asked.

'No, just wondering if Loghlen is about.'

'Yeah, out the back I think, do you want me to—'

'No, I'll just wander through, thanks.'

At a door marked 'Head Honcho', she knocked once, loudly.

'Yo?' Roxy pushed the door open and entered. 'Roxy Parker, good to see ya!' came the thick Scottish accent of the cafe owner. Tall and skinny, Loghlen O'Hare was a geeky looking guy with a propensity for polyester and a head of thick black hair that turned into orange pork-chop sideburns down each cheek and fluffy sandbars above each sea-blue eye. His lily white skin was badly dimpled where acne once reigned, and his temperament as mellow as a sleepy Labrador. In three years, Roxy had never seen him cranky, not even during the frantic lunch-hour rush. He could teach both Roxy and her mother a thing or two.

'Hey, Lockie,' she said, leaning across to give him a kiss. 'How's business going?'

'Oh, greeeaaat, yeah! You?'

'Pretty slowly, actually, although I am working on a story right now and I'm wondering if you can help me.'

'Suuure, suure. Pull up a pew.'

The office was small and cramped with old menus piled up randomly and a paint easel propped against one wall. A half-finished piece featuring yellow sunflowers was resting on the spare chair and Loghlen placed it back on the easel.

'Nice piece,' she said, lying, and he shrugged her off with a giant smile. 'So tell me, know much about Heather Jackson?'

'The artist?'

'Yeah.'

He scratched his head thoughtfully. 'What's to know? She's brilliant. Why?'

'I'm interviewing her tomorrow.'

'Interviewing her? You looky booger! I didn't think she did interviews.'

'That's the problem, she doesn't so I don't know much about her.'

'Well, she's an abstract artist…'

'Oh I know all that. I'm just wondering if you know any personal details? Boyfriends, hobbies, scandals, that sort of thing.'

'Aye, you want the juicy stuff, eh? Let's see… she's unmarried as far as I know and there's never anyone too serious on the scene; her hobby would be art, I guess, and as for scandals?' He brought his long, skinny fingers together in a prayer-like manner and rested his ruby lips upon them, thinking. Eventually comprehension flickered across his eyes. 'Aye, that's right. There was qui' a bit of press about a book that was going to come out.'

'Yeah, a couple of ex-lovers were having a whine.'

'No, no, no' that. There was somethin' else… her maid, or someone like that was about to do a tell-all. I remember it because I was studyin' Heather at art school and, well, to be honest I didn't want to know the oogly truth. I just like her work. Why should anything else matter?'

'And did the maid talk?'

'No' as far as I can recall. Ye know, I have a fuzzy feeling she might even have disappeared. You know, it all went kinda silent after that. But this was at least 15 years ago and me memory's not what it used to be.'

'So how did you know the truth was, as you say, "ugly"?'

'Well if it was nice do ya think she would've vanished? My guess is, Heather paid her off to shut up and leave town. I never heard of a celebrity puttin' a stop to good publicity.'

'Especially Heather "the hedonist" Jackson.'

'Hey, easy there. I have bi' of a soft spot for her, in case you couldn't tell. Even if she can only paint one style.'

'How do you mean?'

'Well she never does anything but abstract portraits. You don't find that a little strange?'

28

Roxy shrugged her shoulders. 'To be honest, I wouldn't know. Is it?'

'I reckon so.' Lockie leant towards a bookcase and retrieved a thick textbook subtitled 'Modern Australian Artists'. 'Take a look for ya'self, around section six, I think. But then what do I know? I'm no art critic, can't even ge' a sunflower right.'

'You could try chopping off one of your ears,' Roxy suggested and Loghlen laughed uproariously. 'Can I hold onto this book for a while?'

'No worries. So, you wan' a cuppa?'

'Already had one, thanks Lockie.' She placed the book in her handbag and got to her feet. 'Gotta go.'

'That should be your second name,' he cried out as she closed the door behind her.

Halfway along Pitt Street in the heart of the city, Roxy located a well-lit shop called 'What A Spectacle!' She entered and, ten minutes later, returned outside with her new glasses firmly in place. They were identical to her last pair, with a tortoise-shell rim that was thick and glossy and shaped in the current wayfarer style. She adjusted them on her nose and headed back down Pitt Street towards her car. She had 20 minutes to get across town and down to Mosman. Didn't want to keep Beatrice Musgrave waiting.

'Good afternoon, Miss Parker,' Beatrice purred. 'Come in, dear, I was expecting you.'

Beattie was well into her 70s, although one or two eye jobs might suggest otherwise, and her pale, bone-china skin was stretched tightly across two chiseled cheekbones. Beside them, on each ear sat two pearl earrings and behind that, her glistening silver hair was cut short and blow-waved back. Today she wore a pale pink silk shirt beneath a thick brown plaid jacket and cream trousers. Add to that brown court shoes and a powdered face and you'd be forgiven for thinking the stylish socialite was about to head out. But Roxy knew better. Beatrice was always well groomed, as though Royalty might drop over at any moment.

Yet despite this impeccable exterior, Beattie, as she liked to be called, was anything but a snob. She lent her name and fortune to a myriad of charities that other socialite do-gooders steered well clear of, from AIDS to Narcotics Anonymous, and was frequently seen dishing out food to street kids and assisting the Salvation Army on their blanket drives. And it was probably because of this, more than the hefty pay check, that Roxy had readily signed up for the job of co-authoring Beattie's autobiography. Of course she needed to pay her bills, but Roxy also didn't suffer fools gladly and she knew that it would have been impossible to work with Beattie so closely if she had turned out to be more fluff than substance.

A housekeeper appeared from behind her to take Roxy's things and then lead them through the spacious lounge room, past antique furniture and extravagant artworks, out on to the balcony where a table had been set up in the shade, complete with a fresh pot of tea and a plate of wafer biscuits.

'We must lap up this splendid day!' Beattie exclaimed as she was helped into her seat. Then, with a quick nod and a smile, she dismissed the housekeeper and prepared the tea herself. Before taking her own seat, Roxy stepped to the edge of the balcony to admire the view. They were perched high above a cliff and the water that crashed against the rocks near Balmoral Beach below was vibrant blue and as frothy as a milkshake.

'Looks tasty down there,' Roxy declared before joining her host at the table.

'Tea, dear?'

'Yes, thank you. Milk—'

'And two sugars,' she interrupted, 'yes dear, I remember.'

Of course you do, Roxy thought, always the consummate hostess. Beatrice Musgrave's life played out like a social climber's fantasy. Born into an upper-middle class family in a quiet, leafy suburb of Adelaide, Beattie Alexander had been sent away to a posh girl's school in Sydney less for the education, it seemed, than the opportunities it allowed to meet wealthy bachelors at the neighboring boys' schools. And by her account there had been several interested eligibles, including a young lad from rural New South Wales whom she was particularly fond of. 'Frank was my first love,' she had said, a little misty-eyed, 'and you can never forget your first love, not even if you try.'

'So what was this Frank guy like?'

She considered this for a moment. 'Sweet. Devoted. And...' she smiled sadly then, 'perhaps a little naïve.'

'How do you mean?'

'Oh dear, let's discuss him later. I want to get on to Terence.'

She was talking about her husband, but Roxy was not particularly interested in him, at least not yet. She nodded politely. 'Of course, Beattie, I understand. But, well, it's important to add some color to this book and it's often the sideline characters, such as the first love, that do that.' She was worried. She didn't just want to write this book, take the money and run. She was hoping that it might actually make a half decent read, sell a few copies perhaps. At this rate, it'd send potential readers into a coma.

Beattie clearly understood her. 'You will get your story, Roxanne, I promise you that. But I need to get the basics down first. Then we'll get on to the juicy stuff. And I promise you, there is some very juicy stuff.'

Roxy must have looked surprised because she burst into laughter. 'Oh dear, you must think I'm such a frightful bore!'

'No, of course not...' she tried some back peddling, 'it's just that—'

Beattie dismissed her with a wave of one paper-thin, elegant hand. 'Now, about my husband...'

And so she continued telling her story, of how she eventually married Terence Musgrave, the wealthy heir of one of Australia's leading department store chains who had been a keen suitor and would make a good match. And so they had married on her 21st birthday.

'A truly pretentious affair, as you can imagine,' Beattie had declared with a throaty laugh, and then hesitated. 'But I guess you'd better not use the word "pretentious". Say…'

'Extravagant?'

'Hmmm.'

'Spectacular, magnificent?'

'Yes, either will do. But boy it *was* a party!'

The party, Roxy understood from her own research, did not last long. Terry Musgrave's enthusiasm soon switched to other women and he became known as a philanderer, as unfaithful in the bedroom as he was in the boardroom. Yet Beattie had stuck by him and, if the newspaper pictures were anything to go by, mourned dutifully at his funeral five years ago when he had dropped dead of a heart attack during a polo match. Their only son, William, was by her side. But, in the photos at least, he was not weeping.

Roxy had heard a little of Beatrice before taking on the job, mostly through the social pages and mostly regarding her charity work. While it was all positive stuff, Roxy wasn't convinced it was worth an entire book, but Beatrice Musgrave had insisted. She wanted her story told, ASAP, and she was paying generously for the privilege. Besides, their meetings, for two hours every Monday morning and Wednesday afternoon, were pleasant enough affairs, Beatrice a gracious host, Roxy an attentive listener. In the four weeks they had been meeting, they had even become quite close. And now, with the turbulent marriage years about to unfold, Roxy wondered whether things might start to heat up.

'Another biscuit, dear?' Beatrice asked, her kindly smile imploring her to accept.

'Oh no thanks, Beattie. I'm fine.'

'Oh but you *must!*' she insisted, placing them down in front of her. And then she added, 'But I do like your new glasses.'

Roxy looked up from the wafer plate with a start. 'How...how did you know they were new?'

'Well aren't they?'

'Yes. But they're exactly the same as my old ones.'

'Yes, but they look new. Now, let's continue shall we?'

Roxy nodded but her mind was now elsewhere. Did Beattie know something about yesterday's incident, she wondered? Was it just a lucky guess?

'Beatrice?' she interrupted, unable to help herself and the older woman looked up, surprised.

'Yes, dear? More tea?'

'No the tea's fine, thanks. Just a question and it might sound a little odd.' She pushed the pause button on her recorder. 'You wouldn't happen to know anyone who *doesn't* want you to publish your memoirs do you?'

Beatrice looked suddenly wary, her chestnut eyes flickering back and forth across Roxy's face, her features now tense.

'Oh, er, it's nothing to panic about,' Roxy stammered. 'I just thought I should check, in case we upset anyone. Autobiographies are personal things, you understand.' But Beatrice did not seem placated. 'What is it?' Roxy asked. 'You can tell me anything, you know that.'

'Well there is one person.' Roxy's heart skipped a beat. 'But...oh, I don't think he's serious. Not really.'

'Your son?'

'William? Oh dear, no, he thinks it's a swell idea.'

'Really?' This surprised Roxy. By all accounts William Musgrave was the quiet, reserved type who rarely made the papers and certainly never attended his mother's high-profile events. He seemed too busy minding his deceased dad's affairs to be interested in publicity of any kind.

'No, it's my grandson, Fabian. William's boy from his first wife, Belinda.'

'Oh?'

'He's a lovely lad, really. Just a little mixed up that's all.'

'How do you mean?'

'Well, he's had troubles in the past, but that's irrelevant here, and I told him so.' She swallowed hard. 'The point is, he's against this book. Says the past is the past. Best left that way.'

'But if it's a past to rejoice in, surely—'

Beattie's frown deepened and she stood up, hugging her jacket around her tightly. 'Oh dear...' she said, clearly agitated. 'It's all such a can of worms.'

Roxy took a deep breath. 'What is, Beatrice?'

The older woman had turned deathly quiet and, clutching on to the edge of the balcony, stared out at the view for what seemed an eternity. When she did turn back, her frown had vanished and her society smile was firmly back in place.

'It really isn't important, Roxanne, dear. We shall talk about it all later.' Her voice was business-like again, but this time uncharacteristically insincere.

'Beatrice you must tell me if there's something wrong.'

'No, no,' she swept a feathery finger up to her lips as if to hush her up. 'We will get on to it all later. Everything in good time. For now, let's keep it light.' She clapped her hands together, 'My marriage!'

Roxy squinted her eyes and considered pushing the point. If Beattie was hiding something, she needed to know exactly what it was. Her own life may depend upon it. But Beattie had already restarted the recorder and was describing, in some detail, her honeymoon home, with its crystal chandeliers and 'exquisite' Persian rugs. As Roxy listened, she softly stroked her facial scratches now firmly believing that the two were related.

After just 20 minutes, Beatrice sat back and began to rub at her temple. 'Oh dear, I feel frightful all of a sudden. I think I've said enough. For today. Do you mind if we finish this another time? I'll pay you for the full two hours, of course.'

'That's not necessary and of course I don't mind. Are you okay?'

The older woman struggled for a smile. 'Yes, yes. Just tired. That happens at my grand old age.'

Roxy switched the recorder off and placed it back in her bag. 'Well, thanks so much for the tea. And take care, okay? I'll see you next Monday? 9.30 as usual?'

'Of course, dear, I look forward to it.'

As she made her way down the steep, paved driveway to her car, Roxy felt her own head starting to throb. It was clear Beatrice was hiding something that she wasn't yet ready to reveal. But what could it be, she wondered, and why was she feeling an odd sense of dread?

4 THE ARTIST

The sun struggled to peep out from behind a thick swell of gray clouds that had hijacked the sky and, by mid-morning, gave up the effort as rain began bucketing down. If there was one thing Heather Jackson hated it was the rain. Not because the thick drops slowed the traffic down or turned normally cheerful faces glum as they scurried for shelter. But because it turned her hair frizzy. And the only thing she hated more than the rain, was frizzy hair. Now *curly* hair, she could handle—although she forced her own into long, straight strands, spending a good half hour each day ensuring it was just right—but frizzy hair was altogether different. It was ugly, and unsightly. And out of her control.

My hair's not even wet yet, and the bloody strands are starting to frizz up, she thought. Like a cheap check-out chick. And where the hell is this cafe Maria insisted she'd find, 'no worries'? Maria Constantinople. What a classless piece of trash. She had been so smug about her little scoop, as if Heather had chosen the cheap rag for her. What a fool. And surprisingly self-assured. But her tone was still reverent, like most people's now, respectful and excited, overawed to be talking to her. Once she could barely get a glance from

36

the average Joe. Now she was an icon. And she hated people for it.

A neon sign flashed 'Lockies' and Heather pursed her lips together. The place looked like a hovel. She had wanted to do the interview at home but her agent/manager, Jamie, was right, she didn't need a sniveling little reporter going through her things. Neutral territory was the best idea. *But this dump?* Briefly, she considered accelerating, but she spotted a parking spot out front and slipped her Mercedes into it. Then she wrapped her hair in a Hermes scarf, grabbed an umbrella from the back seat and stepped out onto the curb.

Inside Lockies, Roxy watched Heather park and felt her stomach lurch. She was not normally star-struck, but this one was an enigma. Roxy couldn't correlate her poignant first portrait with the meticulously dressed woman stepping out of a luxury vehicle, struggling to open her umbrella as though the rain would turn her to jelly. She got to her feet as the artist entered the cafe, shaking her hair out frantically and turning her attention to a blue slip of paper. 'Miss Parker?' she asked, barely looking up.

'Roxy. Yes, thanks for coming, Heather.'

'Oh.' She glanced back at the piece of paper. 'But it is *Roxanne Parker*, right?'

'Well, some people call me Roxanne.' But how unusual, she thought, that Maria would refer to her that way. 'I prefer Roxy. You can dump your umbrella there.'

Heather looked over at an old beer keg cluttered with umbrellas and then back at Roxy. 'Let's get this over and done with shall we? Where do you want me?'

They walked to the back of the cafe where Loghlen had set up a special table, far enough from the other patrons to ensure privacy and quiet enough to get the whole thing down clearly on Roxy's old tape recorder. Apart from one or two half-interested glances from the other diners, no-one seemed to recognize the infamous Heather Jackson. One black-clad woman glared at her Chanel suit and a young man darted a second look but Roxy sensed this was more out of curiosity than anything else. Heather certainly looked out of place in this artists' cafe, and therein lay the conundrum. She was an artist after all.

Choosing the seat facing back into the cafe, Heather placed her jacket on the back of it and her umbrella below, then sat down and removed her delicate, diamond-encrusted Cartier watch, placing it on the table in front of her. She then picked up the menu and began scanning the list.

Roxy took the opportunity to scan Heather. Despite the designer threads and long, richly streaked hair, she was actually a pretty ordinary-looking woman, nose slightly askew, the beginnings of a double chin, a smattering of freckles barely visible behind the make-up, and it heartened Roxy a little. It helped explain all the glamour. She was clearly compensating.

'Ready to order?' Loghlen asked, beaming from ear to ear, his snowy skin blushing red, his hand shaking beneath his pen. He had been ecstatic when Roxy had announced the interview would be done in his tiny cafe—a small gift to an old mate—and she suspected he'd spent half the night scrubbing and preparing as though royalty were about to descend. Heather didn't even bother looking up.

'Yes a decaf skinny latte. And an ash tray.'

'Coitinly,' Lockie replied, conveniently forgetting the smoking ban. 'And would yar like anything wi' tha'? Some home-made cheesecake perhaps?'

'No I wouldn't.' And then a more cordial, 'Thank you.'

'An' you, Ro—, ma'am?'

'Just the usual, thanks Lockie,' Roxy replied smiling warmly at him. She turned to Heather. 'You don't mind if I tape record this?'

'Tape record?'

'Yes.' She had only mentioned it out of politeness. 'Well I can take shorthand if you like—'

'Yes, better.'

Roxy brushed a strand of black hair back from her eyes and smiled. 'No problems, Heather. Of course, it's not as accurate a report of what was said. My shorthand is very sloppy. But we'll get the basics down.'

'Oh the tape recorder will be fine.' Heather looked a little annoyed but, again, tried for a smile. 'Don't want to be misconstrued, you understand?'

'Absolutely.' She pushed the record button down, checked that the tape was rolling and in a clear tone said, 'Heather Jackson interview, Lockies café, May 2nd.'

She could work for the bloody pigs, Heather thought as the journalist placed the recorder directly below her and smiled that, 'Now this won't hurt a bit' kind of smile. She had seen that smile before. Too many times. And it always hurt. But this time she was prepared to pay the price. Everything depended on it.

'Congratulations on your success since the *Sydney Art Gazette* competition,' Roxy began and Heather bowed her head obligingly. Waiting for the kill. 'Did you ever imagine you would end up where you are now?'

Ahh, there it is. She was faster than most, maybe even smarter. She had better watch this one. Heather shrugged her shoulders flippantly. 'Of course not. How could I? I really have been very lucky.' Oops, she shouldn't have used that word. She had left the door wide open. Was out of practice, that's all, but the sea-weed-eyed reporter did not take the bait.

'What did you think when you first applied for the *Gazette* comp? Where did you think you would be?'

'Be?'

'Yes, as far as the success of your art was concerned? Did you always think you would make it eventually? Or did you imagine years struggling to no avail, like most artists do?'

'Ahhh,' Heather said. *The modesty versus pride question.* 'I honestly couldn't tell you. Twenty years ago did *you* have any idea where you'd be today?'

'I think I did, yes,' Roxy replied. 'I always figured I'd be interviewing interesting people for worthwhile publications. It was a lifelong ambition.'

'Then hurrah for you.' She hoped it did not sound mean-spirited, but what was the four-eyes referring to? Instead of answering she asked, 'So *do* you get much work, writing?' Roxy was surprised by the question and nodded yes. 'Interviewed anyone interesting lately?'

Roxy squished her lips up to one side and studied the artist's eyes. She had seen this trick before but the clock was ticking and she was not about to waste time talking about herself. 'Not as interesting as you,' she replied casually. At that moment, Loghlen appeared with their coffees in hand and placed them down. He was grinning like a teenage boy and Roxy quickly thanked him, eager to pick up the pace.

'The *New York Times* art critic calls your most recent work, "A delight in unpredictability and surprise",' she said. 'Tell me what motivates you? What drives that surprise?'

'Ahh.' Heather knew how to respond to this one. It was as though the answer was written on the back of her hand. And indeed, she thought with smug delight, it once was. 'When I first look at a person, nothing much comes from it. They are straight, tangible and, I'm sorry to say, rather uninteresting. But then I *really* look at them, and things start to jumble. The person becomes the puzzle and then, somehow, the portrait. It is as though I were not even in the room. Suddenly they have metamorphosized onto my canvas.'

'And yet, sometimes what you paint is less a metamorphosis than an annihilation,' said Roxy, very calmly, and the artist looked up from her coffee.

'Annihilation?'

'Green skin. Red eyes. Protruding necks. Hardly flattering.'

Her expression relaxed a little. 'Ahh but there is a certain ugliness in us all.'

'Even a handicapped child?'

This caught Heather completely off guard and she dropped her teaspoon against the china saucer so that it clunk loudly, forcing the other patrons to look up. The curious man began to squint his eyes. He recognized her now but couldn't decide from where.

'Ah, the winning portrait,' she said, her composure returning.

'A stunning piece of art,' Roxy offered.

'Some say the best yet.'

'And you?'

'Well I guess I will always have a soft spot for it, how could I not?'

'And where is she now?'

'Hmm?'

'The young girl in the portrait?'

'Oh, goodness, I don't know. Can't even remember her name.'

'Yet she launched your career.'

'No, darling.' Heather's voice was perfectly amiable, but there was a steeliness in her eyes. 'I launched my career. The portrait is one of several hundred I have now completed. Have you seen any others?'

'Of course I have.' Roxy lied, realizing that Lockie's textbook hardly counted. 'Where is the portrait now?'

'I still have it.' *I couldn't sell that one*, she thought, *I'm not that stupid*. 'Do you only write about artists?'

Roxy glowered at her again. 'No, I write about all sorts of people.'

'What sorts?'

'Look, Heather. I appreciate your interest but if we can just get through my questions I'll tell you all about myself at the end.'

Heather shrugged and took a sip of her coffee.

'I'm very interested to know what you were like as a child, Heather.'

'What I was like as a *child*?'

'Yes.'

'Oh, um. Let's think. Tall, skinny. Freckle-faced.'

'Did you paint?'

'I'm sorry?'

'As a child, did you paint?'

'Of course I did. Incessantly.'

'And your inspirations?'

Heather seemed relieved by the question and began rattling off a list of names, expressing their unique qualities as though reading aloud an essay. As she talked, Roxy wondered why the artist was so defensive. What had happened in the past to make her that way? She was about to ask when Heather's iPhone began to ring. She excused herself, turned her chair around and answered. Lockie grabbed the opportunity to clear the cups.

'How's it goin'?' he whispered excitedly.

'Okay.'

'Hey, I've got a bit of a soiree here on Monday morning, a new writer's comin' in. Your cup a tea, I'da thought. Wanna drop by? About 10ish.'

'Would love to,' she said, 'but I've got an interview to do on Monday, and this one I don't want to miss.'

'Oooh,' he said. 'Sounds intriguing! Anyone interesting?'

'Just a client who's been quite dull to date. But I get the feeling things are going to liven up enormously.'

'Good luck then!' he said, and noticing that Heather had now finished on the phone, scurried away.

The rest of the interview went smoothly enough. Roxy asked all the questions she needed to ask and, for the most part, Heather delivered all the answers, her mood now mostly cooperative and congenial. But as she spoke, her eyes frequently darted about the room, sizing up the staff and customers as though she was checking for invaders. She fiddled with her hair, too, releasing it from its scarf from time to time and stroking it straight before tying it back again. During all of this she barely looked at Roxy, only focusing upon her when the questions turned a little deep or probing. Then, Heather's eyes narrowed slightly and her lips pursed together as though sucking on a cigarette. She took her time answering and offered only monosyllabic responses. Yet these were the questions Roxy really wanted answered and, as the interview wrapped up, she felt as though she had learned little more about the elusive artist than when she had started.

Exactly an hour after they had begun, Heather picked up her watch, strapped it back on and declared, 'Well if that's all, I need to be off.'

'Actually, there was one more question.'

'Yes?' *Oh God*, she thought, *I'm nearly away.*

'In your *Gazette* application 20 years ago, you said that you wanted to paint people who matter. I quote, "Not film stars and fluff". Why then have you gone on to only paint celebrities? Do you think now that only famous people matter?'

Heather's lips tightened again and she reached for her jacket. 'We all matter, Miss Parker.' She pushed her chair backwards and stood up.

'Just one other thing!' Heather smiled stiffly. 'Do you have a number I can call—in case I've forgotten anything or need to check something? I like to get my facts straight, I'm sure that's important to you, too?'

Heather considered this for a second and then reached into her bag for a scrap of paper and a pen. She pulled out the blue piece she referred to earlier, and, turning it over, scribbled down the name Jamie Owen, adding a number below it. 'My manager,' she explained, dropping the paper to the table. 'He can help you with anything you need.'

With a swish of her thick locks, she turned away and strode swiftly across the room, past the gobsmacked patron who had finally worked out who she was, and out the door. Within seconds she was speeding off up the road, leaving Roxy alone with her tape recorder and a bemused look upon her face. Loghlen watched his idol drive away and rushed back to Roxy.

'So how'd it go? Get what you need?'

'I'm not sure,' Roxy said, feeling both relieved and rueful at the same time. She couldn't recall ever having done a more difficult interview and was not sure she had got anything out of the acclaimed artist. But she was sure of one thing: that was clearly what the artist had intended.

'What's with the umbrella?' Max asked as Roxy strolled into the bar. 'Rain packed up shop hours ago.'

'Yes, I know, it's Heather Jackson's. She left it behind after our interview, and now I have to take my own advice and get it back to her without running into her.'

'Huh?'

Max was confused and Roxy was too tired to explain it all now. She wedged the umbrella into her handbag and dropped it to the floor, then took a seat, pulling her long scarf off and tucking her brown boots beneath the barstool.

'Get us a drink will you, Max, I'm dying here.'

He motioned for the barmaid and ordered a glass of Merlot and a beer for himself. He didn't push her to explain, that's not what these weekly get-togethers were about. Instead, he dragged a bowl of peanuts towards them and, throwing a handful into his mouth, chewed loudly while asking, 'So how was the meeting with your mum?'

'Disastrous.'

'Same old same old then?'

''Fraid so.'

'So, who's she got you hooked up with this time?'

'Oh some lawyer dude who's no doubt short, fat and extremely dull.'

'Ahhh, but he'd make a faithful husband.'

'Which is more than I can say for most men.'

Max smiled. 'So young and yet so cynical.'

'Not that young,' she corrected.

'Which is exactly why she's setting you up with drongos instead of dishes. Less chance of them running off with the secretary.'

Roxy gulped at her glass. 'God, do people even do that anymore? It's so cliché. Anyway, don't make excuses for her.'

'Just making an observation, Parker, nothing to get in a twist about. You really don't like your mum very much do you?'

'Oh it's not that. I just don't *respect* her. That's much worse. How's your dad going?'

'Grumpy old bastard as usual. I swear, we should be able to put them down when they get to a certain age.'

Roxy laughed and felt her shoulders relax a little. Max and Roxy met weekly at Pico's, a small, candle-lit wine bar, where they left work worries at the door and sorted each other's private lives out instead. They called it their 'sanity date' and often let it carry on into the early hours of the morning, drinking and laughing and forgetting their woes. Or at least making fun of them, which was almost as good. She ran her eyes over her good friend. He had a beaten up leather jacket on tonight, and baggy black jeans. No skinny jeans for this guy. It was too much like hard work. He ran a hand through his tousled hair, only managing to tousle it further and she thought she detected the slight scent of aftershave. Surely not, she thought? It wasn't really Max's style.

'So did you get the jacket back okay?'

'Yeah.' He sounded glum.

'She didn't spot you cowering behind the light box?'

'No.'

'So what's the problem?'

'Oh, nothing.' He drained his beer and ordered another. He was drinking fast, even for a Thursday night.

'What? Spill!'

'She wasn't all *that* bad,' he said.

'What happened?' Why this change of tune?

'Well, I called her up again.'

'After all that?'

'Hey, it's fine for you. You like being single. I hate it.'

'Oh give me a break.'

Max sucked the froth from the top of his bottle. His mood had turned a little sour. 'Tell me, Rox, why exactly do you like being single?'

'Huh?'

'You never need anyone, do you?'

Roxy sensed bitterness in his tone and wondered if he was drunk. 'That's the second time I've heard that in as many days. That's absolute crap, you know that.'

'No, actually, I don't.'

'Well, for starters, I need you or I'd go slowly insane.'

'Bullshit.'

Roxy gulped her drink and felt her shoulders tense up again. But she softened her tone as she asked, 'What is it? If you like this girl, then just see her. It's not a big—'

'Look, I know that.' He was trying to control his anger. Unsuccessfully.

'Good. So how's work? Snapped any big fish?'

'No work, remember.'

'Well what *do* you want to talk about? You're in such a filthy mood.'

Max swallowed hard. 'So I'm gonna see her again.'

'Good! Do it!' What did he want from her?

'I will!'

Roxy rolled her eyes and looked away. Above the bar a small TV screen was heralding the ABC's 7pm news. The lead story was dubbed 'Horror Find Still Unsolved' and, upon her instruction, the bartender turned it up.

'The one-handed corpse discovered at Rushcutters Bay on Monday has still not been identified and Bay police are asking for assistance from the public,' a harried voice declared. 'According to forensics, the victim, whose right hand had been chopped off, was drowned late Sunday night or early Monday morning and they are appealing to any witnesses who may have seen anything suspicious in the area at that time. Please contact your local police station or the police hotline on—'

'Horrible stuff,' Max said, shuddering a little, and Roxy turned back to him, her eyes now twinkling again.

'I read about it earlier this week. Why on earth would you chop a person's hand off?'

'Identification.'

'Oh but there's always the other hand, the face, the dental records. It's quite bizarre.'

'Murder is always bizarre,' Max insisted, crunching on some ice.

'Not at all,' Roxy replied. 'Sometimes it's downright dull.'

He stared at her like she had finally flipped, his thick eyebrows rising, his brown hair flopping down on top of them.

'Oh, you know,' she continued, 'shoot-outs at a 7/11 or pub brawls. That's all pretty ordinary stuff. But killing someone for their fingers, now that's *interesting!*'

'You have always had a macabre interest in death, haven't you?'

Roxy smiled and picked up her drink. 'Not all deaths,' she replied. 'Just the involuntary ones.'

He smiled at that, his large, all-consuming smile, and with it the mood of the evening lightened up. But as they ordered more drinks and a bowl of wedges on the side, Roxy couldn't help a niggling sense of unease. Max wasn't himself tonight, and for some reason—a reason she couldn't even articulate to herself—she was too terrified to ask him why.

5 PLAYING DUMB

'**Hi** Roxy,' Loghlen sang as Roxy pulled up a chair by the coffee bar the next day. 'What can I get ya?'

'I think I'll go for a strawberry frappe and one of your No. 7's,' she said. 'Oh, and a newspaper on the side.' He pushed his bushy orange eyebrows together, curiously, and she quickly added, 'Just need to look something up.'

'No problemo.' He detoured to grab that day's *Herald*, which he dropped in front of her, before placing the order.

Roxy thanked him and then carefully studied the paper from cover to cover. She was hoping to read more about the mutilated body but there wasn't so much as a mention. Lockie returned to the coffeemaker and began frothing the milk.

'Checkin' the Dow Jones?' he asked as she scrutinized the pages.

'I wish, Lockie, I wish.' She tossed the paper aside. 'So, how are you going?'

'Good, good! Hey, the artist was back.'

Roxy was surprised. 'Heather Jackson?'

'The veddy one!'

'Don't tell me she came back for one of your world-famous decaf skinny lattes?'

''Fraid not!' He laughed. 'She was lookin for somethin' but it wasn't my coffee that's for sure. I asked her what, but she wouldn't say.'

'Bit odd.'

'Aye. She obviously left somethin' here but she wouldn't tell me what. I reckon it was probably her umbrella. She did have a bit of a rummage in the old keg up the front.' He placed the frothy brew in front of her just as a small bell rang, and he dashed out the back to fetch her sandwich. After taking a giant bite to quiet her stomach down, Roxy asked, 'But why come all this way for a crummy umbrella?'

'Oh, I don't know,' he said, waving to another patron who had just entered. ''P'raps she's just cheap? What did you do with it, anyway?'

'What?'

'The umbrella.'

Roxy shrugged. 'God, I can't even remember. I think it's at my house.'

'Well you'd better get it back to her. She looked frantic enough. And I can't think what else she woulda left. And here—' he grabbed a shiny black umbrella from behind the counter. 'If you can't find it, give her this one. She seemed desperate for one and I can't have her thinking we're a pack of thieves. This one's brand new, even cost me a bi', but she's welcome to it.'

As he wandered off to tend some tables, Roxy sat nibbling her focaccia sandwich and wondering at Heather's behavior. Why wouldn't she simply tell Lockie what she was looking for? It seemed very odd, but then, Heather was proving to be stranger and stranger by the day.

'Enough about her,' she thought, reaching for her smartphone and scrolling through her contact list. It was several rings before it answered and Beatrice Musgrave's voice was uncharacteristically high pitched.

'It's Roxy Parker, Beattie, are you okay?'

'Oh! Miss Parker. Yes, dear, I'm fine. No, I'm wonderful. It's been quite a day!'

'Really?'

'Yes, I've had the most surprising visitor, you wouldn't believe.'

'Oh?'

'Yes! My long-lost… oh, hang on a minute.' The phone was suddenly muffled and Roxy strained to hear what was going on, but only the scratchy sound of palm against phone could be detected. After a good minute or so, Beatrice cleared her throat and spoke again.

'Look I have to go, Roxanne, I've got someone here. I'll tell you all about it the next time we meet. Are you fine to come in on Monday?'

'Absolutely. Are you sure everything's alright?'

Beatrice laughed heartily. 'Of course, yes! Now everything is perfect. Sorry about the other day, dear, I was a little worried, but now it seems she doesn't mind.'

'Who doesn't mind?'

'My daughter, dear. Oh, I really have to run. We'll get it all out, once and for all, when we meet on Monday. 9.30am still okay?'

'Fine, yes.'

As Roxy hung up, a mixture of excitement and trepidation ran down her spine. Not only was there something strange in the older woman's voice, as far as Roxy knew Beatrice Musgrave didn't have a daughter.

6 SURPRISING NEWS

Roxy awoke late on Saturday morning and, well aware that she should be getting stuck into the Heather Jackson transcript, opted to go grocery shopping instead. 'You can't work on an empty stomach, after all,' she told herself, slipping on brown hipster cords, a floral blouse and denim jacket, and made her way down to her car.

It was close to 2pm by the time the young woman finished her shop and, the car now laden with food, wine and a bundle of tulips, she was about to head home when she remembered. *The bloody brollie.* She took a few minutes to search the car. Damn it, Roxy thought, I must have left it at home. She spotted the black one Lockie had given her on the back seat, shrugged and then turned the car towards the posh Eastern Sydney suburb of Vaucluse. This one would have to do.

Heather Jackson's house was easy enough to find. Loghlen had described it for Roxy the day before and his description was spot on. He was obviously a bigger fan than she realized. When she spotted the 'white monolithic structure with a giant gold fence and a slight view of a mermaid waterfall inside', she slowed her car down and swung it into the driveway and up to the front gate where an intercom and camera were wedged into a wall. She buzzed twice but it was some time before a small voice answered, "Allo?'

'Hi, this is Roxy Parker, here. I have something for Heather Jackson.'

'All delivewies awound the side.'

'Ahh, no, this is personal, it's just an umbrella, she left hers behind the other day.'

There was a long pause and Roxy wondered whether she'd been given the brush off before the gate finally clicked open and swung inwards. She drove through and up the winding driveway to the house, which was grander in size than it appeared from the road. It was not exactly beautiful but it did have a striking presence, and the meticulous gardens surrounding it were breathtaking. There were several impressively sized fig trees on either side of the house and what looked like an orchard to the left. Roxy parked in front of the main door and jumped out, clutching the black umbrella. Before she had a chance to ring the doorbell, a short Chinese woman had swung it open and was reaching for the umbrella.

'T'ankyou velly much,' she said quickly but Roxy did not relinquish her hold.

'Actually I need to speak to Heather. Is she around?'

'She no here.'

'Okay, then I need to write her a message.'

The maid looked uncertain but nodded her head anyway and led Roxy inside the house to the white marbled foyer. It was set around a large courtyard overflowing with ferns and orchids. Two long, carpeted corridors swept off, one to the west wing of the house, the other to the right, and Roxy noticed that there was a row of doors along each one, all heavy timber and all closed shut.

'Here,' the maid said, thumping a note pad and pen down onto a white marble side table.

'Thank you,' Roxy said and began to write: '*Heard you were looking for your umbrella. Here's a new one courtesy of Lockies. If there's anything else, don't hesitate to give me a call.*'

She jotted her home number below and signed off. As she handed the paper to the maid, she thought she detected a door opening to her left. She glanced across and saw a flash of silver before it swung quickly shut again. The Asian woman also noticed the door and glanced from it to the writer's face, her expression growing increasingly more anxious. She grabbed Roxy's arm and pulled her back out the front door.

'You go now,' she urged. 'Goodbye.'

An hour later, while unloading the vegetables into the fridge, Roxy's phone rang. As she had suspected, it was Heather Jackson.

'Lovely to hear from you,' Roxy said, trying to sound casual, a lemon still planted in one hand. 'You got the umbrella okay?'

'Yes I did,' the voice was stiff. 'But it won't do, it's not the one I left behind, you see. Mine was gold, not black.'

'Oh, we could get you a new gold one if you prefer.'

'It's not *mine*, Miss Parker. I'd really like mine back. Sentimental reasons, you understand. If you could take another look for me.'

'Oh, sure, no sweat,' she said, thinking, *but it's only an umbrella.*

'Good. And if you could call me when you find it. I'd rather you didn't just turn up to my house unannounced.'

'Oh, of course. What's your number?'

The woman hesitated before saying, 'You have my manager's number, call him and he'll organize a pick up.'

It seemed like a lot of trouble for an old umbrella. Roxy tossed the lemon aside and marched through the lounge room into her bedroom, flicking the TV on as she went. The early news bulletin would be on soon and she was keen to see if there had been any developments in the case of the mutilated corpse. She located Heather's umbrella, tossed into one corner, and opened it up to survey it in full. The gold was fake plastic, and the handle simple cane. Nothing worth fussing over. And then she saw it. Scratched in very fine print along one side of the cane was the name: *L. Johnson.*

'So that's what all this is about,' she said aloud, swiveling the umbrella in her hands. 'I wonder who that might be?'

Roxy was so engrossed by the question that she almost missed the lead news story booming out from the next room. She rushed out. The body of an elderly woman had been found washed up on the shores of Balmoral Beach very early that morning. Police had not yet released the name of the victim, the perky reporter exclaimed, or the official cause of death. But stay tuned, she gushed, as more details unfolded.

Balmoral Beach. Roxy stared hard at the television, the gold umbrella still open in her hand, the blood now drained from her face.

That's near Beatrice Musgrave's place.

A loud screeching sound startled Roxy from her sleep and at first she ignored it, imagining she was still lost in her dreams. But the screeching persisted. She peeled open her eyes and slowly struggled to her feet, stifling a yawn as she stumbled to the front door and the intercom that was mercilessly loud for that hour of the morning. This had better be good, she thought angrily, pressing the speak button and groaning, 'Yes?'

'It's the police Miss Parker, we need to speak to you. Can we come in?'

Roxy blinked back her surprise and glanced at the clock. It was not yet 8am on Saturday morning. 'Ah, yeah, sure.' She buzzed them through then loped back to her room to put something on. Within seconds they were banging on the door and, after checking their ID through the key chain, she let them in.

'I'm Detective Spicer,' the older of the two men announced after they had made their way to the centre of her lounge room and stood standing in the official 'at ease' position, legs apart, hands behind their backs. 'And this is Detective Valence. We'd like to ask you a few questions regarding Beatrice Musgrave.'

'Of course,' Roxy replied, and felt tears well up in her eyes again. She had quickly dismissed yesterday's news story, determined that the body on the rocks was some other elderly lady, someone other than Beatrice Musgrave. Until Oliver had called with the bad news.

'Looks like you're out of a job,' he'd said and Roxy's heart had plummeted.

'Oh God, no!'

'Fraid so. My friend at the *Herald* just called. Old Mrs Musgrave did the high dive late Friday night or early Saturday morning, they're still working all that out. But it's definitely her, the son has identified the body.'

Roxy was expecting a visit from the police but their haste surprised her. She shrugged back her tears and said, 'Please, take a seat.'

Spicer strutted straight to the dining table and, selecting a chair, pulled it back into the lounge room directly in front of where Roxy now sat on the sofa. Meanwhile Valence, a small man with slicked back hair and the beginnings of a moustache, began to wander the room, peering at her photos and sneaking peeks into the other rooms. It unsettled her but she bit her tongue and raised her eyebrows expectantly at Spicer.

'You've heard that Mrs Musgrave is now deceased?' he said.

'Yes, I heard late last night, my agent rang me.'

'What was your relationship with the deceased?'

'I'm a writer. I was helping her write her autobiography.' *But then you must know that*, she thought, *why else are you here?*

'How long had you known the deceased?'

'I had known Beattie for just on a month. She contacted my agent, looking for a ghost wri—'

'Your agent's name?'

'Oliver Horowitz.'

'Got a number handy?'

Roxy rattled several numbers off, giving them Oliver's home and work details. It was Sunday morning but chances are he'd be skulking about in his office downtown doing whatever he did when he wasn't out guzzling beer or at home trying to sleep. Valence meanwhile had disappeared into the kitchen.

'Looking for something?' Roxy called after him, annoyed, and the officer poked his head around the door, shrugged and then slouched back into the living room and dropped into a chair. 'Do you have any idea what happened?'

'We're still piecing it together, Miss,' Spicer said, 'But it looks like suicide. Pretty cut and dried I believe.'

Nice choice of words, Roxy thought and then snorted. 'You're kidding, right?'

'When do you think you last saw her?' Spicer continued, ignoring her comment.

'I *know* I last saw her on Wednesday afternoon. We had our usual 3pm appointment. It lasted about 20 minutes and then Beattie said she was tired and abruptly ended the interview.'

'How did she seem?'

'Well, as I said, tired.'

'Anything else?'

'Yes, she was wary, she was holding something back.'

'Oh?'

Roxy repeated what Beattie had said regarding her grandson's objections to the book as well as her comment that it was 'all such a can of worms.' As she spoke, she noticed that neither man took any notes.

'You been ghostwritin' for long?' Valence suddenly asked, his accent surprisingly broad.

'A couple of years. Look, that's not all.' Roxy leant forward in her chair, excitement edging into her voice. 'There is one other important thing I should tell you.'

'What's that?'

'Well, I spoke to Beatrice two days later, on the Friday—'

'The day she died?'

'Yes, I suppose that's right. She couldn't talk, said she had someone there—which you might want to check, her maid will tell you—'

'Her maid wasn't working that day,' Valence said.

Roxy glanced across at him, surprised. 'That's odd, I thought she was full-time. Anyway, the point is, she seemed very flustered and said a few things which I believe are quite vital.'

Roxy repeated her final conversation with the elderly socialite including her revelation about a 'surprising visitor' and her almost matter-of-fact admission that she had a daughter. Again, neither officer bat an eyelid. 'Anyway,' she continued, unperturbed, 'she also confirmed that she wanted me back the following Monday to resume the interviews.' Again, neither man reacted, so she helped them along. 'That doesn't sound like a woman who's about to kill herself, does it?'

As if on some silent directive both officers stood up and stepped towards the door. Spicer turned and said, 'Thank you for your assistance, Miss Parker.'

Roxy raced after them. 'But *surely* you still don't think it was suicide?'

'If we need anything else,' Spicer replied dryly, 'we'll be in touch.'

And with that they were gone. 'Bloody useless,' she spat, slamming the door behind them. It seemed to her that the policemen had no interest whatsoever in what she had to say. It was as though they had simply dropped by to check her out, tick her off their list, and get on with their day.

'You certainly had more to contribute than I did,' Oliver was saying over the phone from his apartment an hour later.

'So they came to see you, too?'

'Just been 'round. But I don't know why they bothered. Walked in, looked around, asked my occupation and walked out again. Hardly an investigation.'

'Must be your trusting face,' she replied. 'What do you think they're up to?'

'I *know* what they're up to. Haven't you read the papers yet?'

'Haven't had a chance, why?'

'Go get 'em, it'll explain everything.' And with that he hung up.

Roxy slipped on her Converse sneakers and, grabbing some loose change, dashed down to the local newsagency that was just opening its doors for the Sunday trade.

'Hey Roxy!' the owner called out as she dashed in. 'You're up early.'

'Tell me about it,' she said, grabbing the three main newspapers and handing him her change. 'Have a good one.'

Back in her apartment, Roxy buttered some toast and, with a cup of strong coffee in front of her and a pair of scissors in hand, began to scan the headlines. The articles on Beattie's death were all disappointingly brief, each containing just a few quick paragraphs which paid more attention to her late, roving husband than the woman herself. And, much to her surprise, the police had already confirmed that there were 'no suspicious circumstances'. They clearly believed it was suicide.

'So that's why they were so flippant,' she thought enraged. 'They've already closed the case. They were just here to cross a few Ts.'

Roxy jumped up and began pacing the room, anger swelling up inside her. Surely there needed to be a proper investigation before they could confirm anything, she thought, chewing frantically at her lower lip. She, for one, could not accept it. The Beatrice Musgrave she knew would never commit suicide, and certainly not in such an ignominious way. An overdose of sleeping pills, perhaps. It was clean and dignified. But leaping to her death off the balcony? It was too public, too *messy*. After all, this was the woman who was so into keeping up appearances she wore pearls around the house! Roxy sat down, trying to get her head together. If Beattie didn't kill herself, then it was murder. Either that or a tragic accident. But you couldn't really expect a 70-something to be dangling dangerously over a balcony for no good reason.

'Nup,' thought Roxy, 'She was definitely pushed. Had to be. But by whom? And why?'

She considered that final phone call with Beattie, tears welling up again as she realized that she might have been one of the last people to speak to the poor woman before she died. *Apart from the killer, of course.*

Now what exactly did she say to me? Roxy jumped back up, grabbed her laptop and quickly set up a new file. She needed to get some facts down, and fast, before they soon fictionalized, as facts often did over time.

She recalled her last few conversations with Beattie, tapping the entire thing down, and then underlining the pivotal lines:

I've had the most surprising visitor…you wouldn't believe…My old…'

No, she hadn't said old. What was it? Roxy stared hard at her tulips for a few moments. Ah, that's right! *'my long-lost—'*

That's when Beattie had been interrupted.

'I have to go, Roxanne, I've got someone here.'

Roxy felt a slight chill. Had the murderer been there? In her house? At that exact moment? Was the murderer listening in and ready to stop the old woman before she gave anything away? Roxy shook the thought away and continued scribbling.

'Now everything is perfect…now it seems she doesn't mind.'

'Who doesn't mind?'

'My daughter, dear.'

The daughter. Roxy placed the word in thick bold type and sat back, trying to think. It seemed that the answers to her questions might lie with that elusive daughter. But who was she? Where had she come from? Was she friend or foe?

'Arrrrgh,' she groaned, placing the computer aside and glancing up at the clock. It was only just 10am. She grabbed her jacket and handbag and returned to the street.

'Come on, Olie,' Roxy pleaded, her legs scrunched in front of her, her arms wrapped around them. She was perched on a bright red sofa in his apartment, just one suburb down from her own, and growing quickly impatient. 'You've done it before!'

'Well I don't want to do it again. What are you hiding?'

'Nothing!'

'Then why exactly do you need me to call my mate at Forensics?'

'Because if anyone knows the goss about Beatrice Musgrave's death she will.'

'But why get involved? It's out of your hands now.'

'Beatrice was my client, Oliver, you know that. I was writing her life story for God's sake. I'd just like to know how it ends up.'

'She threw herself off her balcony. It seems pretty clear to me.'

'It doesn't make an ounce of sense,' she retorted. 'I spoke to Beatrice the day before she died and she sounded excited, anxious to meet with me again tomorrow. She confirmed the appointment herself.'

'Sorry, Roxy, but it makes perfect sense to me. Think about it. She's near the end of it, she's had enough, she's given you her life story. Now you can write it with the ending in place. Sounds pretty clever in fact.'

Roxy dropped her feet down and began tapping them anxiously on the parquetry floor. Oliver's apartment, bathed now in orange light, was art deco in design and a little shabby in a kind of charming, indolent way, with unmatching sofas, mismatched rugs and old movie posters taped to the walls. 'But we hadn't *finished*, Oliver,' she said. 'We'd only got a third of the way through.'

He shrugged. 'Maybe she took one look at the rest of her life and felt suicidal. From what I've read, she had a pretty miserable marriage.'

'Or perhaps,' Roxy said, 'she was murdered.'

Oliver shook his head. 'Roxy you really do have a wild imagination. I think you should be in crime fiction not biographies.'

'Oh be serious. There's always that possibility.'

'But who would murder a little old biddie?'

'I don't know, but she was digging into her past, after all. Perhaps someone wanted to shut her up.'

Oliver suddenly squinted his eyes and then surprised Roxy by jumping up and closing the front door, which had been left ajar when she arrived. It led out to the main staircase of his apartment block and she didn't know any of his neighboring tenants to be particularly nosy, so she wondered why he did it.

'What could she possibly be about to tell you?' he asked, his tone now anxious, and Roxy felt her defenses rise up.

'Oh…I don't know. Maybe she wasn't. I'm just guessing here, Oliver.'

'Do you have any idea at all?'

'No.'

He scanned her eyes, as if trying to determine the truth and she stared coolly back. After years as an interviewer Roxy knew that a sudden change of tone was something to be wary of, even in her agent. She tried lightening up. 'Oh you know me, Olie. I'm *obsessed* with death. I just figure your mate might know a little more than the press are letting on, that's all. Aren't you intrigued just a little bit?'

'So that's all this is, morbid curiosity?'

'What else could it be?'

He slowly nodded his head. 'Alright I'll give her a call. But that's on the proviso that if you do come up with anything juicy and decide to write a piece, you sell the story through me. Deal?'

'Ah, there he is, the eternal agent, rearing his ugly head. It's a deal.'

'Good, now get out of here, I got some work to do.'

'Thanks, Olie.'

As Roxy reached the door, Oliver called out, 'Anything in particular you want me to ask about?'

'Yeah,' she replied. 'Ask about palm prints on old Beattie's back.'

7 SEARCHING FOR SUSPECTS

Monday morning dawned bright and cloudless, doing very little to cheer up workers as they made their way back to the grindstone. Roxy congratulated herself, as she often did on Mondays, for not having an office job. She was simply not the nine-to-five type, forgetting as she always did that she tended to do longer hours than that and worked most weekends. As she sat down at her desk and scanned her diary for the week, Roxy's good humor quickly dissipated. She was scheduled to return to the Musgrave mansion for the next installment of Beattie's life story that very morning and for the first time since she had begun, she longed desperately to do just that. She wished she could turn up at the grand old house and find the elegant hostess ready and waiting, eager to share cups of tea and her life story. She sighed heavily. If only Beatrice had not been so determined to tell that story, 'get it all out once and for all', she might still be alive today, spooning some Earl Grey tea leaves into her ivory china tea pot in anticipation of Roxy's visit.

Roxy realized, of course, that it was all conjecture. She understood that she could well be barking up the wrong tree, that the old lady could have done herself in, as others were so quick to assume. But she just didn't believe it. Not for one second. She felt a sudden urge to finish transcribing their interviews together. There were four hours of tape left to write up and it seemed imperative that she do it, and do it soon.

Overnight Roxy had contemplated finishing Beattie's biography for her and had decided to approach the Musgrave family about this very subject. But right now she had a strong urge to see what else was on those tapes, in case there was something important that she'd missed. Perhaps Beattie had made a previous, albeit subtle, mention of another child or given some indication that she was contemplating her own brutal death. If the police aren't interested, she thought striding into the kitchen, I am. She prepared a plunger of fresh New Guinea coffee and fetched the tapes.

As they noisily rewound in her small recorder, Roxy set her laptop up on the dining room table so that she could drink in the view as she worked. She poured herself some coffee, added a few sugars and some milk, took a good long sip and then pressed the start button on her tape recorder. As the ferries chugged across the horizon and the sun beamed down on the ferns just beyond, Roxy ploughed slowly through, noting down anything that rose an eyebrow or tickled her instincts.

By mid-afternoon she had listened to the final tape, the last aborted interview in which it was made perfectly clear by Beatrice that there were, indeed, skeletons in her closet. Roxy pushed the laptop aside, stood up and stretched like a cat easing out the aches and pains of sitting in a concentrated state for too long. Then, needing both a distraction and an outing, she fetched her handbag and rummaged through for the blue scrap of paper Heather had given her with the name of her agent Jamie Owen written on it. When she located it, she picked up the phone and dialed the number scribbled below it. On the first ring a gruff voice answered, 'Owen!'

'Hi, is that Jamie?'

'Yes, who's this?'

'My name's Roxy Parker—'

'This about the umbrella?'

'Yes.'

'You got it?'

'Yes, I had a good look and found—'

'Good. I'll send a courier for it. Give me your address.'

'Actually I'm about to head out. I'm happy to drop it into Heather.'

'Not necessary, thank you Miss Parker. Drop it into my office. 323 Park Street, seventh floor. Leave it with the receptionist.'

'Oh, okay, no probs.'

He hung up without another word.

'As polite as your client, I see,' Roxy remarked into the empty receiver. She flipped the paper over to jot down the address when she noticed the words 'Miss Roxanne Parker' scribbled on it. Again, it surprised her—how strange that Maria would refer to her in such a formal way. This was for an artist, after all, not the Lord Mayor. But there was something else now, too, something about the writing. She couldn't quite put her finger on it. Roxy shrugged and began scribbling down Heather's manager's details, then fetched the gold umbrella, her boots and a jacket. The sooner she was rid of it the better.

Within the hour Roxy had dropped the umbrella off and was back at her desk perusing her notes on Beatrice Musgrave. She felt oddly relieved, now that the umbrella was out of her hands, and fresher, too, for the break. These little outings—to fetch the paper, do a grocery shop, grab a bite at Lockies—were almost ritualistic for Roxy. They helped clear her head and get her out of the house, something she understood was important, even if her heart wasn't in it. She recalled a week some time back when she hadn't stirred at all. She was finishing several big articles, Max was away and the weather had not been conducive, but by the Friday she was crawling the walls and when the takeaway guy arrived with her dinner, she had practically thrown herself upon him, desperate for company and conversation. Perhaps she wasn't the loner she pretended to be.

But now it was time to knuckle down to business. Roxy pressed a random key on her keyboard and the laptop danced back to life, displaying the page titled, 'B. Musgrave' which she had been working on that morning. Unfortunately, as she scanned the transcription, nothing especially revealing stood out. While the older woman had lamented one thing or another, the loss of her first love being about the saddest of all, her tone was otherwise upbeat. If anything, Beatrice Musgrave had sounded like a woman with everything to live for. While she clearly didn't have a very close relationship with her 'workaholic' son, she did dote on her grandson and got enormous satisfaction from her volunteering and charity work.

And then of course there was the matter of the daughter. This was particularly perplexing. If there really was another child, none of the papers had mentioned it. They had listed her son William as Beattie's 'only child'. It was clearly not common knowledge, and Roxy wondered who else in Beattie's life knew about this daughter? Had her husband known? Did William? Was the daughter estranged? Had she been adopted out at birth? It was all very strange and Roxy guessed it could have been the reason Beatrice was writing her biography: to get the truth out at last. It might also have provided a motive for murder if someone had not wanted the truth revealed.

Roxy wondered who else knew about the secret daughter and if any of it was related to the threatening emails she, herself, had been receiving. Certainly none of the names mentioned in Beattie's interviews corresponded with the initials AIL from the Hotmail account. In fact, after four hours of tape Roxy had only noted four names of any interest.

She perused the list. The first was Terence Musgrave, Beattie's husband of whom she said, 'He was not the perfect husband, but then I was not perfect either.' Roxy wondered what she meant by that and if he knew about the daughter but concluded it could now be of little concern. Terence had been dead for five years. She turned to the next name on the list: William Musgrave, Beattie's 'only son'. 'He's a mad workaholic,' Beatrice had remarked. 'I rarely see him.' She had also insisted that he was in favor of the biography. Mentally, Roxy scratched him off the list.

William's son Fabian was also mentioned in the transcript and, while Beattie described him as having 'a lot of growing up to do' she also called him, 'sweet, charming and attentive.' Of all the family he was the only one she had mentioned as being against the book. Roxy wanted to find out why. Perhaps he was the one sending her the threatening messages. She underlined his name and made a note to pay him a visit.

The final name on her list was Ronald Featherby, Beattie's longtime lawyer. 'He's such a dear friend,' Beattie had remarked. 'I'd trust him with my life.' What else had Beatrice entrusted him with, Roxy wondered? Perhaps Mr Featherby was holding the key? Roxy made a similar note next to his name.

The phone let out a shrill cry and Roxy nearly jumped out of her skin. She quickly saved the copy and grabbed the remote. 'Roxy Parker speaking.'

'Hey Parker, how's it goin'?' It was Max and he sounded more cheerful than the last time they had spoken. 'I heard about Beatrice Musgrave. Pretty shocking.'

'Yeah,' she said. 'The police dropped by and it seems they're determined to think it's suicide.'

'And you don't?'

'I honestly don't know.'

'It looks like I've been roped in to cover the funeral for the *Tele*.'

'Really?'

'Yeah.' His tone flattened. 'Let's just say I'm hard up for cash.'

'When is it? You have to tell me how it goes.'

'See if I can spot a murderer wandering about?' He was joking but Roxy had lost her sense of humor. 'Look,' he continued when she did not respond, 'that's not the reason I called, I wanted to say thank you.'

'Oh?'

'Well, after what you said the other night, I took your advice and saw Sandra again.'

'The suede-jacket woman?'

'Yes and, well, suffice to say, we went for dinner Friday and she just left this morning.'

'Good for you.' Roxy felt her stomach lurch. That explained why he hadn't called her all weekend. Max had a new playmate and she was out of the picture again. It didn't happen that often, but when it did, she always felt a little irked. Her mother and Max were wrong, she did need people around. She just didn't like admitting it.

'So what did you get up to over the weekend?' he was asking. 'Working as usual?'

'No I did not work the entire weekend.' Now she was feeling defensive. 'Besides, I've got a hot date tonight.'

There was a brief pause on the other end and then Max said, 'Really?'

'Yes really. Why, does that surprise you?'

'No, no not at all.' Was that ridicule in his voice? 'So who's the lucky guy?'

'I'll tell you all about it on Thursday,' Roxy said, 'that is, if you still want to meet on Thursday?'

'Yeah, what do you reckon?'

'Well, I figured now that you're in love—'

'Who ever said anything about love? See you at Pico's at seven. 'Til then, have a cool week, hey?'

He hung up and Roxy felt hollow inside. It was not that she was jealous, she decided, she just liked having him all to herself. Then she thought about her 'hot date' and cringed. She hadn't lied exactly, she did have a date tonight, but it wasn't exactly hot. It had taken her a few days, but she'd finally worked out why the 'dashing young lawyer' that her mother had been trying to set her up with sounded so familiar. It wasn't his name, it was his company: Featherby & Phillips. It was clearly the firm of Ronald Featherby, Beattie's good friend and lawyer. That's why it had rung a bell. She kept the phone in her hand and pressed speed dial. Her mother answered.

'You still on for dinner tonight?' Roxy asked.

'Naturally! Don't tell me you're going to make an effort and come along?'

'Don't push it, Mum, or I'll cancel.'

'Alright darling, don't get in a tiz. We'll see you at 7.30. Sharp.'

'And Mason what's-his-name is going to be there?'

'Yes.'

'Fine. I'll see you tonight.'

'Oh and Roxanne?'

'Mmm?'

'Try not to wear black this time.'

Lorraine and Charlie Jones lived in the fashionable North Shore suburb of Lane Cove in a modestly sized house that overcompensated with bulky antique furniture and rich, patterned hues intended to suggest English aristocracy. The result was a cluttered, claustrophobic effect, which was exactly how Roxy felt whenever she came visiting. The house she had been brought up in, before her father died, was older, more spacious—rambling even—and settled on a large plot of land in the decidedly unfashionable suburb of Hornsby, much further north. Roxy wondered if her mother ever missed the old place like she did but one look at the woman gliding towards her with her pearly blonde bob and her long gold chains, suggested otherwise. Lorraine had slipped into the life of an upper middle-class gentleman's wife smoothly, never looking back at the teaching career she had given up or the old friends she never seemed to find the time for now. She took Roxy's hands in hers as though greeting a distant friend.

'I'm so glad you came, Roxanne,' she cooed, leading her through the living room towards the kitchen before adding, 'even if you did wear black.'

'It's chocolate brown, Mum.'

'Same difference.' Her eyes swept down to Roxy's flowing brown skirt, buckled at the waist with a thick leather belt, and back up to her creamy cardigan and long chained necklace. 'Charlie's delighted you're here, too. He's mixing up quite a feast.'

'Hi Charlie,' Roxy murmured to a large, well-built man wearing a frilly apron over trousers and a lemon sweater, his hands immersed in a bowl of what looked like turkey stuffing. He waved one crumbly hand towards her.

'How the hell are you, Roxy? Glad you could make it.'

'Thanks for inviting me.' Why is it, she wondered as she always did, why she felt so out of place in what was supposed to be her family home? 'I come bearing gifts.' She produced a bottle of red wine from behind her back and her mother took it from her.

'Merlot...hmmm.'

'It's a good drop, Mum, take my word for it.'

'Thanks Roxy,' Charlie called out. 'Lorraine why don't we crack open the bubbly? There's a bottle of the good stuff in the fridge.'

Roxy watched as her mother slipped the Merlot into a cupboard and retrieved the champagne. She felt her stomach tighten but kept her mouth shut. She did not want to get into a fight tonight.

'Mason is on his way,' Lorraine said and Roxy felt a pang of guilt. She did not ordinarily like using people for information but she *was* doing it in the name of dear old Beatrice. And besides, it was thrilling her mother no end, thinking she was finally making an effort to meet 'dashing' eligible bachelors.

As it turned out, Mason Gower was anything but dashing. He looked handsome enough if you liked your dates straight up—short back and side hairstyles with stiff, overly starched suits—which Roxy did not, but he had pomposity of a male peacock and the personality of a pigeon. He was an arrogant know-it-all and it delighted her immensely. Whatever guilt she was carrying, quickly disappeared. Even better, he was a big mouth and had no qualms discussing his work, his colleagues and his boss, Ronald Featherby. But it was what he had to say about Beatrice Musgrave that left Roxy reeling.

They were well into the main meal, an extravagant duck and sauteed vegetables affair with minted peas and an orange sauce, before Roxy dared to broach the subject.

'So what's your boss like?' she asked as matter-of-factly as she could muster. 'I've heard all sorts of things about that man.'

'Oh yes, Mr Phillips is quite an interesting character—'

'No, I mean Ronald Featherby, his partner.'

Mason looked up from his plate with a frown. 'Ronald Featherby? Why he's a bore. What ever could you have heard about him?'

'Maybe I got it wrong,' she said, adding, 'a bore you say? How do you mean?'

'I mean, dull as a doorknob. Plays by the rules. Never gives anything away. The whole company is terrified of him because of it.' He plunged a forkful of meat into his mouth and began chewing violently. Roxy felt a surge of disappointment. Had this dinner been for nothing? She picked at her food gloomily. She didn't know what she was expecting Mason to reveal, but she was half hoping that Featherby was the philandering type, that perhaps he and Beattie had been embroiled in an illicit affair that he didn't want revealed.

'Roxy's a very clever writer you know!' Lorraine announced and the younger woman rolled her eyes with exasperation. Her mother always did this, embellishing her abilities like a public relations consultant. She didn't really give a toss about her daughter's profession, was never very interested. That is until strangers came along. Then it was boasted about, often in laborious and embarrassing detail. Mason simply shrugged his shoulders and kept right on chewing. Charlie, too, seemed uninterested in conversation. He was too busy admiring his own cooking. Roxy had an idea.

'Actually, now that you mention it, Mum, I was just working on an autobiography with Beatrice Musgrave,' and then almost as an aside: 'Of course it's all over, now that she's dead.'

'Ah,' said Mason. 'Now there's an interesting woman.' Roxy looked across at him, her eyes narrowed with interest. 'Beatrice Musgrave was one of our clients, you know?'

'Oh really?' she feigned surprise. 'So why do you think she's particularly interesting?'

'Well, let's just say she had friends in *low* places.' He placed his fork down deliberately and leaned back in his chair to scan the group, his eyes darting between them.

'What do you mean?'

'As far as I could tell, old Mrs Musgrave had…now, how should I put it?' He stopped to consider this, plucking a bit of food from between his teeth as he did so. 'She had a few dirty little secrets I'd say.'

Roxy could barely restrain her smile. 'Go on.'

'Weeeeeell,' he produced a toothpick from somewhere and began jabbing at his teeth again. 'There was some indication that she had a past. A pretty dark past.'

'Oh you're making all of this up, you big liar!' Lorraine squealed. 'I used to see old Beattie Musgrave around the traps. Not a hair out of place. If she had any past to speak of, it was in a past life! As Queen Victoria! Everyone ready for dessert?'

Roxy could have throttled her mother. She glared at her across the table but Lorraine was already clearing away the plates and had indicated for Roxy to do so, too. Reluctantly,

Roxy picked up the empty serving bowls and deposited them in the kitchen. When she returned to the dining room, Charlie and the lawyer were discussing their share portfolios. She wanted to scream.

It was not until dessert was over and coffee had been served before Roxy had a chance to broach the subject again. With the subtlety of a sledgehammer, Lorraine and Charlie had dragged the couple into the living room, handed them a glass of dessert wine, and then simply vanished. Roxy knew exactly what they were up to and, for the first time in her life, was grateful. She seized the opportunity.

'Tell me more about Beatrice Musgrave,' she implored. 'I'm intrigued!'

'Sure, but first, you tell me, what's a beautiful woman like you still doing on the shelf?'

She swallowed hard, attempted a smile. 'Just fussy I guess.'

'Be careful you don't get left there.'

Roxy kept her smile in place, thinking: *With prats like you around, there's nowhere I'd rather be.* But she bit her tongue and tossed her hair back provocatively instead. Years of watching the likes of Maria Constantinople at work had taught her how and she needed to humor him long enough to get what she came for.

'Perhaps we can do this again some time?' he suggested. 'Outside of your parents' house?'

'Perhaps,' she lied. 'So, Mrs Musgrave?'

'Ah yes, the society queen. As I said, she had friends in low places. *Ugly* places.'

'How do you mean?'

He sipped his glass of wine slowly, stringing out the suspense. Roxy noticed that he had dripped some sauce down onto his starched cotton shirt and stifled a giggle. She suspected he would be livid when he discovered it in the mirror later that night.

'One day, about a month or so back,' Mason began, 'I was working on the People vs Avery case. Did you hear about it?'

Roxy remembered it well. Avery was a pharmaceutical company who, a few years back, had a class action law suit brought against them by thousands of women who had used their diet pills and ended up with chronic, sometimes debilitating stomach cramps. Only a few months ago, Avery had successfully beaten the suit in court without having to pay a cent or make any disclaimers. As far as Roxy knew, the diet pill was still available for sale. It had made her sick to her own stomach at the time but she simply shrugged imploring him to continue. She was not here to get into an argument.

'So I'm standing out in the lobby with the CEO of Avery. The *Chief Executive Officer*, you understand, the top dog.'

Yes, you idiot, I do know what CEO stands for.

'And this hideous woman—if you can call her that—comes hobbling in, smelling up the place like you wouldn't believe, and screaming to God almighty that she wants to see Beatrice Musgrave!'

'Goodness, who was she?'

'Well I hardly know that. She's not exactly someone I'd ever associate with.'

'Of course not. What did she say? Exactly.'

'Oh something or other about Beatrice owing her and how she'd spill the beans—"I'll ring *The Gossip Show*!" she screamed. Which is hysterical, really, because we all know the show's been off air forever.'

'How intriguing!' Roxy felt like a mother humoring her child. 'What happened then?'

'Well, I'm trying to get Mr Daniels— the CEO—out of there. It was hideously embarrassing. And then old Ronnie appears and ushers her quickly into his office.'

'Ronald Featherby?'

'The very one.'

'So any idea at all what she meant? Who she might have been?'

'No idea. She certainly smelt like a derelict but was extraordinarily well dressed. Chanel I believe.'

'I'm sorry?'

'She was wearing a Chanel jacket or some such! Bit dumpy, if you ask me, but the girls in the office were *green* with envy wondering how she could afford something like that.'

'She could have just been an eccentric rich woman.'

'Hardly! I know my derelicts, darling. I get enough of them harassing me every morning on my way to work. No she was definitely a bag lady and a mad one at that. A nasty piece of work. Probably got lucky at an op shop.'

Roxy thought for a second. 'How old was the woman?'

'She looked about a hundred and five—'

'Yes, well, living on the streets will do that to you. But could she have been much younger, given a decent scrub and a bit of make-up? Like, in her 50s or—'

'Good Lord no! Why on earth would you ask? No, no, no, this woman was definitely an old broad, gray hair, bent over, the works. As old as Beattie I'd say.' Mason shivered all over then, as though the mere memory of the woman disgusted him, then he struggled to his feet. 'Time to "make a movie" as they say.' He giggled at his own line. '*Big* case in the morning.'

Roxy nodded amiably and walked him to the door.

'So, we'll talk again. What's your number?'

'Actually Mason, let me take your number instead.'

'Oh, one of those, hey?' He didn't sound perturbed and wedged one of his business cards into her hand before slopping a wet kiss on top. Roxy pulled her hand away firmly and tried for a smile. When he had finally driven off, proudly revving his BMW in the process, Roxy felt a sigh of relief followed quickly by a prickle of excitement. Okay, so the bag lady clearly wasn't the secret daughter, that was clear. So who was she then? And why was she threatening Beatrice

Musgrave? Did she also know about the daughter, or was Beattie hiding something else? And was she the one who killed her? Roxy slipped back into the house, fetched her keys and then slipped quietly out again. It was late and she wasn't in the mood for her mother's endless questions.

8 THE FUNERAL

Beatrice Musgrave's funeral was held at the prestigious St Mary's Cathedral in the city at 9am the Tuesday morning after her death, but Roxy was not invited. It was a strictly private affair. She begrudged her exclusion. Not only would she have valued the chance to pay her last respects but, if truth be told, she was also hoping to check out the family close up, to look for signs of guilt or remorse. At least Max would be there taking photographs for the *Tele*, she told herself, he could fill her in. In the meantime, she turned her attention elsewhere. She still had the Heather Jackson interview to transcribe and write up. It would be a welcome distraction.

Just as she had done with Beattie's interviews, Roxy rewound the Jackson tape and, setting up her laptop in the dining room, began to type the full interview into a file she marked 'H files'. Many of Roxy's colleagues hired typists to transcribe their interviews but Roxy liked to do it herself. While she detested the grind—a 20-minute interview could take well over an hour to transcribe—she felt it was essential that she listen back to her interviews personally. Not only did that ensure the job was done properly but she could also note down mood changes, lengthy pauses and even the odd giggle or sigh, all things that added the real flavor to any good story. After she had transcribed the full interview, Roxy spent the rest of the day constructing it into a feature that Maria Constantinople would approve of. By sunset the article was done and she padded into the kitchen to pour herself a glass of Merlot. She then swung open the fridge and pulled out some chicken breasts, zucchini, a clump of broccoli, bok choy and carrots, and, after rinsing them, began to chop them into smaller pieces on her wooden chopping bench. She dribbled a little olive oil and a tablespoon of red curry sauce into her wok, turned on the gas and added some coconut milk. As the mixture sauteed and the rich aroma filled her small kitchen, she switched off her mind and concentrated on her cooking.

She hadn't managed to step out today, but she found cooking was almost as therapeutic, allowing her to tune out and give her brain a break. If she was ever struggling for a line or an original start to a story, it often provided one, or at the very least, gave her the sustenance to continue on.

When the sauce was thick and slowly simmering, she added some cut onion, garlic, lemon juice, fish sauce, bamboo shoots and the chicken, stirring the mixture around and then, reducing the heat, returned to her computer to read over her story. Roxy kept her own words as objective as possible, letting the artist's actions and answers speak for themselves. And she couldn't help but smile. On the surface, the piece was complimentary, meriting the woman's talent and emphasizing her early declaration that she wanted to make a difference in the world, to paint truly important people. This was then followed by an intensive description of Heather's 'magnificent celebrity-centered' works, her 'opulent' appearance—'the latest in designer couture'—and the 'magnificent, sprawling mansion' in which, it seemed, she lived all alone. On a deeper level, it was clear Heather Jackson was as far removed from her original intention as she could get. Heather had provided her own noose. The reader could decide whether to hang her.

As Roxy watched the automatic spell check whiz across her words, she wondered whether Maria would catch the irony, but was in no doubt that Heather Jackson would. And it made her pause for just a moment. For some reason it didn't seem like such a bright idea to get on Heather Jackson's bad side.

Roxy shrugged and closed the file down. She needed to sleep on it, now, so that she could give it a fresh read in the morning. It was the perfect way to catch any sloppy sentences and spot anything that needed changing. She dialed the office number for Maria Constantinople and reached her voice mail instead.

'Leave a message!' the brassy editor bellowed. Roxy waited for the beep and then said, 'Hey there, it's your favorite freelancer. The Jackson interview will be with you by Wednesday pm. Call me after that.'

She then dialed Max's number and invited him for dinner. 'I'm cooking your fave,' she teased.

'You just want the goss on the funeral.'

'Funeral? What funeral?'

'Very funny. I'll be there in ten.'

Max was wearing a sloppy pair of cords and a paint-splattered, long-sleeved T-shirt when he arrived and his hair looked like it hadn't been washed for weeks.

'Not getting much sleep these days are you?' Roxy commented as she took the bottle of Verdelho from his hands and let him in.

'What can I say? Sandra's an animal.' His face crinkled into his trademark smile and she rolled her eyes at him.

'Spare me the details, please. You want me to open this or you want to join me in a Merlot?'

'Merlot will do, thanks.'

They moved to the kitchen and, as Roxy poured him a glass, Max had a pick at the curry. 'Looks delish, Rox.'

'Naturally.' She threw in the rest of the vegies, stirred the wok a few times, then reached for a bag of jasmine rice. 'Can you fetch the cooker from the cupboard below you there? I'll put some rice on.'

As the rice bubbled away, the friends moved into the lounge room to enjoy their drinks and chat.

'So it's getting pretty serious between you and Sandy?'

'Sandra, -dra! Yeah, well, as serious as I can get, and we both know that's not saying much.'

'Well give this one a go, okay? Don't run off the second you think she's hooked.' Roxy didn't know why she was encouraging him except that she wanted the best for her good friend and if Sandra made him happy, she was happy. He stared at her for a few moments, his smile now missing, and then just shrugged.

'So you want to know about the Musgrave funeral.'

'I never said that.'

'This is me, here, Rox. I know you too well.'

She shrugged, 'Alright, alright, give me the goss. Did you bring the pix?'

'Aw, shit, I knew I'd forgotten something. They're on my computer back at the warehouse.'

She tried to hide her disappointment, and wondered for a moment if it wasn't deliberate. 'No worries. So, what was it like? Anything interesting happen?'

'Not really. But I can tell you one thing, there wasn't a lot of crying going on.'

'Not even her great mate, the lawyer, Ronald Featherby?'

'Nope, he was pretty subdued. As for the son, William, he barely changed expression all day. Serious but subdued I think they call that. Now, the grandson—'

'Fabian?'

'Yeah, something like that, he looked a bit sad but I have to say his wife was practically beaming. She's not losing any sleep over the old lady's demise.'

Roxy's ears pricked up. 'I didn't realize Fabian was married. What's she like, this daughter-in-law?'

'Scrawny in that inner-Darlinghurst kinda way. Had some tight leather number on. Looked like she was going to a dance party not a funeral. I tell you, Rox, I've photographed a few funerals in my time but this one was depressing for all the wrong reasons.'

Roxy jumped up and checked the rice, then threw two placemats on the table, some cutlery, a plate of sliced lime and the newly opened bottle of wine. She lit a candle and placed it in the middle and then returned to the kitchen to fetch the food. As Max helped himself to a hefty plateful, Roxy pondered his account of poor Beatrice's funeral.

'You're telling me that not a single soul seemed sorry to see Beattie go?'

'Well, there were a lot of old ladies I assumed she played Bridge with or something that were a little tearful. Oh and some old guy in a beat-up suit and an Akubra hat. Now he was miserable, that's for sure. But, no, as far as funerals go it was pretty tearless. Cheerful almost. I guess she was getting on in age, maybe old people's funerals aren't such a tragedy?'

'They should be if that old person supposedly killed herself.'

Squeezing some lime over her plate, Roxy couldn't help frowning. Perhaps she should have gate-crashed the funeral and given the old woman the tears she deserved.

'And tell me, any woman there in her 50s who didn't seem accounted for?'

'How do you mean?'

She swallowed a good mouthful of curry before relating her final conversation with Mrs Musgrave in which she had let slip about a daughter. He scratched his messy hair, trying to remember.

'I honestly couldn't tell you. There were a lot of people there I didn't recognize, most from charity groups I gather. Certainly there was no such person in the family section.'

'Yes but I doubt she'd be sitting with them. My guess is, if they even knew about the daughter—which they may not have—they mightn't be exactly accepting. She might even be the reason Beattie was killed.'

'Killed? Roxy you don't know that for sure.'

'Yes but—'

'But *be careful*. Murder's a big call.'

'I know, I know.' She returned to her food and ate sullenly. Max was right. What did she have to base her assumptions on? An old lady's last-minute declaration about a daughter who may, or may not, exist? The fact that she may, or may not, have been blackmailed by a strange old woman dressed like a socialite and smelling like a derelict? Or the abusive emails which, Roxy had to concede, might have absolutely nothing to do with Beatrice at all. And yet she hadn't received one since Beattie had died, and this seemed to indicate that the two were indeed related.

'You're right,' she told Max as she filled up his glass. 'I'm assuming too much and not checking the facts. I need to check the facts.'

'Look, drop by my place one day and check the pix out for yourself. Something might stand out. I'd email them to you but there's hundreds. They'd crash your hard-drive. In the meantime, lighten up!'

She did as suggested and by the time Max had departed she had determined to put the Musgrave case aside for a while, get on with her own life.

And then Oliver Horowitz called.

'I'm meeting my friend in Forensics for lunch tomorrow at the Fountain Cafe, 1 pm. Wanna drop by?'

'Damn right I do,' she replied without hesitation. 'See you then.'

9 THE JANE DOE DONS DESIGNER

The Fountain Cafe was Oliver Horowitz's favorite haunt. Nestled in the heart of Sydney's seediest suburb, Kings Cross, and next to the iconic El Alamein Fountain, it offered a lively view of neon-lit Macleay Street with its sleazy strip joints and 24-hour bars, and the hoards of ogling guys and giggling tourists who wandered through all day and all night as though on some perverse pilgrimage. Roxy wasn't particularly fond of the place which fringed her own suburb like cheap, unwashed lace, and usually walked the extra distance along the back streets to bypass it altogether. But today was unavoidable. Oliver Horowitz had a soft spot for the 'Cross. As an ex-newspaper man it once provided him with a good deal of his material, and he still enjoyed watching news in the making.

Roxy increased her speed as she maneuvered her way through, the crowds heavy despite the hour. She spotted the police station and then the spurting fountain, which served to split the area between Kings Cross and the once posh suburb of Potts Point. Of course it had gone the way of its neighbor soon enough, but several stately old brick buildings reminded anyone who cared to notice that it once had class, too many broken promises ago. Oliver was sitting on the seedier side of the fountain. Two plates of half-eaten sandwiches were in front of him but he appeared to be alone and Roxy frowned as she pulled up a plastic chair beside him.

'Relax,' he said, pushing his untouched water glass towards her. 'Kay's just powdering her nose. Be back in a minute. You been jogging?'

'Speed walking, actually.' She tried to regain her breath. 'What has she said so far?'

'Oh, well, she's breaking up with her boyfriend, which is kinda exciting because—'

'About the Musgrave case.'

'Nothing.'

Roxy's eyebrows furrowed.

'I was waiting for you. Didn't want to seem obvious.'

'Oh I'm sure she won't suspect a thing.' Roxy took a good gulp of the water and then frowned again. 'It's not even cold, tastes like chlorine.'

'I'll tell you what is cold, the friggin' service around here. Hopeless today. Where is that bloody waiter? You want something? Coffee? Oh, here you are, Kay.' He made a feeble, fat man's attempt to pull out her chair and the petite Asian woman sat down, glancing curiously across at Roxy and poking her cat's-eye spectacles back into place.

'Kay, this is my friend—'

'Hello,' Roxy interrupted. 'I'm Roxy. I was just walking past and saw poor old Olie here sitting all alone.'

'Oh,' the woman stammered, 'Really?'

'Yep.' It wasn't such an unlikely coincidence. Roxy and Oliver frequently ran into each other. His art deco apartment was on the other side of the Cross, in the terrace-lined Victoria Street that overlooked the city.

'You into walking?'

'Um, no, not really.'

'Roxy's a mad walker,' Oliver chirped, trying to do his bit.

'Mmm,' Roxy glanced at her watch. She didn't have much time for small talk. She decided to plunge right in. 'Oliver tells me you work in forensic science?'

The woman nodded yes.

'I am *intrigued* by your sort of job. I was thinking about taking it up myself, except I just don't think I'd be strong enough, you know?' She patted her stomach. 'Or smart enough. You guys must be just so cluey. Worked on any exciting cases lately?' She tried not to wince as Oliver kicked her under the table.

The woman, who was probably more accustomed to looks of abhorrence when she mentioned her profession, blushed a little, flattered. She cleared her throat. 'Oh there's always something exciting going on,' she said. 'What do you do?'

Roxy hesitated, she didn't want to scare her off.

'Rox is one of my clients, she ghostwrites autobiographies,' Oliver replied quickly. 'People's life stories, that sort of thing.'

'Yes, in fact, I just lost a big job.'

'Oh?'

'I was going to write the biography of Beatrice Musgrave. But she recently died, so…'

Mrs Musgrave's name did not bring any change in Kay's features and, instead, she seemed more interested in the menu than the conversation.

'Yes I read about that,' Oliver was saying. 'Suicide.'

'Mmm. Very shocking, quite unexpected. You didn't happen to work on that case did you, Kay?' Roxy tried to keep the eagerness out of her voice but the other woman shrugged no and turned towards the waiter who had miraculously—inconveniently—turned up to take their orders.

'I would like the iced chocolate please.'

'A latté for me,' Roxy added, feeling bitterly disappointed.

As though sensing this, Kay announced, 'But I did work on the mutilated corpse that has been in all the papers. The Jane Doe.'

Roxy cheered up enormously. 'The one-handed corpse!? Now that was fascinating. And you got to perform the autopsy?'

'Well, I assisted. But you know, she—the deceased, that is—did have both hands, it was just the fingers on the right hand that were missing.'

'Had they been cut off? Or was it a deformity she already had?'

Kay looked at her surprised. 'That's a very good question because, actually, the answer is, both.'

'Huh?' Oliver was not keeping up. The smaller woman cleared her throat and edged her spectacles back on her nose.

'It's hard to explain, but Dr Omah, my boss, he said that it looked like the hand had already undergone surgery and, judging from the scar tissue, some of the fingers had probably already been removed.'

'When? How?'

'Oh many, many years ago, probably from an accident or something.'

Roxy's lips pursed a little and nudged to one side. She wanted to get it straight.

'So her fingers weren't cut off by the murderer at all?'

'Oh yes they were cut off, well, *some* of them were freshly cut off you see? The others had been removed earlier. We concluded that at least three fingers were not there to begin with.'

'So let me get this straight. Three had been removed a long time ago, and then the last two were sliced off before she was killed?'

'Got it in one,' said Kay. 'Very strange, hey?'

They all nodded their heads and then the waiter appeared with their drinks, lazily placing them down.

'Have they identified the body?' Roxy asked when he had gone.

'Not as far as I know,' Kay replied, scooping some cream from her drink. 'And I doubt that they will.'

'Oh?'

'Well, she was clearly a derelict of some sort. Probably had no fixed address and relatives close by.'

'How did you know she was a derelict? Her clothes?'

'Oh no they were very flashy.'

'Flashy?' A thrill ran down Roxy's spine.

'Yes, good quality material, obviously quite new.'

'Really?' Oliver was showing interest now. 'Then what makes you think she was homeless?'

Kay gulped her drink down and smiled widely, proud to have them both intrigued. This was her defining moment, her chance to impress. 'Because her body was filthy and covered in ulcers and other skin conditions you find on people who have lived on the streets for too long.'

During this exchange Roxy had almost forgotten to breathe and she gulped the air in hungrily before asking, 'But she *smelt* like a derelict, right?'

'Oh Roxy,' Oliver chided, 'I reckon anyone would smell like a dero' when they've been decomposing on the banks of Rushcutters Bay for half a day.'

'No, Roxy is right,' the scientist replied. 'She had a definite derelict aroma. Decaying flesh is quite a different scent altogether.' Her eyes began fluttering then. 'This is all top-secret, you know? I get in big trouble if you tell anybody, especially you Mr Agent Man.'

'Hey, discretion is my middle name,' he replied with a suave smile.

All of a sudden, the sky gave out an almighty roar and then broke into giant sobs of rain, forcing the trio to abandon their drinks and seek shelter under the cafe's awnings.

'I'm going to make a dash for it,' Kay was saying, groping for her umbrella and acting as if she had not just made the most astounding announcement. 'Nice to meet you Roxy.'

They shook hands and then Oliver leant down and planted a quick kiss on her cheek. Kay smiled meekly and skipped off into the rain.

'I'll call you later in the week,' Oliver called after her and then, 'Thanks, Roxy! You said one question. Not a hundred.'

'Sorry, Olie, but that was fascinating what she said about the poor old lady.'

He shrugged. 'But you didn't get anything on your other old lady, Beatrice Musgrave.'

'Oh, I wouldn't say that exactly.' And to his perplexed expression she added, 'I'll explain it all later. I gotta go, too. We'll talk.'

He waved her goodbye and called out, 'Be careful!' as she dashed back past the fountain, across the cement park and the police station and on to Elizabeth Bay Road again. Oh she'd be careful, alright. She had lovely long, thin fingers and she intended to keep them. All ten of them.

Later that afternoon as lightening and thunder played havoc with the sky, Roxy read through her Heather Jackson feature and, feeling somewhat pleased with the result, emailed a copy to Maria at *Glossy*. Then she shut the computer down, brought out her journal and began to jot down her thoughts. She had embraced the computer age wholeheartedly but there were times when scribbling words on a blank page provided all the clarity in the world. She jotted down the words 'Beattie' and 'Derelict' and then drew bold black lines from each word towards a box in which she wrote 'Ronald Featherby'. From the moment Kay had described the mutilated corpse's clothes as 'flashy' she just knew it had to be the same woman Mason Gower had spotted cursing Beattie's name and threatening to 'spill the beans' in the lobby of Ronald Featherby's law firm. How many designer-clad bag ladies could there possibly be wandering the streets of Sydney?

The real question was, what was the woman's connection to Beatrice Musgrave? It seemed pretty obvious she had something over the socialite and Roxy suspected it was linked to her supposed daughter. Perhaps she was blackmailing her. That would certainly explain the fancy threads—they could have been hand-me-downs from Beattie, intended to appease her. Blackmail might also explain why the woman had been murdered. But it didn't explain the chopped fingers. And none of it, not one little iota, sounded like something Beatrice Musgrave would ever be party to. Roxy had only known Beattie a month but she couldn't see her carving off a woman's fingers and then holding her down in the murky bay. She didn't have the strength for it, let alone the character. And she couldn't see an old, faithful lawyer friend doing it for her either. Besides, Beattie was clearly intending to tell all. She'd hardly kill, or ask Featherby to kill, for a secret she was about to reveal just a few months later in her own autobiography. Roxy knew all about exclusive rights to a story, but that was too ridiculous a notion.

She drew another black line down the page and underneath it wrote the word 'police'. Had they already connected the two women? Had they, like Roxy, jumped to the seemingly improbably conclusion that Beatrice killed the homeless woman to shut her up and then, out of remorse, threw herself into the sea?

Roxy tossed her pen down impatiently. It was all so absurd. Beatrice Musgrave was not a murderer. She glanced back at the page. *Ronald Featherby*. She picked up her pen and circled his name over and over and over. He might not be a murderer, either. But he might know someone who is. Perhaps he had set the whole thing up, as a favor to an old client? She needed to see him and soon. But first, there was the matter of the unfinished biography.

10 THE SON

It did not take long to track William Musgrave down. It was now after 8pm on Wednesday night but, with Beattie's description of him as a 'mad workaholic' in mind, Roxy had a feeling she knew just where he'd be, even so soon after his own mother's funeral. Donning a warm overcoat, Roxy headed out into the chilly night, dashing to her car and turning the heat up a little as she drove along Botany Road to the grimy industrial suburb of Mascot where the head office of Musgrave Incorporated was located. She parked in the empty car park and strode up to the main entrance, almost knocking the lone security guard to the floor as she buzzed on the intercom.

'Office hours are nine to five,' he stammered, holding the glass door ajar, unwilling to let her in.

'Yes, I'm aware of that. I need to see William Musgrave. I believe he's here now?'

'Well, yes, but *Mr Musgrave*? You can't disturb Mr Musgrave.'

'It will just take a minute. If you could tell him that Roxy Parker wants to see him, explain that I'm an associate of his mother's.'

Of course she could have called by in the morning, or better yet, made an appointment, but Roxy knew she could only get face to face with someone as busy as William Musgrave through drastic measures, like daring to interrupt him out of hours. And it worked. The guard was so overawed by Roxy's audacity, he let her in and, leading the way past the polished lobby to the information desk beside the elevators, picked up the phone.

Pulling her beanie off and loosening the scarf around her neck, Roxy strained to hear what he was saying, but it didn't really matter. She had a hunch William Musgrave would soon be down. He may have given his mum very little of his time, but Roxy suspected William still kept one eye on her affairs, and would certainly have known something about the autobiography. You don't run a family corporation so well by letting things like that slip. The guard's sudden look of relief confirmed her thoughts. Within moments he was leading her to a cream suede sofa along one wall.

'Please take a seat, Miss, Mr Musgrave will be with you shortly.'

Roxy thanked him and did as instructed, dropping her bag to the floor. The lobby was large and sterile with the information desk on one side and a shiny metallic sculpture on the other. A large gold and black billboard listed the various departments and senior staff, noting which floor they could be located on, and Roxy considered jumping up for a closer look. She was keen to see what floor Beattie's grandson Fabian worked. But before she had a chance, the elevator bell let out a loud 'bing!' and William Musgrave stepped out.

Beattie's only son was the antithesis of his father. He was rake thin, with long, gangly limbs and pale, almost sallow skin, the kind you get when you spend too much time indoors, doing the books. By contrast, Terence had been a tanned, almost portly fellow who looked like he knew exactly how to have fun.

Roxy jumped to her feet and extended one arm. 'I'm Roxy Parker,' she said, taking his limp hand in her own. She noted a barely constrained frown on his face. 'I was a friend of your mother's and, first of all, please let me pass on my sincerest condolences. She was a good woman.'

'Thank you, Miss Parker. I believe you were helping her with the autobiography?'

'That's right.'

He indicated for her to take a seat and then asked, 'What can I do for you?'

'Well forgive me for the timing, so soon after the funeral, but it's about the book—'

'The autobiography? What about it?'

'Well, we hadn't finished and as you're her next of kin, I wanted—'

'Oh, I see,' he said, cutting her off and producing a business card from his pocket. 'Call my office in the morning and speak to my personal assistant Anabell Lorrier. She'll see about squaring up outstanding payment.'

'I'm not talking about payment, Mr Musgrave, although that would be good, thank you. The reason I'm here is to seek your permission to continue writing it. After all, it was your mother's final wish to have her life story published.'

William let out a little, mocking laugh then, his thin nose crinkling as though he'd just heard something particularly distasteful. 'Yes, well I really don't know that the fading memories of my dear old mother are really worth sharing with the entire world. After all, it's not like she had anything particularly titillating to say, right?'

Roxy stared at the businessman blankly. Was he fishing for information, she wondered? In any case, if William Musgrave knew about his secret sister he was not owning up to it and she wasn't about to break it to him, at least not until she had proof.

'Besides,' he continued, 'I thought you'd only just started.'

'We were a third of the way through, but I could quite easily continue the research on my own.'

'What on earth for?'

'To cherish her memory, for starters.' She didn't try to hide the disdain in her voice but he seemed unperturbed.

'No, no,' he was saying in that conclusive way businessmen have of finishing things up and shutting you down. 'But thank you anyway, Miss Parker. As I say, call Anna tomorrow and you will have your money. We'll cover all your expenses, don't worry about that.'

Roxy was infuriated. That's what William Musgrave thought this was all about, a last pitch effort to profit from his mother. It rattled her nerves but she let him steer her through the shiny lobby, past the guard now standing to attention like he was at Buckingham Palace, and out the exit into the damp outdoors.

'Would you like the tapes back, then?' she asked, testing him and, once again, he passed with flying colors.

'No, no I don't think that's necessary. Just dispose of them, that would be fine.' Roxy smiled to herself. If William had killed his own mother to shut her up, or at the very least sent Roxy the threatening messages, he'd hardly be so relaxed about the interviews. Surely he'd want to get hold of their conversations to determine exactly what Roxy knew.

'Perhaps,' Roxy continued, 'I could give them to Mrs Musgrave's lawyer?'

'Why would you want to do that?'

'Well it seems foolish to trash them in the light of her, um, suicide. They may hold the key to it all. It just seems the right thing to do.'

He was growing quickly impatient and, glancing at his thick, gold Rolex watch, nodded his head and said, 'Fine. Good idea. As I say, speak with Anabell in the morning and she'll give you the details for a Ronald Featherby.'

Roxy thanked him and, as she watched him stride quickly inside the building, it occurred to her that William Musgrave was simply not very interested in his dead mother. In fact, he'd probably not given her a second thought since they dragged her lifeless body from the shores of Balmoral Beach five days ago. Beattie's son was not only harmless, Roxy concluded as she started up her VW Golf, he was heartless, too.

The following morning, Roxy picked up the phone and dialed the number William Musgrave had given her.

'Good morning, Musgrave Incorporated, Anabell speaking.'

'Hello Anabell, Roxy Parker's my name, William—'

'Oh yes Miss Parker,' she said, cutting her short, 'Mr Musgrave told me to expect your call. Can you hold?'

Roxy indicated that she could and waited just three seconds before the assistant returned, providing her with the account department's details for invoicing, and a phone number for Beattie's lawyer, Ronald Featherby.

'Was there anything else I could help you with?' Her voice was polite but there was a slight edge, too, and Roxy suspected the efficient PA was not exactly happy about Roxy's unsolicited visit the evening before. It undermined her authority. Roxy had had plenty of experience with executive assistants, her step-dad Charlie had one of his own. Her name was Jenny Golden but they called her 'the pit bull' and she more than lived up to her name, refusing anyone, including Roxy and her mother, access to her boss until they had gone through her. It gave her a sense of purpose.

'Well, actually there was one other thing,' Roxy said cheerfully.

'Yes?'

'I was hoping to get in touch with Fabian Musgrave. Can you put me through to him?'

There was a brief pause before she replied, 'Fabian does not work with the firm anymore.'

'Oh, then if you could give me his number that'd be great.'

'We are not in the habit of handing out personal numbers, you understand?'

'Oh, of course. Well perhaps, if you do happen to see him, you could pass on my details? Let him know I was hoping to have a chat. My number here is—'

'I have your details, thank you Miss Parker. Good day.'

Roxy smiled as the line went dead. Anabell Lorrier had obviously been to business school with 'the pit bull'.

11 THE LAWYER

Ronald Featherby was the antithesis of his young protégé, Mason Gower, and this disheartened the ghostwriter who suspected from their first handshake that afternoon that he would not be of much assistance at all. Featherby was quiet and assured in a manner only achieved from years of legal wrangling. And he chose his words carefully, deliberately. Well into his 60s, he was semi-bald with gold spectacles on his nose and a suit that was stylish without being showy. His handshake was firm and friendly.

'I'm so glad to meet you,' he told Roxy, after offering her a seat and sending his assistant for coffee. Ronald had been most obliging on the phone and asked Roxy to come straight in with the tapes. She thought his urgency odd, but did as he asked and, upon her arrival was whisked straight into his stately office. 'Beatrice told me quite a bit about you,' Ronald was saying. 'She was very fond of you.'

'Well, thank you Mr Featherby, I'm flattered.'

'No need to be. I'm sure her faith was not misplaced.'

Roxy wondered if there was a subtle threat in there somewhere. Or was she just being neurotic? 'Beatrice also spoke highly of you,' she said. 'She called you her "saving grace".'

He leant back in his large leather chair and placed one hand under his chin, as though contemplating, but did not acknowledge the compliment.

'Not that anything could save her in the end,' she continued, undeterred. 'Poor Beatrice. I was so shocked to hear of her…death.'

'I believe you have some tapes for me?'

'Yes.' She fetched them from her bag and placed them in front of him on the desk noting as she did so that it was completely clear of paper, just host to a small laptop, two telephones and several photo frames, which were facing his way. She wondered if he turned them round to face clients when he wanted to give a friendly impression. The assistant appeared with an espresso coffee, which he placed before her, and in his other hand he produced a small silver mug of milk and a silver sugar bowl. He placed them beside the coffee and promptly departed.

'Thank you!' Roxy called behind her and then turned back to the lawyer. 'You're not joining me?'

'No, but please enjoy.' He took up the tapes and scrutinized them. 'Are these the only copy in existence?'

'Yes.' She was lying, of course. Experience had taught her to duplicate everything, no matter how meaningless they appeared to be. The lawyer didn't need to know this. He studied each tape carefully and then placed them in a drawer to his right before turning his gaze back upon her.

Ronald Featherby was clearly one of those people who had a tendency to allow long gaps in the conversation, knowing only too well that the likes of Roxy Parker would feel compelled to plug the silence with small talk. This time, however, she bit her tongue and simply sipped her coffee, staring straight back at him. *Two can play this game, she thought, and if you're not giving anything away, neither am I.*

'Are there any outstanding invoices you need me to take care of?' he said at last.

'No, thank you, Ronald. William is looking after that.'

'Fine.' There was a sense of finality in his voice, although his face retained its warmth and, leaning back in his chair casually, he looked like he had all day. She decided it was time to show her hand.

'Ronald, I wanted to ask you a question regarding your client.'

'Go ahead.'

'According to Beattie you were one of her dearest friends and, being her lawyer you'd be in the best, most objective, position to answer this.'

'Yes?'

'It was perfectly clear to me that she wanted her story told. She came to me to write it. She had organized another interview with me just before she died. I understand that death has prematurely silenced her, but I wonder whether I should…whether *we* should fulfill that wish posthumously.'

'What exactly do you mean?'

'I mean finishing the book. Researching it myself. Getting her life story told.'

'I see.' He rocked a little on his chair as though giving her suggestion considered thought. After several seconds he sat upright and, his hands interlocked on the desk before him, said softly, 'I understand your concerns, Ms Parker, and I appreciate them. I'm sure dear Beatrice would, too. But you seem to be forgetting one rather important detail.'

'Oh?'

'Beatrice Musgrave—may she rest in peace—*chose* to end her life. I don't believe there can be any clearer statement that, in fact, she did not want to finish the book.'

'Yes, but do we really know it was suicide?'

He did not flinch. 'That's the official report. I have no reason to question the police, the forensic scientists, the coroner. Perhaps you do?'

'No, not really, it's just a hunch.'

'On what evidence is your, er, hunch, based?'

Roxy slammed her lips shut. She debated whether to tell him about the daughter Beattie had mentioned. Roxy had carried the burden of Beattie's secret around since her death and was desperate to share it with someone who might be able to shed some light on the truth. She wanted so much to confide in this polite old man with the gray hair and the Grandpa specs. But, again, her instincts begged for silence. So she shrugged her shoulders and said, 'No evidence. Just a hunch.'

'I see. Look, Ms Parker, I do appreciate your concern but there is no scoop here.' He smiled warmly enough but there was a slight cynicism to his tone. 'Beatrice's beloved husband died five years ago to the week that she died. Did you know that?'

'No, I didn't.'

'She may not have told you, but she never really recovered from the loss. I think, if anything, her final wish was peace, and silence.'

Roxy did not believe him for one moment. In the interviews, Beattie had made it perfectly clear that her marriage was a loveless one. Why, then, would her husband's death destroy her? No, she knew he was throwing out red herrings and was now thankful she had stayed silent. The lawyer was hiding something and she guessed it had everything to do with the well-dressed derelict and Beattie's secret daughter.

'You're a journalist, too, I believe?' he said.

'Yes I am.'

'I'd like to make one thing crystal clear.' His tone had turned icily formal. *No more Grandpa Ronald, she thought.* 'The information that you retrieved from Beatrice Musgrave was given in good faith and for the sole purpose of her authorized biography. Now that we have *agreed* that the biography is to be aborted, and I believe her next of kin, William Musgrave has also stipulated this, I expect the information to be concealed and any notes that you have made destroyed immediately. In other words,' and he paused then, as though for effect, 'it would be morally and ethically reprehensible to use any of the information for your own purposes.'

'I see.' She understood him perfectly. He was warning her to shut up. To give the story away. To let sleeping dogs lie. He clearly didn't know who he was dealing with. In fact, Beatrice Musgrave had signed no confidentiality or exclusivity agreement nor could there be a copyright on her life story. 'I won't be using any of the information Beatrice provided to me in our interviews,' she said calmly, wondering if that was a glimmer of relief that she spotted flickering across his face. 'But I can't promise you I won't be writing about Mrs Musgrave somewhere down the track.'

His eyes turned stony then and she quickly added. 'I'm not out to hurt anyone Mr Featherby, least of all Beatrice, but I have reason to believe there is more to her death than a case of lovesick suicide, and if my hunch is correct, it is the right of the public to know that. Quite frankly I find it abhorrent that not one of Beattie's relatives or close friends has questioned this. That you're all just willing, hell you're *eager* to accept that someone as full of life and as dignified as Beattie would throw herself, willy-nilly, over a bloody balcony! It's ludicrous, and about as likely as you becoming a hip-hop star!' She took a deep breath, tried to calm down her tone while the old lawyer simply glared at her from the other side of the desk. 'Now, your power and standing in society may help you to quash the truth, but I'm a journalist, Ronald and I smell a rat.'

He paused, took a deep breath of his own, then said very softly, very sweetly, 'If there is a rat, Miss Parker, it might end up biting you back.'

'Is that a threat?'

'Oh no my dear, just a warning from one friend of Beatrice Musgrave's to another. I know it's hard for you to understand this now, but I am acting solely in my dear friend's interests. Not mine. You need to take a good, hard look at your own motives and decide in whose interests you are working.'

Roxy shook her head and stood up. 'Thank you for your time, Mr Featherby. It has been most…enlightening.'

She left the office as calmly as she could but Ronald Featherby's warning echoed loudly in her ears and by the time she reached the elevator, Roxy was shaking from head to toe. The truth was, she wasn't exactly sure why she was pursuing the woman's death so passionately. Why couldn't she just let it go and get on with her carefree existence? Deep down she believed it had more to do with a sense of righteousness—of finishing the job Beattie had hired her to do—than the newspaper scoop he had accused her of seeking.

But was it worth the headache?

Roxy massaged some rich moisturizing cream into her black locks and then swept them up into a warm bath towel. Fastening her bathrobe tight around her waist, she stared hard at her reflection in the mirror. Jet black hair, porcelain white skin, glossy green eyes. It was a striking combination and she was looking okay for 30, she knew that. Few wrinkles remained when her smile dissipated, and she credited good sun-sense and, she had to concede, excellent genes. Her mother was also relatively blemish-free for her age. Still, Roxy wasn't about to rely on that—she hadn't been able to rely on her mother in years—and so she picked up some nourishing night cream and applied a little around her eyes, mouth and forehead. Just in case. Then she padded out into the living room, pushed open one window slightly to allow a cool breeze to trickle through and pressed 'play' on her stereo. As Nina Simone belted out a sorrowful tune, she made herself a herbal tea and then collapsed onto her sofa to think.

Now that she had calmed down, she had to concede that however odious Ronald Featherby appeared, he was most likely just protecting his client posthumously. It was clear from Mason's banter at her mother's dinner party that Featherby knew all about the derelict and her threats against Beattie. In turn, he probably knew about Beattie's little secret. And now that both women were dead he probably wanted the truth to die with them. The big question was, how much, if anything did he have to do with one or both of their murders?

Roxy stretched her legs out before her and considered the phone message she had received from Maria Constantinople while she was out. In her trademark gruff way she had said simply: *'Got the piece, it's good stuff. Didn't like her much, did ya?'*

Roxy cringed. She had hoped her disdain was not so obvious. Heather Jackson did not seem like the sort of person you'd want to make an enemy of.

12 THE GRANDSON

While combing her newly washed hair through, Roxy's doorbell buzzed. 'Who is it?' she said into the intercom.

'Fabian Musgrave,' came a lazy drawl and the writer blinked back her surprise. It was Beattie's grandson.

'I'll just be a second!'

With the lawyer's subtle threat clear on her mind, Roxy's nerves began to jangle and, trying to remain calm, she slowly made her way to street level. This time the fuzzy glass entrance door revealed a slim figure leaning to one side. She swung it open to find that Fabian Musgrave was not so much slim as painfully skinny with a greasy mop of blond hair and the same high cheekbones as his grandmother. In his early 20s, he wore black skinny jeans with a ripped white T-shirt and a dark jacket over it. The jacket looked a little old, ratty even and he appeared more like a down-and-out rock star than the heir to a vast fortune. His face was unshaven and his biker boots were old and scuffed. Only his voice gave him away, it was well-spoken in the same Private-school-boy way as his father's. He thrust one hand out to shake hers.

'You're not what I was expecting,' he said, giving her the once-over, then added, 'Can I come in for a minute.' It wasn't a question and he was already halfway through the door.

'Sure, help yourself,' Roxy replied. 'I'm on the fourth floor. You up for the walk?'

'I think I can manage it.'

Once inside Roxy's apartment, Fabian immediately took a seat, choosing the largest sofa chair and almost falling into it. Her nerves relaxed considerably. This guy didn't look strong enough to swat a fly.

'Can I get you something? A coffee, tea? Orange juice perhaps?'

'Got Scotch? On the rocks, thanks.'

Roxy glanced at the clock, it was not yet 4pm. She found an old bottle of whisky in the back of a kitchen cupboard, made him a drink and sat down, facing him across her lounge room. He lit a cigarette and dragged on it between sips and she noted that he didn't bother asking her permission. She got up, opened a window and fetched him a saucer for his ash.

'Dad's secretary said you were looking for me,' he said eventually.

'Yes I was, but I didn't mean for you to come all the way over—'

'Well I'm here now. What's up?'

'Nothing really. I just wanted to pass on my regrets.'

'Oh.' He sounded disappointed.

'Yes, your grandmother was a great woman and, as you probably know I was writing her biography.'

'Yes I did know.' His sudden smile looked strained. He drained his whisky in one gulp. 'Speaking of which, what did old Bet' have to say?'

'She said you were charming, always popping in, paying your respects.'

'I mean about life in general.'

'I'm sorry?'

He got to his feet and walked towards the window where he took long drags on his cigarette, staring out at nothing in particular. 'I mean, how was the story going? Did she say anything profound, something I can take away with me now that she's… you know?'

Roxy was not clear what Fabian was driving at but had a feeling it had something to do with the daughter. She wondered if he knew. 'Not really,' she said instead. 'We didn't get very far, you understand, before she was…well, before she died.'

'Nothing too exciting then?'

'Nothing you wouldn't already know.' Roxy eyed him from her sofa. What was his game? 'Perhaps if you're so interested in her story,' she said casually, 'you could give her lawyer a call, he has the original tapes of the interview.'

'Yes, I know.' He returned to the sofa and ran one hand through his scraggly hair with what seemed like exasperation. 'Why did you have to give them to him? He's not even family, man.'

'Your dad okay'ed the move. Surely he'll let you have a copy?'

Fabian sat upright. 'Look, here's the thing. She probably told you I was against the book?'

Roxy remained quiet, waiting for him to continue.

'It's just that, well, it's about all of us, you see. It's all very well for old Beattie to bare her soul in her autumn years, but it's the rest of us that pay. That is, if she did have anything, you know, *interesting* to reveal?' He was probing again and she just shrugged back. 'So I just want to know if there's anything she said that might, um, shall we say, affect the rest of us?'

Roxy leant back in her chair as casually as she could. 'Fabian, apart from how extravagant the wedding reception was, your Grandmother never revealed anything very interesting at all during our taped interviews.' Strictly speaking that was not a lie, but the young man did not look convinced. 'Honestly, it was just standard stuff about her childhood. Why? What could she possibly be hiding?'

He considered that for a few seconds and then stamped out his cigarette and lit another. 'As I say it's my life, too, I'd just like to know what's out there.'

'Well, so far, nothing. Your grandmother's death put a stop to the book, remember?' She scanned his face for signs of remorse but it was more like relief that flooded his eyes. He stood up, the cigarette hanging in a kind of James Dean way from his mouth and she wondered how long he'd practiced that.

He shook her hand again, then with a puff of smoke he was out the door and had disappeared back down the stairwell without so much as a thank you. Roxy locked the door behind him just as her smartphone beeped loudly. She had a text message. She dashed into the sunroom and scooped it up, tapping at the numbers until her heart skipped a beat. It was another threatening message:

'Warning!!! We won't give you another chance. Drop the story or you die.'

She stared at the screen and shook her head furiously. Roxy had honestly believed the threats would stop now that Beatrice was dead. Had she been on the wrong track all along? And if so, what story were they referring to? In any case, one thing was perfectly clear. There was no way Fabian Musgrave could have sent it.

'Of course Fabian could have sent the message,' Max chided as he handed Roxy her glass of Merlot and pulled his own beer, something tall and foreign, up close.

'How?' she asked incredulously.

Once again, the good friends were wedged at their usual spot at the far end of the bar in Pico's.

'He could have typed the message into his mobile phone before he got there and then just clicked send the second you closed the door on him. It did come after he left, right?'

She thought about this for a moment. 'Yes, but only just.'

'Or he could have got someone to send it for him while he was conveniently hanging at your house. Gets him right off the hook.'

'So he gave himself an alibi.'

'Yep. That is, if he did send it. You still don't know that.'

Roxy gulped her wine and shook her head. 'But what's the point? Beatrice is already dead. Why threaten me now?'

'Dunno, maybe he's just stupid.'

'Or maybe he—or any of them, his dad, the lawyer—is worried I still might write the piece. It could be a warning to let sleeping dogs lie.' She considered that for a moment. All three men knew she was still keen to get the story told.

'Yeah that's possible. So you're determined to believe Beatrice Musgrave was murdered?'

'I just *know* she was. Her lawyer practically threatened me to butt out today and I have a feeling Beatrice was somehow connected to the Jane Doe found in Rushcutters Bay last week. It could be the same woman who was threatening her at Featherby's office. How many Chanel-dressed bag ladies can there be? Argh, it's all so exasperating! In any case, if I could just work out the identity of the people who've been emailing and texting me, I might get a few answers.'

'People?'

'Yes, well the third message used the term "we".'

'You should check the return number.'

'I did. Zip.'

'Jesus, it's quite a tangled web you've woven yourself into here, Parker!'

'Tell me about it. You hungry? Let's eat.'

Roxy signaled the waiter for a bar menu and, while she scanned it quickly, Max reordered drinks.

'I'm gonna go the Nachos,' she told the waiter.

'And a steak sandwich for me,' he said. 'So, Rox, when are you going to tell me about your hot date?'

'Nothing to tell. How's your new woman?'

'Oh no you don't!'

'What?'

'You always do this.'

'What?'

'You change the subject. For a woman who spends her life trying to get straight answers out of people, you sure do avoid giving them yourself.'

Roxy played with her drink for a minute and then rolled her eyes resignedly. 'There was no hot date, Max. It was just that lawyer guy my mother wanted me to meet.' His jaw dropped and she quickly added, 'It's not what you think. I thought he could help me with the Musgrave case, he works for Beattie's lawyer.'

'Oh that's real decent of you.' He ran a hand through his hair, shaking his head at her.

'Well I'm being honest.'

'You're being manipulative. And you accuse me of being heartless.'

'Look, it was a harmless dinner.'

'Yeah, under false pretenses. The poor guy gets all excited, thinks he's got a chance, and actually he's just being used for journalistic purposes.'

'He's a lawyer, Max, hardly a lamb to slaughter.'

The food arrived then and they ate in stony silence for several minutes. Max ordered himself another drink.

'You're drinking a lot lately, you know.'

'When did you become my keeper?'

'Just mentioning it.'

They fell silent again and then Max pushed his plate towards her. 'Want some chips?' It was his way of calling a truce and she scooped a few up, trying for a smile. But she was feeling a little forlorn. These weekly drinks were fast losing their sense of fun. They seemed to be arguing all the time, constantly picking at each other, just like she imagined married couples did. She tried changing the subject, she was good at that.

'Did you bring the funeral photos?'

'Some of them. I downloaded the rest. They're on my camera in my bag. I'll get it in a minute.'

'Thanks, Max, I appreciate it.' But there was something in his sad brown eyes that suggested he did not believe her.

The next morning, Roxy awoke with a vicious hangover. She'd downed one too many Merlots the evening before in an attempt to keep up with her drinking buddy and because she hoped it would lighten the mood. She had also resisted, with considerable effort, the temptation to ask for his camera straight away, to scan the pix he took at Beattie's funeral. The very subject seemed to send his mood southward and so she had decided to wait for another time, when he didn't have alcohol fuelling his emotions. But, despite her efforts, the evening had remained strained and she wondered, for the first time in a year, whether they ought to catch up the following week. It depressed her enormously but she charged into a steaming shower and tried not to think about it. It was her way.

As the water pumped down upon her, Roxy turned her attention to last night's text message. She could not be sure who had sent it (again, the return number came up as unlisted) but, even worse, she still could not be sure *which story* they were referring to. That was the most exasperating part, they could be referring to some other story, not the Musgrave one. The only other option was the Heather Jackson interview. It didn't seem likely but Roxy had to maintain an open mind. Perhaps someone had it in for the yuppie artist? A rival painter envious of her publicity, perhaps? It seemed like a stretch but she had better look into it, just in case.

Once she was dried and changed, Roxy pulled up Heather's file and began to re-read the interview transcript, searching for clues. Unfortunately, not one suspicious name came to light and certainly none that correlated with the initials 'AIL' from the Hotmail address. She clicked the file closed and then fetched the folder that Maria Constantinople had given her. It was more promising.

Amongst the snippets on Heather's nightclub antics were two stories about a past lover called Rocco. He was a little-known art model, the image of a Greek Adonis and had been Heather's lover for just on a year. Their split was supposedly acrimonious and Roxy made a note of his name. Perhaps he was still bearing a grudge? Another lover was mentioned, a rock star called Zuban Z. *(what was it with these names?)* but he had gone on to marry a soap actress. Roxy doubted he'd be bothered with the artist now. But she noted his name, too.

Finally, of course, there was the disgruntled maid Loghlen had mentioned. According to him, she had threatened to write a 'tell all' about the artist and then simply disappeared into thin air along with her book. Roxy wondered if Loghlen could recall her name and decided to pay him a visit. Besides, she could do with some fresh air and something greasy to take care of her hangover.

Lockies was bursting with patrons when Roxy pulled up and, seeing how busy Loghlen was, opted for a back table and some lunch first. She would try to speak to him when things settled down. But it was a good hour before the Friday lunch crowd dispersed and Lockie found a few minutes to dedicate to his friend.

'Sorry 'bout that,' he said, pulling up a chair beside her. 'The salami focaccia okay was it?'

'It hit the spot, actually. Crazy today, huh?'

'Friday's always a bi' mad. You get the umbrella back to wacko Jacko okay?'

'Heather Jackson? Yeah, and here's your black one back.' She retrieved an umbrella from her bag and handed it to him. 'Now, I've got some more questions to ask you.'

'Ever the journo. Wha' is it?'

'Remember you were telling me about the maid who threatened to write a book about Heather?'

'Aye, that's right, the one who disappeared. Wha' about her?'

'Can you recall her name or any more details about her?'

He stroked his chunky orange sideburns slowly, deep in thought. A sudden swarm of new patrons entered the cafe and he looked around anxiously.

'You'd better get back to it, Lockie, but if you do recall the name, please give me a buzz. You've got my number, right?'

'Sure do. No probs. I'll talk to you later.' He dashed off to see to his customers and Roxy paid up and returned home.

At her mailbox she stopped, tapped it and then opened it up to reveal a variety of bills and some junk mail. There was also a letter from a childhood friend who was now living overseas. They hadn't seen each other in years but were faithful correspondents. And that's when it hit her. She bolted up the stairs, let herself into her apartment and headed straight for the Jackson folder, which was still spread out on her desk. Flipping through each page, she quickly scanned the interviews and studied Heather's biographies in detail. She wondered why she had not noticed it before. *Heather Jackson had no past.* At least not one anyone had written about. And that was odd. Even Heather's very first interview, with the *Art Gazette*, offered not a shred of information about her family, her birthplace, her life before her infamy. And it seemed no journalist since had managed to find out. Or perhaps, like Roxy, they hadn't thought to ask, assuming foolishly, that it was all old news by now.

Roxy turned to her computer and clicked on the icon for the World Wide Web. Once the Google search engine appeared on her screen, she typed in the words 'Heather&Jackson&artist' and then clicked, 'Find'. Her screen went blank and then a few seconds later alerted her that there were multiple entries for that name. She scrolled down the list to the one that read 'Official Home page' and opened it. It started with a reproduction of one of Heather's latest works, an abstract portrait of a well-known Australian actor, followed by a list of exhibition dates and five further categories to explore. Roxy clicked the 'Bio' box. A good second later, Heather's face appeared in multicolor and clearly airbrushed on screen. She was smiling but the usual coldness in her eyes was not lost in the translation.

Roxy scrolled down the page to the copy below and scanned through it. All Heather's basic statistics were listed, from her height to her weight *(yeah sure you're just a size 8, Roxy sniggered)* to the color of her eyes. It also included details of her numerous awards and the various international cities in which she had exhibited. But there was not a thing about her real self, outside of the art world. And certainly nothing pre-*Art Gazette*. She clicked on the 'back' button twice, returning to the list of search options. She scrolled down them again, this time clicking on a home page called 'Heather's Horror: the unofficial fan club site'. It boasted the 'world's ugliest pictures of the world's most abstract artist' and was followed by a stream of unflattering shots of Heather getting out of cars or sneering at paparazzi. It also included less than glamorous reviews of her work and her persona, but, again, it was all post-*Gazette*. Heather's two most disgruntled ex-boyfriends were mentioned in the copy numerous times, as well as several more, but nothing about a maid, a tell-all book or anything of the kind. And not one word about her childhood.

Roxy was about to log off when she noticed another site dubbed, 'Heather's Home: Her Secret Haven'. It was a reproduction of a trashy magazine article that had run some years back about the artist's 'brand-new McMansion'. *'Riddled with hidden tunnels, mysterious doorways and secret rooms!'* screamed the main headline, and the copy proceeded to quote 'inside sources' and 'close friends of the reclusive artist' who, in their anonymity, divulged all sorts of juicy details about her sprawling abode. Apart from the rumored hidden rooms, the sources said that Heather ran her home like a fortress. Much of the property was out of bounds, even to her staff, and one wing, the story claimed, had never been seen by anyone but Heather. Roxy clicked off. Scandal rags like that one gave her profession a bad name and she was not about to give them any more attention than they deserved.

There was one person who would surely have information on Heather Jackson's past, Roxy decided: her manager, Jamie Owen. She would call him up and demand a comprehensive biography. She glanced around her desk for the blue slip of paper on which Heather had scribbled her manager's details and, locating it, was about to call the number when she noticed the handwriting on the back again: *'Miss Roxanne Parker'*.

This time a bell began clanging loudly in her head.

She raced to her old steel filing cabinet and searched for a folder labeled 'Invoices'. Flipping through them, she located one for Beatrice Musgrave and pulled it out along with a copy of a check Beattie had made out to her in lieu of their first two sessions together. She compared it to the blue slip of paper and a shiver ran down her back.

The writing was identical.

Roxy began rustling through her files for more examples of Beattie's handwriting. In every instance, the older woman had written the name 'Miss Roxanne Parker', just as her name appeared on Heather's blue slip of paper, and in exactly the same scribe. Roxy had assumed Maria Constantinople had written it down, now she knew better. Had Beatrice and Heather known each other? She put a call through to *Glossy* magazine.

'Lookin' for more work?' Maria asked, cutting to the chase.

'No, Maria, I'm ringing about Heather Jackson.'

'I got the copy—'

'Good. Now tell me how you got the interview in the first place.'

There was a slight pause. 'What's the problem, Rox?'

'It's a simple question, Maria. How did you get the interview with Heather Jackson? And I want the real version this time.'

There was another pause, this time longer, and eventually Maria replied, 'Hang on a sec', I'll close the door.' A minute later she was back. 'What have you heard?'

'Maria!'

'Okay, okay, don't freakin' spit chips. She rang out of the blue last week offering us the exclusive. Said she needed it done ASAP.'

'Why? What was the hurry?'

'No idea, love, but I wasn't looking a gift horse in the mouth. We've been trying to get her for a decade. She suddenly wants a bit of publicity who am I to question her?'

You're an editor who should have been more inquisitive, she wanted to say. Instead she asked, 'So what happened next?'

'I said I'd get a reporter over there within the hour.'

'Is that when you called me?'

Her tone was suddenly defensive. 'Er, well, no, to be frank, I was gonna get Jack to do it.'

'I suspected as much.'

'Now hang on a minute, Jack's a bloody expert when it comes to the art world. He knows his shit, Roxy, which you don't. Even you admitted that.'

'I'm not arguing there. So why *didn't* you send Jack?'

'Because she didn't fuckin' want Jack. She asked for you!'

Roxy caught her breath. 'And why on earth would she do that? I didn't even know the woman.'

'Search me! I was flabbergasted, myself. No offense, darl' but you're hardly Lois Lane.'

'So she didn't tell you where she got my name from?'

'Nuh-uh. Just said, "I want that Roxy Parker woman." I guess she saw you listed as one of my contributors, or maybe she liked something else you'd written for me?'

'Did she call me, "Roxy" or—'

'Oh, no, you're right. She said "Miss Parker" if I recall rightly. I had to think for a minute who she was talking about. Then she said, "Miss Roxanne Parker"—I remember because I haven't heard your full name used in yonks. Made you sound very sophisticated. I might start calling you that, myself!' And she let out a teasing chuckle then, trying to lighten up the conversation. Roxy was not buying it.

'Right, now tell me about L. Johnson.'

There was a brief pause on the other end before Maria hurriedly said, 'Look, Roxy, hang on a minute.' She dropped the phone and it was some minutes before she returned.

'Morons, I work with a pack of morons,' she wailed. 'Now, where were we?'

'You were going to tell me about an L. Johnson.'

'No I wasn't. Never heard of him. Look, Roxy, what is this all about?'

Roxy sighed. 'If I knew, Maria, I'd hardly be telling you.'

'Geez, thanks. Okay, well I really gotta go, you know how it is.'

'Sure, Maria. Just one other thing. Has Heather insisted on signing off on my story?'

'What do you reckon?'

'Have you sent it to her? Has she seen it yet?'

'No it's still with the subs, why? Want to lighten your tone? Pretend you actually like the woman?'

'Not going to happen, Maria. What you see is what she gave me, I didn't have to elaborate a bit. She's a dark horse that one. But listen, could you do me a favor? I think you owe me one.'

'Shoot.'

'Can you hold off sending it to her until I call you back? I need to get some more info out of her agent first, and he may not be so obliging if he knows the story is already out of my hands.'

There was another one of those pauses. 'What are you playing at, Roxy? What the fuck is going on?'

'Probably nothing but just hold off, please, until I give the okay?'

'Fine, fine. Look, I really gotta go, the cover's just come in and it looks like a friggin' dog's dinner!'

'I'll leave you to it then. Thanks.' She hung up, more confused than ever.

As far as Roxy recalled, only two people ever used her full name. Her mother, who knew squat about the artist and whose handwriting was as far removed from the writing on the blue paper as her own, and old Mrs Musgrave. And her writing was a perfect match. Beattie must have recommended Heather. *But why?*

Roxy sat back and gave it some thought. She had to confess, it was not such an unlikely scenario, and it could well have been perfectly innocent. Heather may have been looking for a reliable writer to give her some publicity; it had been five years, after all, since her last interview. And, if Beattie and Heather happened to know each other—for whatever reason—the former could easily have suggested Roxy. The mystery was, how did they know each other? And what, if anything, did Heather have to do with Beattie's murder? Roxy needed to have another conversation with Beattie's son, but this time she needed to be a lot more discreet.

In the flesh, William Musgrave's personal assistant, Anabell, looked just as she sounded, like a giant brick wall, with thick, Rugby-style shoulders squeezed into a well-made but matronly suit, and brown hair that had been cropped into a neat, boyish style. No fuss, no fun, no breaking through. She would have been in her forties and, judging from her sudden frown when Roxy introduced herself, was still smarting from Wednesday's impromptu visit.

'I'm sorry to drop by unannounced,' Roxy said with a smile, her own hair clipped back off her face with blue butterfly pins which perfectly matched the blue Fifties-style dress she was wearing over long, black boots. 'I was passing by and wondered if I could have a quick word with William?'

The assistant pursed her lips together and asked, 'How did you get up here?'

'Oh the security guard and I go way back.'

'Mr Musgrave is very busy today.'

'I do not doubt it for one moment. I just need to ask him a very quick question for a magazine article I'm writing—'

Just then William stepped out of a room marked 'Conference' and turned towards his office. He didn't seem to notice Roxy but she grabbed the opportunity and called out, 'Mr Musgrave! Hello again,' and, in reply to his puzzled expression, added, 'Roxy Parker. Remember I was writing your mother's book?'

'Of course, Miss Parker.' He seemed friendly enough but Roxy thought she spotted a quick, irritated glance in Anabell's direction. She would no doubt pay for this one later.

'I'm sorry to disturb you again, William. But I have a completely unrelated matter to speak with you about.'

He hesitated and then waved one pale, skinny hand towards his office. 'Certainly, come on in. I have about one minute to spare, I'm afraid that's all.'

'That'll do it,' Roxy replied, following him through. William's office was more stylish than Roxy expected with a large black desk in the centre, two black leather chairs in front of it and a large oil painting hanging on the wall behind him. The west side featured several enormous, tinted windows looking down on the busy street below, and on the east was a bright orange sofa shaped like a giant jelly bean with a chrome, oval shaped table in front of it. It could have been straight out of *Vogue Living*.

'Have a seat,' he was saying. 'What is this about?'

'It's actually regarding another story I'm writing for *Glossy* magazine.'

'Oh?'

'About Heather Jackson.'

'Heather Jackson?' He was confused at first and then a look of comprehension crossed his face. 'Oh, the artist? The Australian woman?'

'The very one. The thing is we're doing a bit of a tribute to her and are getting a list together of the various celebrities and well-known Sydney names who may be fans of hers. I was wondering whether you were a collector or at least a fan of some sort?' She was lying of course and hoped she sounded convincing.

'I'm afraid not. Does that mean I'm out of the article?'

'Looks like it. For some reason I picked you as an abstract art kinda guy.'

He seemed flattered by this and let out a loud chortle, his pointy nose crinkling up in an almost witch-like fashion. Roxy concluded that he probably didn't have much time for laughter and figured it was a good thing. He didn't suit it one bit.

'Do you mind me asking, then, if maybe your mother had been a fan?'

He paused for a few seconds before saying, 'I really wouldn't know.'

'She didn't collect any of Heather Jackson's art works or ever work with her on any charities?'

'Not that I know about. My parents, in fact, were both more in favor of the traditionals.'

'Oh?'

He pointed to the painting hanging on the wall behind him. It was a dusty paddock, somewhere, Roxy guessed, in outback Australia.

'A leftover from my father's days. He and my mother shared a fascination for late 19th century Australian landscapes.'

'Mind if I have a look?' Roxy jumped up and moved around the desk to peruse it more closely. 'It's beautiful.'

'Not really my thing but then I haven't had the heart to take it down. They had another two at home, I'm surprised Beattie didn't point them out. She was very proud of them.'

'Now that you mention it, I do recall some beautiful art works at your mother's house.'

'But nothing too abstract, eh?'

'No, not at all.' As Roxy moved back towards her seat she spotted a large silver photo frame on William's desk with what looked like a family portrait inside. 'Is that the Musgrave family in its entirety?' she asked.

'The whole lot of us, I'm afraid, and one or two ring-ins.' He sprang from his seat, blocking the picture from her view and leading her to the door. 'I do need to get back to it now if you don't mind.' He led her out into the corridor where Anabell had remained standing beside her desk. She did not look happy. 'Anna, can you recall, at all, whether my mother ever called the artist Heather Jackson to help out with her charity work?'

Anabell shook her head slowly. 'No I don't think so, sir. I sent most of her celebrity request letters out and the name certainly doesn't ring a bell.'

William turned back to Roxy. 'There's your answer. Looks like the Musgrave family are out.'

'Never mind,' Roxy chirped. 'I thank you for your time.'

'Not at all. But next time, Miss Parker?'

'Yes?'

'Please pick up the phone and make an appointment, first? That's the way we like to do things around here.'

She promised that she would and, throwing a wide, victorious smile in the direction of the scowling pit bull, charged out of the office. She wasn't any closer to working out the Beattie-Heather connection but she had just spotted the large, hairy guy who had shoved her into a bus on Elizabeth Street not so long ago. He was standing next to Fabian Musgrave in the portrait on William's desk.

He was clearly part of the Musgrave clan.

Like Roxy, Max also lived alone but his place was enormous by comparison. It was an old warehouse he had converted into his home and studio, with one large room boasting giant windows from floor to ceiling that drenched the room in sunlight almost the entire day. There were skylights, too, and all manner of lighting and camera equipment spread strategically around the room. Several brightly colored tarpaulins hung from one wall and various props, including an old steel fan and a Chinese umbrella, were scattered throughout the room. Max had converted one wall into a workable kitchen and what was once a small office loft high in the far corner was now his bedroom. The place was usually jumping with models, make-up artists and various hangers-on, so Roxy was surprised to find it empty when she arrived. She was panting from her speed-walk and took a few gulps before calling out Max's name.

'Hang on a minute!' came a groggy voice from within the loft and, a few seconds later, a disheveled Max poked his head out at the top of the stairs. 'Rox!' he cried and then jumped the stairs two at a time to give her a hug. 'How'd you get in? Don't tell me I left the door opened again?'

'Fraid so. Is this a bad time, or—'

'No, no, just catching up on some shut-eye. I cancelled all this morning's bookings. Need a quiet one.'

'Too many heavy nights?'

'Something like that. To what do I owe this visit? Ah, don't tell me!' He lifted one hand to her lips to quieten her. 'The so-called "Beatrice Musgrave murder", right?'

'Yes, but that's not the main reason I dropped by. I wanted to say hi and apologize for Thursday night.'

'No, I should apologize, I'm a dick when I've had one too many beers. Come in, I'll make some coffee.'

She sat down in a sofa and looked about the room. Three brightly painted papier mache mermaids were leaning against each other on one side and she was going to comment on them when he called out, 'Say hi to my new girlfriends, Mary, Mertle and Merrilee.'

'Very beautiful.'

'And completely unthreatened by you.'

Roxy's thick eyebrows knotted together, confused and, when he had returned with two mugs of coffee in hand, she asked, 'What's going on?'

He handed her a cup and then slumped into a chair beside her. 'She dumped me.'

'Sandy?'

'Sandra. Yep, that one.' He tried scraping his fingers through his matted hair and then gave up. He offered her a lopsided grin instead.

'When? Why? What happened? You sounded so happy.'

'I kinda was. But, well, she was all upset that I saw you the other night instead of her.'

'You're joking, right?' Roxy reached for her coffee and blew at the top before taking a sip. She suddenly felt very tired and realized that she had a throbbing headache, she'd just been too preoccupied to notice it. 'You don't have some Paracetamol do you?'

He grabbed some pills from the table and flung them towards her. 'Be my guest. I've practically OD'ed this morning.'

She swallowed two and then shook her head at him, trying to understand. 'You did explain we're just friends?'

'Yes.'

'That we've been getting together every Thursday night since forever, that she needn't be threatened?'

'Yeeess…well, kinda.'

'Kinda?'

He jumped up and began pulling at a white canvas on the wall. 'I gotta prepare this for the arvo, the gang'll be in soon enough.'

'You need a hand?' He was changing the subject for a reason and she wasn't up to finding out why. Not today. Not with her thumping headache. She helped him roll the canvas up and they placed it along the back wall out of the way. Then, together, they hung a large turquoise colored sheet in its place and placed the mermaid props below it.

'Very classy,' she lied. 'Vogue? Harper's Bazaar? Tacky Monthly?'

'Oh some arty street rag, they think it's kitsch.'

'Well, it's certainly something.'

His deep brown eyes caught hers and he held them for just a moment. 'Thanks for your help, Parker. I'll do the lights later. So, what did you want to ask me?'

'Oh, never mind, it can keep.'

She went to turn away but he grabbed one hand and pulled her a little closer, looking up through his unruly fringe. 'I'm sorry I've been such a jerk lately. I've just got a few issues to sort out in my head and I'm taking it all out on you, the very last person who should have to deal with it.'

'You liked Sandra a lot, didn't you?'

'Let's just say, I needed her.' He dragged Roxy back to the sofa and they fell into it together, Max still holding Roxy's hands tightly in his. 'So fire away, what do you need?'

She took a deep breath. 'I wanted to take a look at the funeral pix, especially the out-takes.'

'Beatrice Musgrave's?'

'Yes.'

'Sure thing.' He didn't ask why, simply jumped up and retrieved a laptop which he placed in front of her, clicking away at the screen until a file of images marked 'Musgrave Funeral' leapt to life before her eyes. As he disappeared upstairs, she began opening each jpeg, scanning them carefully. She was looking for two faces in particular: Heather Jackson and the Greek guy from the Musgrave family portrait. The artist was nowhere to be seen but the latter was featured in several shots, standing beside Fabian and a tall, skinny woman with fluorescent red hair. *Bingo!*

'That's the grandson, Fabian, and his wife, Sofie or something like that,' Max told her when he returned. He'd straightened himself up a little, changed his shirt and looked like he'd even combed his hair.

'Thought as much. And who's the other guy? The dark, hairy one?'

'Can't recall his name but I would've written it down somewhere, hang on.' He rummaged around and located a small notepad that he began flipping through. 'Ah, here it is, um, Fabian, Sofia and…God my handwriting's crap. I think it says Angelo Linguine?'

Prickles of excitement ran through the writer. It looked like she had stumbled upon the likely identity of her blackmailer. AIL. Were they Angelo's initials?

'Who exactly is he, do you know?'

'I think—and I can't believe I didn't jot it down, I'm getting sloppy in my old age—but I think it was Sofia's brother or cousin or something. Definitely a relation of some sort, but on her side. He's no blue blood.'

That would make sense, Roxy thought. Fabian had been the most vocal critic of Beatrice's biographer so it made perfect sense that someone closely connected to him, his brother-in-law for instance, had tried to help him put a stop to it by scaring the ghostwriter off. The pieces were beginning to click into place. Roxy felt anger swelling up inside again. That was her life he had been playing with that day on Elizabeth Street. If she had been pushed just a little harder, she might have been struck by a passing bus!

'Do you know him from somewhere?' Max asked, his voice laced with concern.

'Yes I think so, but I need to double check it all first.' If there was one thing she had learned from her years as a reporter, it was to get her facts straight before pointing the finger. 'Can I copy some of these?'

'Sure thing.'

She went to work on the computer while Max wandered off to brew more coffee. 'Thanks, Maxy,' she called after him, 'you've been an enormous help.'

13 THE FOURTH LETTER

On Monday morning the sky outside Roxy's window looked impossibly blue and birds chirped cheerfully from a distance, but it was an angry ghostwriter who reached for her laptop and began to get to work. The weekend had been relatively—blessedly—uneventful. She had put all thought of Beattie and Heather out of her mind and focused on Roxy, instead. She gave her home a scrub, caught up on her laundry and then spent the evenings concocting original story ideas for her magazine clients. The death of Beattie meant the death of several months work and, she realized with a start, she would have to hustle up some more or she'd be lucky to meet the mortgage. Roxy was a good saver, but she enjoyed the finer things in life, too: designer glasses, dinners out, decent wine. The only way the two could be reconciled was to work hard, and it was something she was happy to do. By late Sunday, the story ideas had been slotted into menus and emailed off to her respective editors. Now all she had to do was sit back and wait. It sometimes took days to get a reply, but she almost always hit the bullseye. Finding work was never a real problem for this talented writer.

In the meantime, she would do a little research, starting with Heather Jackson. She put a call through to the agent Jamie Owen and left a phone message: could he email Heather's detailed bio ASAP? 'I particularly need to fill in the early years, especially her childhood,' she said, leaving her email name.

The Musgraves were next, and she opened the Google home page and typed in the words 'Angelo Linguine&Fabian Musgrave&Sofia'. And presto! The first of thousands of entries sprang up before her and she tapped on one. It was a gossip page from a daily tabloid with a small snippet about the Beattie funeral.

It read, 'Accompanying the grieving grandson was his model wife Sofia and her brother, Angelo Linguine, an importer/exporter by trade.'

She glanced at a few other pages, not finding too much more about the man, and was about to quit the internet when she spotted a familiar name. Tina Passion. She recognized that name, had been staring at a life-size cut out of the woman just days ago in her agent Oliver Horowitz's office. Tina Passion was a romance writer and Oliver was her agent. *What was she doing linked with Angelo?*

Roxy clicked on the entry and waited for it to render, then speedily scanned the information. According to the newspaper snippet, Fabian's 'dodgy' brother-in-law was causing yet more embarrassment to the elite Musgrave name and now dating "trashy" model/writer Tina Passion. She glanced at the date. It was six months ago. Were they still together? And what if anything did Tina have to do with it?

Roxy scrunched her lips to one side. Things were getting increasingly complicated. She tapped at the keyboard with one nail. Was this just another coincidence, or was her agent somehow connected? She recalled their meeting at his office, just minutes after she'd been pushed over in the city, and how Oliver had seemed overly protective, had even asked her to hand Beattie's biography back. Why? *Was there something he wasn't telling her?*

She couldn't believe it of her agent, but she didn't know what to believe anymore. She stood up with a start. 'Time to eliminate some suspects,' she said aloud, 'starting with the least likely.' She decided to set Oliver a trap, and she needed Max's help to do it.

Several school groups were being shepherded through the west gate of the Botanical Gardens when Roxy arrived and she tagged on the end like a teacher rounding up the strays. She had no idea whether he would come but she was not taking any chances. The less she stood out the better.

The school kids meandered along the main pathway, stopping every now and then to observe a particular plant species being pointed out by their droning teacher. Most paid no attention, preferring to tussle and poke at each other as they walked along. Roxy checked her watch. It was just on midday and they were nearing the duck pond now. Earlier she had enlisted Max to send a text message to her agent asking to meet at the main pond at 12 sharp. Max was to address it from 'AIL'. Roxy figured that if Olie recognized the initials, he'd show up as instructed. If he didn't, he'd most likely call Max's number, a number he wouldn't ordinarily recognize, to enquire further. At this stage, Olie had done no such thing.

She scanned the area for a familiar face but no-one stood out. Several old men were feeding the ducks and various couples, mostly Japanese and European tourists, were leaning over the pond bridge, watching the ducks battle for the crumbs. The school kids had now dispersed in every direction and Roxy took a seat at the far right of the pond, in a leafy alcove that provided some coverage while she watched and waited.

Ten minutes later, feeling somewhat relieved and ready to depart, Roxy stood up. That's when she spotted the familiar face she had been dreading. It was her agent, Oliver Horowitz, wearing a trademark bowling shirt. He was circling the duck pond, clearly on the look out for someone.

She watched as he consulted his watch and then walked up to the top of the bridge and waited. No-one approached him so Roxy stood up and walked towards the bridge. She was halfway along when he saw her and he waved casually at first before a look of confusion crossed his face.

'Fancy meeting you here,' Roxy said, leaning against the post beside him.

'Roxy, baby, what's going on?'

'I should be asking you that.'

'Did you get a message, too?'

'I sent that message, Oliver. Or, rather, Max sent it for me.'

His small, brown eyes zigzagged across her face, confused.

'Let's go and get a coffee,' she suggested, leading the way down the bridge. 'We've got a lot to sort out.'

In the heart of the botanical gardens, shrouded in lush forest and set beside a pond bursting with brilliant green water lilies and mud-brown ducks, sits a magnificent octagonal wooden structure. One section is home to a stunning five-star restaurant and the other, a sprawling outdoor cafe. They chose the cafe and ordered. Oliver was sweating a little through his shirt and sweat was gathered on his brow.

'How do you know Angelo?' Roxy asked presently.

'Angelo?'

Roxy cocked an eyebrow at him. 'Don't even try to deny it, Oliver, I'm losing patience.' He looked genuinely confused so she said simply, 'AIL.'

'Yes, AIL. I got a message from some AIL character who asks me to meet here at noon.'

'And you don't know who AIL is?'

'Well, since you're here, I'm guessing it's you.' The perplexed look on his face seemed sincere.

'No, Oliver, it's not me. So, let me get this straight, you get a message from someone you don't know and you turn up anyway.'

'Well…' he hesitated. 'It wasn't exactly the first message I got.'

'Really,' she said flatly, not surprised. He hesitated again, taking a long sip of his latte before saying, 'I got it the day you showed up at my office with the gold glasses on. It was a threat saying I had to get you off the Musgrave biography or we'd both pay for it.'

'Why didn't you tell me this?'

'I didn't want to scare you.'

'Scare me?! Oliver, that was a legitimate warning. I was nearly shoved into a bus. I could have been killed.'

'Hey you were the one acting all nonchalant that day. And remember, I did try to get you to give the bio to Klaus. But to be honest, I really thought it was just some silly prank.'

'Did you get any more messages?'

'No…until the one that came in today. It freaked me out. I thought I'd better find out who sent it.'

Roxy stirred her coffee around. 'Which brings us to Angelo Linguine.'

Oliver sat back. 'That's who you think it stands for? Linguine… Linguine… How do I know that name?'

'Tina Passion's other half. Or, at least, he was.

He sat back with a thud. 'That's right. Slimy bastard, real eye for the ladies. Penchant for gold bling and leather vests. I had to wonder what Tina was doing with him.'

'Yes, because she's all style and grace,' Roxy replied deadpan and he just ignored her.

'Anyway, luckily, they split up months ago. You really think that's who's sending the threats? What the fuck for?' His anger was finally overtaking his surprise as the realization that a real, human being had been threatening his favorite ghostwriter.

Roxy quickly filled her agent in on the details thus far, explaining the connection between Angelo, Sofia and Fabian. 'Surely in the light of that you can understand why I sense foul play with Beatrice Musgrave's death?'

'Now I do, yes. How many messages did you get?'

'A few.'

'And you're certain Angelo's behind it?'

'I'm sure of it.'

'So what happens now?'

Roxy considered this for a moment. 'I've got someone else I need to talk to.'

'Hey, be careful, Roxy. From what I recall of Angelo, he's no gentleman. An oversized oaf in fact. He could be very dangerous.'

'Don't worry, I have a totally different oaf in mind.'

The bill suddenly appeared and Oliver leapt on it. 'Here, let me get this. It looks like I owe you one.'

'It's gonna take more than a coffee, mate,' she replied with a wink.

14 COMMISERATIONS

Oliver's words played havoc with Roxy's stomach all the way home. His story sounded credible enough but she knew there was only one way to sort it out once and for all. She had to confront Fabian Musgrave. If only she knew where he lived.

Back at home, Roxy put a call through to Anabell Lorrier. This time the assistant made no effort to hide her displeasure, barely grunting hello.

'I need to speak with William,' Roxy announced casually.

'He's not actually available now Miss Parker. I don't think you've quite cottoned on but he's a very busy man.'

'Well, you know what, Anabell, I'm busy, too and I really do need to speak with him.'

'Impossible. Can I take a message?'

'I'm after his son Fabian's address. He dropped by my place the other day and left his jacket,' she lied.

'Fine, I'll organize for a courier to come and collect it from you.'

'No, no, I think it's best I speak with William.'

'There really is no need—'

'I'll call back if you like. Say, ten minutes? Oh, better yet, I'll just drive in now, bring you the jacket in person. Maybe even run into William while I'm there. Won't that be fun for us all?!'

There was an impatient sigh on the other end and the assistant finally said, '235 Thomas St, Paddington. That's Fabian's address, you didn't get it from me.'

'Get what?'

'Good day, Miss Parker.' She hung up with a thud and Roxy grinned to herself. It was very easy to annoy information out of people, she had learnt that trick from her mother.

After quickly downing a tuna sandwich and several glasses of water, Roxy grabbed her bag again and in it she placed her phone, a small tape-recorder and a personal security alarm she had found on eBay a few years ago. It was a small device that emitted a giant sound, a kind of piercing siren that she could activate should she ever feel under threat. Of course she'd never had to use the portable device, only trusted that it worked, but it was still reassuring just knowing it was there. She gave herself the once-over in the hall mirror, applied a little lip gloss, removed her dangly earrings—they were way too ditzy for this particular assignment—and made her way outside.

It was close to 4pm by the time Roxy's old Golf turned off Oxford Street into the thin, winding back streets of Paddington. She was not even sure if Fabian Musgrave would be home now but she had to try while her courage was up. She spotted Thomas Street and, noting that its narrow gutters were cramped with cars, drove down several blocks until she found a spare spot. She reversed the car in with some difficulty and frowned to herself. There would be no quick getaways today.

It took some minutes to locate No. 235 and not because most of the terrace houses along Thomas Street were unnumbered or had lush vines covering them up. It was because Fabian Musgrave's house was not at all what Roxy had expected. Rundown and unpainted, the old terrace was in desperate need of repair and was hardly the kind of place you would expect to find the heir to a giant department store chain. She wondered briefly whether Anabell had given her a bum steer, but doubted the assistant would risk another pesky phone call.

The front door was crammed with waterlogged junkmail and cobwebs, and looked like it hadn't been used for years so Roxy made her way along the side towards the back of the house from which music was now emanating. It sounded like a *Smiths* tune. *Bit retro for Fabian,* she thought. There was a small, overgrown garden back there and an old outhouse, but not a soul about. She opened the screen door and knocked hard. No answer. As the '80s band sang about suffering children, Roxy banged again, to no avail. Half relieved, she turned to leave and came face to face with Fabian Musgrave. He was holding a bag of groceries in one hand and a cigarette in the other, and he did not look pleased.

'Roxanne isn't it? What the hell are you doing here?'

'Oh, Fabian, good you're home. Can we chat?'

He hesitated. 'Why?'

'It's important.'

He stubbed out his cigarette, unlocked the door and led the way in.

A damp, musty smell hit Roxy's nostrils as she followed him inside and she noticed that he had to switch several lamps on to lighten the place up. Terraces were notoriously dark but this one was cavernous. He dumped the groceries on the kitchen bench and then led her through to a dank living area with fading wallpaper and a motley collection of second-hand furniture. He cleared a chair and offered her a seat. Roxy noticed that he was less self-assured now as he lit up another smoke. The ashtray on the table was cluttered with old butts and an empty gin bottle was lying on its side next to a collection of candles and incense. Roxy looked into the young man's eyes and sensed something else, too. It looked a lot like embarrassment. She wondered if he ever brought his dad back here, and doubted it. As if reading her thoughts, he growled, 'How'd you get my address?'

'I have ways and means,' she replied. She was not exactly fond of Anabell but she wasn't into betraying her sources either.

He thought about this and said nothing more, waiting for her to speak. He seemed uneasy, too, and she suspected why. She looked about the room and spotted a picture of the woman Max had called Sofia. Her hair was bleached white in this picture and, up close, Roxy could see fine, elegant features. She had a tiny stud in her nose and thick, black eye make-up, not unlike the heroin-chic look of teenage street magazines. Roxy wondered if she was a model. She certainly had the body for one.

'Your wife?' she asked

'Yes.'

'Very attractive.'

'So they tell me.'

Roxy got up and wandered about the room, peering at other picture frames placed on the mantelpiece.

'You don't happen to have a picture of her brother, Angelo, do you?'

'Angelo?' His voice croaked a little then and he shook his head quickly. 'No, no I don't think so. How do you know Angelo?'

'Now that's a good question,' Roxy replied, positioning herself between the lounge room and the kitchen, her best exit out of there. 'Let me think. I guess we first met—not properly you understand—in the city.'

'Oh?' Was that sweat appearing above his lip?

'Yes, Elizabeth Street to be precise. Oh, no, I tell a lie. We first met, indirectly, about a week before that when he sent me an email. A lovely little note threatening my life.'

Fabian's eyes rolled back into his head and he shook his head several times while Roxy pulled her handbag closer to her. There was an alarm in there and she was not afraid to use it. When he spoke, he sounded surprisingly incensed. 'What did he say?'

'He insisted I drop your grandmother's biography "or else".'

'You're shitting me, right?'

''Fraid not.'

He was shaking his head again and his eyes were darting about with anger. 'The A-class dickhead. I am going to kill that guy.'

'Hopefully before he manages to kill me. So let me get this straight. Are you trying to tell me that you *weren't* involved?'

He seemed taken aback by this. 'Of course I wasn't!'

'Well, sorry, Fabian, but I can't see why a distant in-law of your grandmother's would care one iota about the book. You on the other hand—'

'What about me?'

'Well, let's think about this shall we? You tried to convince your grandmother not to write the book, and you even came to me, to make sure I wasn't pursuing it. I think your grandmother had a secret and you didn't want the world to know.'

'Yes, that's true… but I wouldn't push you into a bus for it.'

'Who said anything about a bus?'

He sat back in his chair. The radio was now playing a Nick Cave tune and Roxy was feeling strangely unthreatened, despite her circumstances. 'Look, Fabian, I know about the daughter.'

His eyes darted back at her. 'What do you know?'

'I know that Beattie had another child, she told me as much, just before she died.' His eyes had blanked out. He looked almost detached now. 'And I know that Beattie wanted to spill the beans about her daughter but that you were against it. Perhaps you were terrified that you'd get less inheritance if another sibling entered the picture.'

'It wasn't that.' She raised surprised eyebrows at him. 'Well, not just that. I thought Grandma would be ostracized by the revelation. I thought one scandal in the family was enough.'

'Scandal? What scandal?'

He sniggered. 'Damn, you're not as savvy as you try to make out.' He pointed one long finger at himself and mocked a smile.

Roxy sat down with a thud. He was a junkie. Daddy's little drug addict. She should have spotted it from the start, the bad skin, the gaunt look. The truth was she hadn't wanted to see. This was Beatrice Musgrave's grandson for Christ sake. She said simply, 'How long?'

'Close to three years. I went through rehab two months ago, no thanks to Dad.'

'He's thrown you out?'

'Not so much as a nickel.'

'Was this before or after you met Sofia?'

'During. I've been hooked on smack since we met. But she stuck by me, yeah? She's still here. Which is more than I can say for my fucking father. He found out last March and hasn't spoken to me since. Wouldn't even pay for my rehab, grandma gave me that. A parting gift I guess you could say.'

'But there was plenty more where that came from, wasn't there? The problem was granny wasn't putting out enough and the sudden appearance of an Aunt was certainly not going to help.'

'Look, I didn't threaten you, alright?!'

'No you got your brother-in-law to do the dirty work for you. He was supposed to scare me off and, when that didn't work, you had your own grandmother killed.'

'Hey!' he jumped up as if he'd been stung and Roxy reached into her bag, the alarm button at the ready. 'Hang on a minute,' he was crying, 'that last bit's absolute crap.'

'So you don't deny that you set Angelo upon me?'

'Yes, I mean, no!' He was pacing the room. 'Look, give me a second to explain, okay?'

'Take your time.'

He sat back down, lit himself a cigarette and then placed his head wearily in his hands. It was some time before he spoke again. When he did, his voice was considerably calmer. 'Bet', my Grandma, called me to her house a few months back. She wanted to tell me about the biography, get my blessing as it were. This made me want to laugh because, as far as the rest of the family are concerned, I don't even exist anymore.' He dragged on his smoke for a while. 'That's when she spilled the beans about her first child. Man, I thought I was the only black sheep in the family. Who'd have thought old Bet'ed have it in her, eh? No wonder we got along so well.'

'So she told you about the daughter?'

'Yeah, said she'd had a kid by someone else, before she met Gramps and, well, the days being what they were, was forced to give it up. Her parents wouldn't let them marry or something. I think they whisked the baby away before she even saw the bloody thing.'

Roxy felt a pang of grief for the poor woman. 'So you never knew about the child until then?'

'No, and as far as I could tell no-one but Beattie did. It was her little secret, and might have stayed that way, had she not caught a sudden case of the truths.'

'She wanted to reveal all in the book we were writing.'

'Yeah.' He scoffed. 'Made my scandal look a little menial. Terence would have turned in his grave.'

'So you asked her not to write it?'

'Yes and she insisted. She said she owed it to "all three of us". I guess she meant Grandad, as well. So, yeah, I was irate. I tried to get Dad to talk her out of it but he didn't seem to care.'

'But why wouldn't he care? I find that so hard to believe.'

'Oh, you'd be surprised. My dad hasn't much of a heart, I can tell you. It's all about the business to him, couldn't care less about the rest of us. To him, old Bet' was a bore and well, if this "little book", as he called it, kept her out of his hair, all the better.'

'But surely the scandal—?'

'What does he care? He only ever reads the business section of the newspaper. Besides, in this day and age it was hardly going to affect the business. His precious bloody business.'

'Who else knew about the daughter?'

'Just Dad, myself and Sofia. Oh and Angelo because Sofia can't keep her big mouth shut. He came bowling over one day with all these grand plans to shut my Grandmother up; including scaring you off. He said he'd follow you, work out where you worked and give you a fright. He said a little shove would do it, just something to get your attention and get you to drop out. He figured Bet'ed give up after that. I thought it was just bluff, I didn't realize he'd really do it.'

'He could have killed me, Fabian. I nearly hit a bus, you know?'

'I'm really sorry, man, I honestly thought he was all talk. He was just angry about the book, that's all.'

'But why on earth would your brother-in-law care?'

'Because less inheritance for me means less for Sofia... and, I guess, indirectly, less for him.'

'That's a little far-fetched.' Roxy wanted to believe him but she had known some junkies in her time. They could be expert liars when they needed to be.

'It's the truth. I tried to talk him out of it and I thought I had. I'm really sorry. He didn't hurt you did he?'

'I came close to being mince mint, Fabian. What's to say he didn't go all the way with your grandmother?'

'That's insane. He might be willful but he's not violent, not really. He wouldn't have hurt my grandmother. No way.' His tone wasn't a hundred percent convinced.

'What about this secret daughter?'

'What about her?'

'Did Beattie tell you who she was?'

He shook his head. 'Not a word. Grandma promised she'd tell me as soon as she'd spoken to her. I gather she'd located her but hadn't revealed herself yet. Man, what a nice bit of news: Oh, hello, guess what, you're my missing daughter and you'll be inheriting $20 million when I cark it.'

'So as far as you knew Beattie had not spoken to the daughter before she was killed?'

'No. Well, she hadn't spoken to her a fortnight before, of that I'm certain. Who's to say Grandma didn't find her, tell her the good news and then the daughter popped her? She was probably feeling pissed off about the adoption anyway!'

'No,' Roxy said. 'That doesn't make any sense. Why kill Beattie *before* she revealed your name? Now she'll have to go to all the trouble of a DNA test to prove her right to the inheritance. No, it can't be the daughter. It has to be someone else, someone who'd stand to lose by the revelation.' Roxy got up.

'What are you going to do now?' he asked nervously, following her out and down the side of the house towards the street.

'I don't know, Fabian, but I'd appreciate it if you kept your brother-in-law away from me in future. If he didn't hurt Beattie then he's in the clear, I'm not after vengeance. I'm just trying to get to the bottom of her murder. That's all.' And then she paused. 'Why haven't you asked me why I think it's murder? According to everybody else the verdict is suicide.'

'That's crazy talk, man,' he snorted. 'Bet' couldn't open a can of tomatoes without putting on an apron. She'd hardly split herself open on a pile of rocks below her own house!'

As they reached the street, it occurred to Roxy that Fabian understood his grandmother better than the rest of them, and, in his own misguided way, had probably loved her more, too. She couldn't imagine him killing her. But then he was a recovering addict and sometimes there was no stopping a junkie in search of his next hit. If he needed money and Beatrice had the means to provide it, nothing would stand in his way.

'I really am sorry about Angelo,' he was saying as he leant on the rusty gate. 'Both Sofia and I begged him to leave you alone. I really thought we'd gotten through.'

She shrugged, it was no longer the issue. 'Just two more things,' she said and he raised his eyes uncertainly. 'How do you know Oliver Horowitz?'

'Who?'

'My agent. Angelo sent him a message, too.'

'Never heard of him. Angelo must have looked him up.'

'And the bag lady?'

'Huh?'

'The designer-clad derelict. You know? The old woman in Chanel?' The look of complete confusion that had hijacked his face satisfied Roxy and she waved him goodbye. He clearly didn't have a clue what she was talking about.

15 REVELATIONS

The phone rang shrilly as Roxy entered her apartment and she flung the door closed as she ran to answer it. It was her mother.

'Hi, Mum,' she said sullenly. She wasn't in the mood.

'Why haven't you called Mason?'

'What?'

'He's been waiting for your call all week. Don't tell me you've been too busy.'

'Alright then I'll tell you it's because I don't like the guy. He's a pompous prat.' She dropped her handbag and then slid down the wall to join it on the floor. Her meeting with Fabian had gone well but she was emotionally drained, unable to cope with Lorraine's meddlesome ways.

'You seemed to be getting on really well over dinner. Why the change of tune?'

'Mum, I don't like him, end of story. He's not the man of my dreams, we're not going to end up married, we're not even going to end up on a second date. If you want me to call him and tell him so, I will.'

'Oh *dear* don't do that, he'll be devastated.'

'Somehow I doubt it; too big an ego for that. Was there anything else?'

'Well, no. But I've been waiting for you to call me.'

'Why?'

'About Beatrice Musgrave, of course. She died, dear.'

'Yes I am aware of that. I mentioned it over dinner, remember?'

'Yes, but I didn't realize it was suicide.'

'That's what the cops say. What did you think it was?'

'You just said she had died, I assumed from an accident or old age or something. And then I was playing tennis with Janey Swan, you know the one who's husband works for—'

'Cut to the chase, Mum, what did Janey Swan say?'

'She said the woman killed herself, threw herself over a cliff or something.'

'In any case it's very tragic,' Roxy replied.

'It's pathetic, that's what it is!' Lorraine's voice had grown agitated, she seemed upset. 'Suicide is a form of weakness. I've always told you that. It's a coward's way out. The stupid, stupid woman.'

'I agree, Mum, but we don't know the full circumstances.'

'I don't care, it's irrelevant. What about the people she left behind? Did she think about them when she slit her wrist?'

'Slit her wrist? What are you talking about? Let's stick to the facts, Mum, apparently she threw herself off her balcony. And quite frankly I don't think anyone left behind really gives a shit—'

'Well you don't know that!' The woman was almost hysterical and it surprised Roxy. Her mother didn't usually spare her emotions for anyone besides Charlie and herself. 'Anyway,' she continued, a little more calmly, 'mind your language, dear.'

'Sorry, Mum. Are you okay?'

She heard a sniffle on the other end of the phone. 'Fine, fine. I have to be off, Charlie will be home soon and I haven't even started dinner.'

'You sure you're okay? I didn't know Beattie was a friend of yours.'

'She wasn't. I didn't really know her, not to speak to, anyway. I used to see her about. It's just tragic that's all. She was probably more loved than you realize.'

They said their goodbyes and as Roxy made herself a cup of tea it dawned on her that her mother was right. Someone at that funeral did love Beatrice Musgrave very much.

Roxy deserted her tea and dashed to the bedroom to retrieve the funeral photographs she'd taken from Max. She spread them out on the dining room table anxiously. At first she could not find him and she groaned with exasperation. Then she saw him, standing just out of focus in the background to one shot, holding his battered hat, his gray hair wispy around his temples, his black suit sitting awkwardly on his lanky frame. Despite the fogginess of the focus she could tell he had the weathered complexion of a man accustomed to a lot of sun. This had to be the 'old guy in a beat-up suit and Akubra' that Max had mentioned, the only man weeping over Beattie's coffin. She wondered why Max hadn't taken a close-up picture and, wanting to know more about him, dialed the photographer's studio. The answering machine clicked in so she hung up and tried his new smartphone. It took several rings before he answered.

'Can I call you back in a couple of minutes?' he asked, a little breathless. 'I'm in the middle of a shoot.'

'No prob's, I'm at home.'

She scooped up the photos and returned to the sunroom to switch on her computer. Clicking open the Musgrave file, she began to scan through the transcription of Beattie's last interviews. As soon as she saw the words, 'first love', she stopped and read the paragraph out loud.

'Oh yes I had my fair share of admiring bachelors,' Beatrice had said and Roxy had noted that there was laughter in her voice, 'almost like a giggling school girl!' she had typed in brackets.

'Anyone in particular?' Roxy had prompted.

'Yes, one very special lad. Frank. He was a dashing farmer's son from Macksland, a small country town. Strong hands, soft nature. I met him nearly 50 years ago. He was my first love and you can never forget your first love, not even if you try.'

Beside this Roxy had written the words 'misty-eyed'. It was intended to add color to the manuscript but she wondered now whether there was more to the man from Macksland than she realized. She had a hunch it was the same guy wandering about all alone at Beattie's funeral, the man Max had captured despite himself. And if so, he must still hold a soft spot for Beatrice Musgrave. She had just looked up Macksland on Google Maps and it was in rural New South Wales, 700 kilometers from Sydney. That's a long way to travel for someone you hadn't seen in 50 years.

Roxy sat back in her chair and began playing with her hair, twirling the black strands in one hand. Was this old country guy the father of Beattie's secret child? Had they seen each other since? Perhaps they'd been secretly meeting all along? And what, if anything, did it have to do with Beattie's death? Roxy was about to reach for her journal—to get her thoughts into some sort of order—when the phone rang. It was Max.

'Sorry about that,' he said, the sound of traffic almost drowning him out. 'The model's being a complete prima donna and I don't know where we dredged the make-up artist from, he's useless. We're on our way to the last location now so I've got a few minutes. What's up?'

'Just a quick question about the funeral again.'

'Jesus, Roxy, you still obsessing about the old woman? Are you getting paid to do that?'

'That's not the point. You mentioned an old guy—'

'Hey? I can't...you, what...say—' The line was breaking up so Roxy spoke as quickly and clearly as she could.

'I want to ask about the old man you saw at the funeral!'

143

'Goldman? Who's that?' He could hardly hear her. 'Oh damn, Roxy, it looks like we're gonna…out…you there? Hello?'

'Max, yes, I'm here!'

'I'll try you later, we're in a dodgy transmission area…I'll…you later.'

'Okay!' she called back, exasperated.

'Hey wanna catch…at Indi…light… cheapie tonight? 8 o'…?'

'Indian Delight, at 8pm?'

'Roger!'

'Okay, Max, see you then!'

She hung up disappointed. Her questions about the farmer would have to wait. In the meantime, she had to get her thoughts on paper before she went insane.

Journal in hand, Roxy jotted down the 'facts' as she saw them.

• Beatrice Musgrave had an illegitimate daughter of whom most people, certainly outside of immediate family, had no idea. Fabian had confirmed it.

• Beattie was about to reveal the name and whereabouts of this daughter. She had told Roxy as much.

• Just days before she was due to spill the beans, she ended up dead.

• Beatrice Musgrave had almost certainly been murdered. The police might believe it was suicide but Roxy was not convinced. As Fabian had concurred, Beattie wasn't the suicidal type.

• Who ever killed Beattie intended for it to look like suicide. If not, they were lucky bastards. *I wonder if there was a note?* There had certainly been no mention in the media.

• Beattie may have been killed to hide the truth about her daughter.

• The secret daughter may or may not have been alerted to the real identity of her birth mother before Beattie died.

She drew a circle around this last point and then added a bunch of question marks. Surely, if the daughter had been told, she would have put her hand up by now? Shown up at the funeral? Claimed her stake in Beattie's fortune? As far as Fabian knew, she had not. It had all been silent on that front.

Roxy groaned and stretched, then stared at her notes again. For now she had to assume that the daughter had not been told. The real question then was: who wanted to shut old Beattie up? Roxy suspected that Fabian and his brother-in-law Angelo were not the only ones who would have liked the secret to remain just that. Roxy turned over a new page and jotted down the names: William Musgrave, Ronald Featherby and The Man From Macksland. The son, the lawyer and the first love. Had any of these men wanted to silence the society matron for good?

She considered William first. Was his apparent disinterest cloaking something deeper and more sinister? After all, he lived for the business his father had left him, the business he had successfully built into an even bigger empire after his dad's death. Sharing it with a stranger was surely unthinkable. His own son had thought him heartless. But did he have murder in him?

Next she considered Beattie's lawyer, Ronald Featherby. He had been one of her closest friends, had acted in her best interests for over 40 years. How far did his loyalty extend? Did he kill the old derelict to save his client embarrassment and then her, too? Perhaps he felt death was preferable to the scandal that her revelation would unleash.

It all seemed too outlandish to the young writer, so she turned her attention to the third suspect, the man from Macksland. Perhaps he had come to Sydney to try to dissuade Beattie from writing the book? If the missing daughter was his, and he had a family or some sort of reputation to uphold, then he may not want the truth to be revealed. But surely if he had killed her he wouldn't have shown up at the funeral, and he certainly wouldn't have looked so sad.

'Arrrggh!' she screamed, throwing her journal aside. It was all just speculation; her mind was running away with her.

None of it made sense and there was still so much she did not know, such as the identity of the missing daughter and what connection, if anything, this had to do with the well-dressed derelict. 'And who, pray tell, would have the stomach to slice off her fingers?' And why?!

Roxy thought then of the aggressive Angelo and his waif-like sister. Were they in it together to rob Fabian blind? And how, if anything, was the mysterious Heather Jackson connected? Roxy had still not worked that one out but couldn't be sure there was any involvement. Heather could be the secret daughter, of course, her age certainly corresponded and they obviously knew each other. At some point Beatrice had given Heather the ghostwriter's details and Heather had arranged the interview. But why? Perhaps they had simply shared the same hairdresser?

She let out an enormous sigh, checked her watch and then jumped up and began gathering the photos together into a neat pile. She had to get ready for her dinner date with Max. As she placed the pile neatly in a folder, she glanced again at the top picture of the old man in the beat-up hat. Roxy had a feeling he was more than that and made a mental note to ask Max about him that night.

The rich, spicy aroma of chicken korma wafted towards them as the waiter placed a well-heaped plate on the table and Roxy pushed the Indian Naan bread aside to make room for it. She was planted across from Max in a booth at Indian Delight, a cheap Indian restaurant in the grungy heart of Darlinghurst. Dozens of brightly dressed couples, mostly gay, wandered arm in arm on the street outside and the dull thud of the nightclub upstairs could be heard over a tinny tune now coming from a small stereo by the kitchen. Like Pico's, this was one of Max and Roxy's favorite haunts.

Tingling with chilled Semillon and hungry as hell, the friends dug into their food and savored the taste, the 'Delight's delectable cuisine a conversation stopper every time. Eventually, when she had had her fill, Roxy relaxed into her chair and watched her friend eat.

He had combed his hair today and his long-sleeved, red T-shirt looked freshly washed. He was chomping away at the bread with all the enthusiasm of a kid at McDonald's and she felt a glow of warmth inside her. Max had been her sanity stick for so long she didn't know what she would do without him. Secretly, she was pleased he was single again but she would never admit that, certainly not to him.

'You seem more relaxed tonight,' he said, stopping to gulp his wine.

'I feel great.'

'Any special reason?'

'Well, Maria Constantinople emailed this afternoon with a bunch of stories she'd like me to do.'

'Excellent.'

'I know. They're all your usual women's stuff, and they're not due for a while, but it's good to have a solid stack of work lined up. I think the Heather Jackson feature has booted me up a few pegs in Maria's eyes at least.'

'She really liked it, huh? You want anymore?' He was already scraping the dregs into his bowl so she didn't bother answering.

'Actually, I think she was mainly impressed by the fact that Heather came to her demanding that I do the interview. Suddenly I have some clout.'

'Heather Jackson came to you?' He looked up, surprised.

'Yeah, weird, eh? I think she got my name from Beatrice Musgrave before she died.'

'Ah, there's that name again.'

Roxy sipped her wine quietly. Max was being protective and she could understand his concern. To the outsider she certainly must appear obsessed, frantically trying to find foul play where none might exist at all. Roxy sat upright and looked her friend square in the eyes.

'Can you let me try to explain it to you? I really need you to understand this.' He shrugged, looking far more interested in the food than anything she might say, so she continued, choosing her words carefully. 'Beatrice Musgrave revealed her secret daughter to me the day before she died. I believe she had her reasons. She might have foreseen her death and thrown me this clue to set me on the right track, or maybe it was pure coincidence. In any case I owe it to her memory to check out every lead. If nothing comes of it, at the very least I have honed my investigative skills. At best, I might put a murderer away and pay homage to her memory. Which, right now, is in tatters.'

'And you're not doing it for the scoop? The great story at the end of it?'

'Christ, you sound like Beattie's lawyer!' She paused. 'To start with, maybe I was, I dunno. But now, no, I'm honestly not. In fact, if my investigations uncover something that is of no interest to the public and does not serve to respect Beattie's memory, than I'll let the whole thing drop. Not give it another thought.'

'And if you stumble upon the murderer?'

'I call the police and they take it from there.' He looked hard into her eyes. He was clearly worried and she tried for a confident smile. 'I'm not an idiot, Max, you know that. But I can't just let it drop, not when my conscience tells me otherwise. Can't you see? I'm doing it for Beatrice, and because it just seems the right thing to do. It's that simple. Do you understand?'

He sat back and smiled. 'I understand that you're a better person than me, Parker. If there wasn't money in it, I don't think I would bother.'

'I don't believe that for one second. You underestimate yourself, Max. You always have.'

He blushed a little at this and looked away. 'So, Miss Marple, what now?'

She reached for her handbag and retrieved his funeral shots. 'That's why I was calling you this afternoon.' She placed the clearest picture of the old man in front of him. 'What can you tell me about this guy?'

'Country bloke,' he said, stopping to take a closer look. 'On his own as far as I could tell.'

'Did he appear to know the family?'

'Again, not that I could tell. Actually, no, that's right Sofia and Fabian said they didn't know him, in fact, they were particularly interested in who he was, even asked me to photograph him and get his name for them. Apparently he'd gate-crashed, he wasn't invited.'

'So where's the photo?'

'That's just it. He refused, wouldn't let me snap him, not even unposed. He seemed friendly enough, but said we were there for Beatrice, not for happy snaps. Now let me think. He did tell me his first name.' Roxy went to speak but held her tongue. And then he said it. 'Frank someone-or-other, I think that's right.' She could have reached across the table and kissed him. 'Anyway,' he was saying, oblivious to her joy, 'he said he was from the country and that he and Beatrice went, "way back".'

'Did he mention that he was from Macksland?'

He shrugged. 'Dunno, sorry. What makes you think he's from there?'

'Beattie told me her first love was a guy called Frank from Macksland. It has to be the same guy, it just has to be. And I reckon he's the father of her illegitimate child. In any case I am sure he holds some of the keys to this mystery.'

'So where to now?'

'Macksland, of course!' She took a long sip of her wine and beamed at him across the table, her green eyes twinkling with excitement under her straight black fringe.

'You're kidding, right? That's a fair hike to go on a hunch.'

'Well, sweetie it's not like I've got anything worth hanging around for.'

'I'll take that as a compliment shall I?'

'You know what I mean. The first of the *Glossy* stories aren't due for another fortnight—'

'Parker, Parker, Parker,' he said, cutting her off and pushing his own messy fringe out of his eyes. 'It's always about work for you isn't it?'

Roxy signaled for the bill. She was in a good mood, she didn't want to spoil it, not tonight. As Max walked her to her car she could tell he had grown sullen again. He had been sullen a lot of late and she wondered if there was some horrible secret that was bringing him down. Perhaps he's suffering from depression, she thought.

'Can I score a lift?' he asked. 'Left the old Holden at home, it was full of equipment.'

'Of course, jump in.'

They didn't speak much during the drive but when they reached Max's warehouse he sparked up. 'Wanna come in? I've got something I want to show you.'

Roxy hesitated. She was tired and she needed to get home and book a flight for Macksland. But there was something in his eyes, a kind of eagerness that she could not refuse. She parked in a side alley and followed him inside. A dim lamp barely illuminated the studio, but he did not attempt to turn any other lights on, simply lit some candles instead.

'Do you want a drink?'

She shook her head no. 'What did you want to show me, Max? I can't stay long, I've got to book a flight remember?'

He considered this for some time and then produced a photo from the table and held it up to her. It was a picture of them together at some party they had gone to several months before. They were smiling and their arms were slung casually across each other's shoulders.

'What do you see there?' he asked. Roxy stared at the shot, trying to spot something out of place, to make sense of her friend's strange mood. She flung her hands up, flustered.

'Never mind,' he said and placed the picture back down. He took a deep breath. 'Roxy, you know how I've been a bit weird lately?'

'Yeees,' she said cautiously.

'I need to know if you have any idea why.'

'Are you depressed? Do you have a drinking problem?'

Max's eyebrows shot up with surprise and he laughed a little too loudly. He shook his head slowly as he slipped down into the sofa. She sat down, too, confused. When he spoke again his voice was softer, more controlled. 'You really don't know, do you?'

Roxy blinked and could feel her own defenses rising. 'I know that you've been preoccupied with something, and defensive...all the time. And I know that I can't do a single thing right and I don't understand why. You won't tell me what the problem is, you just shut yourself off.' Then she had a thought. 'Is it that woman, Sandra? Were you in love with her?'

He laughed again but there was a real bitterness in the tone, and she folded her arms around her, unsure what was happening. When he had finished he rested his head on the back of the sofa, closed his eyes and said in a voice so quiet it was barely audible, 'No, Parker, I'm in love with *you*.'

Roxy's heart seemed to stop and she remembered forcing herself to breathe. She was speechless and then suddenly very angry. Was he making fun of her? Or was he just plain drunk?

'I think I need to go,' she said suddenly, certainly, and stood up trying not to catch his eye. He leapt up then and blocked her path.

'So that's it? I say I love you and you do the bolt?'

'I'm tired, Max, I need to go home.' When she dared to meet his eyes she saw misery. He looked like a wounded animal, his fringe hanging down across one eye, his hands thrust defensively into his pockets. Shaking his head sadly, he stepped to one side.

'Run Parker, run. It's what you do best.'

But she was out the front door before she even heard him.

16 THE FIRST LOVE

The alarm bell pierced through Roxy's sleep like a butcher knife through silk and she sat up with a start, feeling anxious and unrested. She had hardly slept a wink, Max's words circling manically through her brain, and as she peeled the sheets away and slipped under the shower, she could not thrust his face, his sad, defeated face from her mind. 'Damn you, Max!' she hissed into the water as it sprayed down upon her.

She switched herself on autopilot, thrusting a spare set of clothes and some toiletries into an overnight bag before catching a cab to the domestic terminal of Sydney airport. She had lucked upon an early morning seat to Macksland and didn't want to miss it. In the cab she sent a text message to her mother letting her know she'd be out of town for a while and promising to call when she got back. 'Just work stuff, nothing to worry about!' she lied. She also checked her inbox and couldn't help feeling a wave of relief. There were no new threatening emails. It looked like Fabian Musgrave had called off his gorilla of a brother-in-law.

The plane was on time and as soon as it departed, she dropped her seat back and fell instantly asleep. An hour later the captain woke her with the announcement that they were fast approaching Macksland. 'We'll soon be starting our descent,' the flight attendant proclaimed afterwards. 'Please ensure your seat is in the upright position and that your seat belts are securely fastened.'

Roxy did as instructed then peeped out the cabin window to see the wheat fields turn to roads and then into a small tar airstrip onto which they landed. Once they had made their way inside the tiny terminal, Roxy continued straight towards the exit sign, her bag already in hand, and towards a waiting bus.

'You going into town?' she asked the large, rosy cheeked woman behind the wheel and then clambered aboard. The airport was just five kilometres from the heart of town and, within ten minutes, Roxy found herself wandering its wide, ute-filled streets in search of the Information Office.

'Lovely weather we're havin', eh?' the small man behind the counter enthused when she strolled in.

'Yes, beautiful,' Roxy replied. 'I'm wondering if you can help me, I'm looking for some accommodation.'

'Not a problem. What kinda digs you lookin' for?'

'Oh, pretty basic, just pub accommodation will do. Got any recommendations?'

'Damn straight I do.' He produced a tatty map from below the desk and, spreading it before her, circled one street corner with a capital H printed on it. 'The Shearer's Hotel is a beauty. Thirty-five bucks for a room and breaky in the mornin', can't do much better than that.'

'Sounds great.'

'You might have to share a bathroom but the rooms are clean and, well me missus says they look like something out of a Laura Ashley catalogue book. I think that means they're pretty as a postcard.'

'Great,' Roxy repeated, 'point me in the right direction.'

The Information Officer's wife was spot on and Roxy cheered up enormously as she entered her spacious room above the old pub. A giant four-poster bed dominated the room and, beside it, sat an antique dresser with a china water basin on top and, beside that, an old milk jug filled with wild flowers. The walls were plastered with dainty floral wallpaper and two French doors opened out to a wide wooden veranda which, Roxy noticed as she stepped out to take in the view, encircled the whole hotel. There wasn't a soul about and she guessed the unseasonably warm weather had lured everyone elsewhere.

She decided to put all thought of Max aside and get on with the job at hand. It was not yet 10am and she had a full day ahead of her. After freshening up in the communal bathroom down the end of the hall, Roxy gave her glasses a good scrub, applied a little lipstick and brushed her black hair down. Then, swapping her bulky jacket for a light red cotton cardigan, made her way back to the reception desk in the pub below. The woman who had signed her in was nowhere to be found so she wandered into the main bar, which was already occupied by a motley group of men, despite just opening. She spotted a young man working at the bar and marched up.

'G'day,' he said, clearly surprised to see a woman in the pub so early. 'Did ya want a drink?'

'Yeah, give me an orange juice, thanks.'

As he poured the juice, the bartender kept one eye on the young woman, as though sure she were a mirage about to vanish before his eyes. When he placed the glass down, he offered a sheepish grin and it was obvious he liked what he saw. Roxy grabbed the opportunity and pulled the picture of the old country guy from her handbag.

'I'm hoping you can help me.'

'Sure,' he said, widening his smile.

'I'm trying to locate this man. He's from here and I think his first name's Frank, but that's all I've got to go on. You don't happen to know him do you?'

As the barman examined the picture, Roxy crossed her fingers. If she could locate him by lunchtime, she could be out of there in time to catch the 6pm flight back to Sydney.

'Yeah I know him,' the barman said and Roxy looked at him, excited. 'He looks like every second guy who comes in 'ere.' He liked the look of the woman but she wasn't real bright. It was now Roxy's turn to smile. The guy was right. According to her own research, there were over 10,000 people in the Macksland region and a good number of them no doubt wore beat-up Akubras and answered to the name Frank.

'Okay, smart-ass,' she retorted. 'I thought I'd try my luck. How much do I owe you for the OJ?'

'Buck, twenty.' He offered her another smile, his white teeth flashing brightly in his tanned face. He could have passed for the Marlboro Man, she thought and paid him in change. As he spilled it into the till, he drawled, 'Why don't you ask old Bluey over there. If anyone knows him, he will.'

Roxy nodded her head appreciatively and made her way over to a side table where a group of men were perched on stools staring out at the street beyond.

'Bluey?' she asked, her eyes wandering over the four weatherbeaten men, almost identical but for the size of their beer guts and the color of their shirts. The oldest and smallest of the group tipped his head at her and grunted. She placed her things on the table and produced a free hand to shake his.

'Hi, I'm Roxy Parker. I'm looking for someone and the barman suggested you might know him—'

'Awww, you lookin' for a man are ya love?' bellowed another man, younger, flabbier with a wicked smirk across his face. 'Bluey gets that all the time! Don't ya Bluey?!'

The men erupted into peals of laughter and Roxy smiled patiently. *Ah, country blokes,* she thought. *What a riot.* She thrust the photo in front of him. 'All I know is he's from Macksland and his name's Frank.'

Several of the men continued to chortle but Bluey took the picture and stared at it hard. 'It's old Frankie O'Brien,' he said matter-of-factly and then handed it to the man next to him, the one with the faded flannelette, for verification.

'Yeah, could be,' the man said, 'but then again. What ya want him for?'

'Just looking him up on behalf of an old friend,' Roxy said.

'Who's Frankie O'Brien?' came the young, flabby guy and for a few seconds nobody answered. Roxy noticed that Bluey and his flannelette-clad friend exchanged cautious glances before the former said simply, 'An old timer is all.' Nobody uttered a word.

'Do you know where he lives? Where I might find him?' asked Roxy.

'Two different questions,' Bluey said, before dragging on a rollie cigarette as though he had all the time in the world. Out here, she thought, glancing about her doubtfully, he probably did. 'He lives way past the Wilo turn-off. Get on the old highway and head north, take the Wilo exit and keep goin' until you see a dirt road called Possum Shoot Road. Lives down there yonder, don't know the property name, don't know the number. But that's Frankie's place.'

Roxy scrawled this all down on the back of a beer coaster, not wanting to fluff about with the memo page on her smartphone, not in front of these potential Luddites.

'But you won't find him there now,' Bluey continued and Roxy glanced up.

'Oh?'

'They tell me he spends his life in church, prayin' for God knows what. I don't *want* to know. The nearest church to his place is the old Anglican just south of the turn-off. I'd bet me hat that's where you'll find him.'

The two younger men guffawed again but Bluey was not laughing. As she walked away Roxy thought she heard him say, 'Poor bastard. Been off his rocker for 50 fuckin' years.'

Within the hour Roxy had hired a rental car and, with the help of the GPS inside, found her way on to the old highway on the road to Wilo. Bluey's directions seemed simple enough but no church was indicated on the map and the man at the rental yard had laughed at her suggestion.

'There's no church out there,' he said, looking at her as if she were half-mad, 'nothing but cows and dust.'

She set out anyway, what did she have to lose? Besides it was a beautiful day for a drive. The journey seemed to take forever and, as the rental man had warned, the road stretched for miles in a colorless collusion of dusty hills and lethargic cows that barely bat an eyelid as the weird white woman sped by. She passed few cars on this road and wondered, as she usually did, whether she had been sent on a wild goose chase, whether the blokes back at the pub were pissing themselves laughing at the stupid city chick chasing after ghosts.

'Why do I do that?' she suddenly cried aloud, smacking the steering wheel with both hands. 'Why do I instantly mistrust people?' Did she get that from her mother, too, she wondered? Or had she developed it, like her ironclad independence, so that she could never be let down. If you expect the worst from people, you were never disappointed.

When Roxy reached the Wilo turn off she felt her heart sink. It was just as she'd been warned, not a church for miles. She turned the car around and slowly retraced her drive, scanning the road for any signs of life. About ten kilometres back, she spotted a thin dirt road leading towards a clump of trees, and brightened up. She had noticed the trees on her way through but the dirt road was so overgrown it was almost obscured from view. She signaled right, despite the empty road around her, and turned slowly up the track.

As she neared the forest of gum trees, she spotted a splash of white and what looked like a steeple, and then she saw it, a small wooden church, almost consumed by the trees around it. She maneuvered her car carefully across a thin wooden bridge towards a dirt clearing in front of the church. Once it must have once been packed with cars, today it was empty, except for a dusty ute which she knew just had to belong to old Frankie. Her heart leapt. Luck was finally going her way. She parked her car beside it and, switching the engine off, sat for several seconds transfixed by the quiet and the peeling dereliction of the unused church before her. How perfect a place, she thought, to hide away and pray.

She stepped out of the car and closed the door quietly behind her, almost tiptoeing up to the entrance. It wasn't secrecy she was after—Frank had no doubt heard her pull up—but there was a serenity about this place that she was reluctant to disturb. Roxy straightened her hair and pulled her cardigan sleeves down. The surrounding trees had starved the area of sun and it was suddenly very cold.

She strode up to the old wooden doors and creaked one carefully open, then, hugging her cardigan closer, stepped inside. The church, which was deathly quiet, was as ice-cold as a butcher's freezer, and just as dark. A sudden chill ran down her spine, but it wasn't from the cold. She knew, almost immediately, what she would find, even before the rotting stench hit her nostrils, even before her eyes had adjusted to the darkness and she spotted him kneeling there, all alone.

Roxy wanted to turn away, then, to run like a mad woman out the front doors and away. But she found her feet moving despite herself, striding calmly down the aisle, as though to take communion from some imaginary priest waiting up the front. But there would be no priest today, just an old man and his hat. She focused on the beat-up Akubra as she walked, one hand covering her nose and mouth, the other clenched in a tiny fist to her side.

When at last she reached him, she willed herself to look, to face what she feared she could not face. He was slouching a little to one side, his hands still clasped in front of him, his head resting silently on top. She whispered, 'Frank?' knowing it was too late, and then a blur of blood, a neck slit from ear to ear and fleeing frantically back down the aisle and out, where the birds chirped carelessly in the branches above. And the horrible knowledge that she was just days too late as a stream of yellow vomit hit the side of the old ute.

The Macksland police chief was not surprised to hear that Frank O'Brien was dead, simply asked Roxy to stay put, he'd be there 'in a sec'. Twenty minutes later, Chief Butler arrived in a cloud of dust and informed the young woman that his deputy and the county coroner were on their way. 'Just finishin' their lunch,' he remarked as he shook her hand, 'Now let's see the old bloke.'

Roxy lead the way inside but stopped before the pews and, as he went to inspect the corpse, returned outside to the fresh air. What she didn't tell him was that she had already returned inside, despite her stomach's objections. She wanted to study the crime scene before the cops came and whisked it all away.

'They can't put this one down to suicide,' she told herself as she stared at his gaping wound, the flesh curling up at the corners where it had resisted the murderer's knife. She could not see the murder weapon anywhere and doubted that she would. It had probably been thrown into a lake by now, or was lost in the fields beyond. It struck her that this was the perfect place for a murder and felt a pang of sadness for the old man still praying in death before her. Whatever he had known, whatever his secrets, they were not worth this. Surely they were not worth dying for.

Ignoring the stench of his decaying corpse, she had taken a pen from her handbag and used it to inspect his hands, making sure she did not leave her mark. She could not see any fresh skin under his nails or any scratching to indicate a struggle. There were no cuts under his knuckles or across his inner palm, which you would expect if he had tried to fend off a knife. In fact, he looked like he had been taken by surprise. Roxy stepped around his body to the most likely vantage point for the kill and noticed the old floorboards creak loudly beneath her feet. How had he not heard his assailant approach? Was he in such a deep trance, praying for whatever it was he needed to pray for, that he did not notice another person sneak up inside an empty, unused church? Or had he just let it happen, like a penance from God?

'Now that's a nasty bit of work,' the police chief was saying as he stepped out into the sunlight again. He was a large man with a stocky build and a face that was scarred from skin cancer. A small round indent on the side of his nose showed where a deadly chunk had once been removed and he had the habit of stroking this while he talked, as though playing with a war wound. 'He's just as you found him?'

'Of course.'

'And you'd never met the man, you say?'

'No, he was a friend of my client's, Beatrice Musgrave—of the Musgrave department stores? You see, I'm a writer and I was writing Beattie's biography. That is until she, um, died two weeks ago.'

'And what were you doing here, why did you come?'

'Well, Beattie had spoken about Frank fondly, they'd been friends since way back, and I was hoping, foolishly perhaps, that he could shed some light on the whole subject. Could help me understand her death.' The policeman seemed content with this and pulled out his notepad to take down her details. She gave him her home address and the name of her hotel.

'I'm gonna need to get an official statement from you back at the station.'

'That's fine.'

'And I'm afraid, for now, we'd really appreciate it if you could hang around, probably just for a day or so, until we, ahhh, clear a few things up.'

'That's fine,' she repeated unperturbed. She had not yet obtained the answers she was after and this new death only made things murkier. 'You don't happen to have an address for Frank's wife or any kids I can send a sympathy card to…later, of course, once you've spoken to them?'

He looked at her surprised. 'Oh he never married, no. Bit of a loner old Frankie. Mad as a hatter, they say. Actually it's a good thing you happened by. He might have turned to dust before anyone noticed he was gone.' He said it so matter-of-factly, as though that was just the way things were, and Roxy looked away sadly. 'I won't be back for a little while but just drop by the station before 5pm.' He slammed her car door behind her. 'We'll get the details down and then you can go and enjoy the night.'

I'm not here to have fun, Roxy wanted to tell him, but nudged her lips into a small smile and drove slowly away. When she reached the main road she hesitated, checked her rear vision mirror making sure she was out of sight of the police chief, and then turned left, back in the direction of Wilo.

She had a house to check out.

At the Wilo exit she turned off and, as Bluey had instructed, located the dirt road to Frank's house and headed north. As she drove along she checked the empty postal barrels that teetered on the edge of the road from time to time with their hand-painted lot numbers and flowery property names. But nowhere did she see the words 'Frank O'Brien'. She was beginning to wonder if she was chasing ghosts again. At one point she spotted a beat-up four-wheel drive plowing towards her in the opposite direction. She considered stopping the man behind the wheel to ask for help but couldn't risk drawing attention to herself and whizzed past him waving one hand in front of her face concealing it from view. After several more kilometres she spotted an unpainted barrel brimming over with mail. The number '64' had been painted across it in a shaky hand and she was about to look away when the penny dropped. The other mailboxes were all empty. Roxy pulled over to the side and, placing the car in park, jumped out to check the letters— mostly bills and junkmail—that were poking out from within. Just as she suspected, they were addressed to Frank P. O'Brien.

Roxy reversed her car and then turned up his dirt road checking her rear-vision mirror constantly. Chief Butler would still be busy with the coroner at the crime scene and she estimated that she had at least half an hour up her sleeve, but she wasn't taking chances. When she reached what looked like the main house, she pulled up at the front door, switched off the engine and jumped out. She needed to hurry.

Like the mail barrel, the farmhouse was old and falling down in parts, but it looked like it had been freshly painted and several empty paint cans piled under the house confirmed this. What looked like a new set of steps lead up to the main verandah and a brand-new welcome mat sat below the door as clean as a whistle. Pulling the edge of her sleeve up over her hand, Roxy banged on the door several times but it was clear the place was empty, she could hear her knocks echo across the wooden floorboards inside. Keeping the sleeve in place, she tried the handle and smiled. Thank Goodness for country living; it was unlocked. She pushed it open and entered.

Just like the exterior, the interior had been freshly painted but the job had not been finished and several cans and brushes sat just outside one of the bedrooms. She glanced inside and noticed how shabby it was. It looked like it had not been cleaned, let alone painted, for over a decade.

'Why the sudden reno'?' Roxy whispered aloud, making her way down the hallway to the living room. It sat across from the main bedroom and a quick glance in both revealed that Frank O'Brien had had another uninvited guest recently. The two rooms were a mess. Clothes and personal affects were strewn around the room and every drawer had been tipped over, the contents clearly searched. Someone had been here looking for something, and it was most likely the same person who'd slit the poor man's throat. She wondered if they had found what they were looking for. *And if they were still around.*

Roxy hesitated briefly before shrugging off her fear. There wasn't time for trepidation. She swiftly scrutinized each room, trying to get a picture of how the old man had lived and what, if anything, was missing. If there had been any incriminating material, love letters from old Beattie, perhaps, she realized with a sigh that the murderer had no doubt taken them or destroyed them somehow. She stepped towards the main fireplace hoping to find the evidence half burned inside and scowled at its emptiness. It was worth a try. Then she noticed the mantelpiece. It was covered in dust except where several thin, rectangular items had once stood. A quick look at the floor revealed two photo frames, both smashed where the burglar had dropped them. She glanced back at the mantelpiece. There were five dust-free marks. Where were the other three frames? Carefully she checked the contents on the floor, but the pictures were nowhere to be found. They had probably been taken.

Roxy glanced at her watch and then returned to the hall, following it down to an old kitchen at the back. It was surprisingly tidy with a small wooden table in the middle and an old fridge and cooker leaning against each other on one side. Nothing seemed amiss and she was about to turn back when she had an idea. She crossed to the fridge, which, predictably, had an assortment of pamphlets, bills and a postcard dangling precariously beneath old magnets. She scooped the lot up and scurried back down the hall and out of the house, careful to cover her hand up before closing the door.

Back in her car, Roxy roared the engine to life and swung it around and away. Within minutes she was back on the old highway and heading towards town.

17 GOOD COP/BAD COP

'What can I get for you, love?' The waitress looked like someone straight out of a B-grade American flick, peroxide blonde hair piled high above an overly made-up face, enormous hoop ear-rings and a tiny pink uniform barely covering her dimpled thighs. She was 40 going on 20, mutton dressed up as lamb, and she was the perfect bit player in the drama Roxy had stumbled into. Concealed in a back booth with her spoils spread out on the table before her, Roxy ordered a toasted cheese sandwich and a coffee, and then turned her attention to the table. She shrugged off a feeling of guilt, knowing only too well she should never have taken the items, and tried to justify it by assuring herself it was all for Beattie's sake.

There were seven items in all and she studied each one carefully, starting with the bills. Frank O'Brien couldn't have been that much of an 'old timer'. He had a Visa card and had purchased several lavish meals with it. She checked the locations: they were all fashionable Sydney restaurants, and they had all been eaten in the space of one week. Roxy checked her diary. That was the week before Roxy had been employed by Beatrice to write the biography, a week before the whole mess started. There was also a rather modest bill for a week's accommodation at a Sydney hotel, and a bill from a jewelry store for a 'personal item' worth $260. Roxy wondered if this had been a gift for Beatrice Musgrave. She had no proof of it, of course, but she was getting good at making hunches. She put the bill aside and consulted the next one, from the electricity company. The amount owing was small, too small for anyone but a bachelor. She put that aside, as well.

There were a few pamphlets, one about pesticide, the other advertising a Chinese restaurant in town, as well as a postcard and Roxy picked it up hopefully. It wasn't from Beattie and her heart dropped. No-one said it was going to be easy. It featured a picture of the Sydney Oprah House on the front, was dated about a month back and had been sent by a chirpy sounding 'Sally Duffy'. 'Having a ball!' it read, then went on to mention a few tourist haunts she'd just checked out before finishing with the line, 'Missing you, xoxo.'

Perhaps the old man was not as lonely as everyone assumed. Roxy made a note of the name and then turned to the final items. One was a clumsily drawn newspaper cartoon about a National Party politician that she guessed farmers might find amusing and, concluding that it could be of no consequence, put it aside. The final item, however, got Roxy's heart racing: it was titled, 'Society Queen's Tragic End'.

'Here you go then,' came a loud voice to Roxy's left and she sat back with a start. 'Aw, sorry dear, didn't mean to scare ya!'

'Oh, God, no, sorry. I was miles away.' Roxy gathered the items together hastily as the waitress placed the food down before her.

'Lucky bugger,' the waitress said with a dramatic sigh, 'wish I was a miles away.' She wandered off, wiggling her bum behind her.

Roxy added sufficient sugar to disguise the bitterness of her so-called 'latte', and then devoured the sandwich as she read the news article through. It was about Beatrice

Musgrave's 'suicide' but provided no more information than Roxy had already learnt and certainly made no mention of Beattie's relationship with Frank. It was from a local newspaper and, if she was correct, it at least proved one thing: whatever Beattie and Frank's relationship, it was obviously not public knowledge in these parts.

She finished her lunch, placed the items back in her bag and paid the bill.

'Do you have some local phone books I can take a look at?' she asked the waitress as she handed over the change.

'Sure thing, love.' She produced one very thin, very ratty phone book from beneath the counter. 'Small town,' she said and winked again.

Roxy thanked her and looked up the name Duffy. There were half a dozen names listed but only one with the first initial S. *Bingo*. She made a note of the address and phone number and then placed the book back on the counter, waving to the waitress as she left the cafe. It was now close to 4pm and, with directions in hand, Roxy made her way to the local police station. There she was ushered straight to the police chief's office, a pokey room with a cluttered desk facing two gray plastic chairs. Chief Butler motioned Roxy into a chair and sent his deputy, a man called Dougie who looked barely out of his teens, to fetch the coffees.

'I'm gonna be taping this conversation,' he told her, when the deputy had returned, 'and we'll type it up later for you to sign.'

'Fine,' Roxy replied feeling suddenly nervous. Did they consider her a suspect? Chief Butler smiled reassuringly and pressed the record button. 'Roxy Parker interview, Macksland station' he muttered, adding the time and date and the names of himself and his deputy, who was perched in the other chair staring intently at Roxy.

'Okay then,' Butler said, 'Let's start from the beginning. What are you doing in Macksland Miss Parker, and how did you happen upon the deceased, Mr Frank O'Brien?'

As Roxy told her story both men watched her closely, firing questions from time to time, and it occurred to Roxy that they were playing the oldest game in the book: Good Cop/Bad Cop. The police chief was on her side, he wanted her to understand that. But his deputy, the pimply faced kid beside her, was less amiable. He would need convincing.

'You're trying to tell us you just rocked on up and found him lying there dead. Is that correct?' he said, sneering a little.

'Not quite,' Roxy replied coolly. 'He wasn't lying anywhere, he was propped up against the pew. I thought at first he was praying.'

'As you would,' Chief Butler soothed. 'And you'd never met the deceased before?'

'Never. But I had heard him mentioned by a client of mine, Mrs Beatrice Musgrave.'

'Yesssss,' the younger officer hissed, leaning towards her, his small eyes constricted suspiciously. 'And what happened to that client of yours, Mrs Musgrave?'

'She killed herself two weeks ago.'

'She killed herself.'

'Well, that's what the police say. Except I found that a little strange—it seemed out of character—so I've been doing a little checking of my own. That's how I came to be here. I believe that Frank and Beatrice were once good friends. I was hoping he could shed some light on her death.'

'Is that right?' It was the young policeman again, his voice stained with disbelief. Roxy was growing quickly impatient.

'Yes it is,' she turned back to the police chief. 'Look, I don't like his tone. I came here in good faith to explain myself and suddenly I feel like a suspect. If I am one, I'd like to know about it and I'll end the conversation here and get myself a lawyer.'

'What you got to hide, Miss Parker?' It was the deputy again and Roxy sighed loudly before the police chief butted in.

'Okay, easy does it, Dougie, why don't you step out for a bit.

'Oh, boss!'

'Doug, just flamin' do it!'

The young cop blushed crimson red and loped out of the office glumly, closing the door behind him.

'I'm sorry about that, Miss Parker,' Chief Butler said. 'Dougie gets a little too enthusiastic. Watches too much *Law & Order*. As far as I'm concerned, you're not a suspect but, well, look at it from our point of view. You rock up out of nowhere, suddenly there's a dead body.'

'But I arrived this morning, as far as I could tell the body had been dead for well over a day.'

'Yes well I've got Shirley checking the plane records and, as soon as we get confirmation on that, you're off the hook. That's not to say, of course that you couldn'ta snuck in earlier, killed him, flown out and back again.' Chief Butler was stroking his nose gently and staring at her.

Roxy was stunned. 'What on earth for? I didn't even know the guy, why would I want to kill him?'

Butler held a rough hand up. 'It's okay, it's okay, I don't reckon ya did do it and I'm usually a pretty good judge of character.'

'That's a relief! Look, I understand your suspicions but I can prove my exact whereabouts over the past week if need be.'

'No need for that. Not yet at least. For now I just have to get some basic details down, I hope you don't mind.'

Roxy nodded her consent, trying to seem detached, but she was starting to regret poking around the dead man and his house. She may have contaminated both crime scenes and it looked like a stray black hair hanging over the corpse was all Dougie needed to lock her up and throw away the key. Chief Butler continued the questioning.

'Had you met, seen or spoken to the deceased before you found him in the chapel?'

'Never. Well, maybe, I mean…'

'You either have, or you haven't. Not a trick question Miss Parker.'

'Sorry, it's just that I had seen him, sort of. I have this photo.' She produced the now crumpled print from her bag. 'My friend, Max Farrell, was official photographer at Beattie's funeral. He mentioned Frank first and, when I suspected that this was the same Frank that Mrs Musgrave said was her first love, I decided to come and find out for myself.'

Chief Butler stared at the shot for some time. 'So Frankie showed up at the Musgrave funeral, eh?'

'Yes, he did.'

'Mind if I keep this?'

'Not at all.'

'Also, if I could have a transcript of exactly what it was your client had said about Frank, that would help.'

'No problem, I have my laptop with me at the hotel. I can print you out a copy of the relevant quotes when I get back.'

'No rush, tomorrow will do.' Glancing at the clock on the wall he said loudly, 'Interview aborted, 4.55 pm.' Then he switched off the recorder and sat back in his seat with a sigh. 'Ugly, ugly business. So you're a biographer you say?'

'Well, more a ghostwriter actually.'

'You write spooky stuff?' He looked confused and she had to laugh.

'Sometimes, yes. But no, I help people write their life stories and then they put their name to it and get all the credit, and I get a decent sized check in the mail. That's how I met Beatrice, and why I'm here at all. I also write for magazines and newspapers, interviews, features that kind of stuff.'

'So you usually play Sherlock Holmes on the side?'

'In my line of work, Chief Butler, we call it investigative reporting. If, like Frank O'Brien, Beatrice Musgrave was murdered, then I think the public have a right to know.'

'Yes, yes, I agree with you.' This surprised the writer and now it was his turn to laugh. 'You can pick your jaw up off the floor, Miss Parker. My wife's the editor of the local rag. I get her "right to know" rant about 10 flamin' times a week!'

'Well that's lucky for me,' she quipped. 'You won't think I'm so strange.'

'Oh I didn't say that!' He boomed with laughter again and pushed his chair out behind him. 'Okay, you can run away now and enjoy the great Macksland hospitality.'

'Thank you, but can I just ask: Did you know that Frank and Beatrice were once lovers?'

He looked surprised 'You sure about that?'

'Pretty sure.'

'Now that's one for the cards. Who'da thought? Old Frankie and the rich bird! Hell, my wife'll be steaming when she finds out she missed that little scoop!'

Roxy opened the office door. 'So, can you recommend anywhere special for dinner?'

'Lucy's at the Royal Hotel. Can't beat it for taste and price. Tell 'em I sent you, you'll get looked after.'

'And some suspicious stares, no doubt.'

'Oh you'll get those anyway, Miss Parker, this is a country town, remember? Everyone's a stranger until they've lived here a lifetime, and not even then half the time.' And with that the interrogation was over.

As Roxy changed her clothes for dinner back at her hotel, it occurred to her that, in fact, the ordeal was only just beginning. Frank's murder clearly opened a whole new chapter. Later, as she sliced into her minted rack of lamb, with the patrons of Lucy's restaurant stealing glances at her from time to time, she lapped up the anonymity almost as much as the warming glass of Merlot she'd ordered. Here no-one expected anything of her and she did not have to try to please. She did not have to explain herself to her mother or fend off Oliver's questions or feel yet again that she was disappointing her best friend who, in his loneliness had mistaken affection for love. Why couldn't Max see that? He craved love so badly, he was willing to destroy their friendship in pursuit of it.

Later, as she struggled her way to sleep, it was not the lifeless face of Frank O'Brien that haunted Roxy's dreams. It was Max Farrell, his eyes imploring, his hands reaching for her as she fled towards the dark gray beyond.

18 FRANK'S BEST FRIEND

The phone rang many times and Roxy glanced again at the number she had scribbled down for S. Duffy, chewing on her lower lip nervously. She groaned and was about to press 'end call' when it picked up.

'Hello?' The voice sounded young, male and croaky, and she suspected that whoever it was, she'd just dragged him out of bed.

'Oh, hello! Is Sally Duffy there please?' Roxy crossed her fingers.

'Hmm? Sally? No, mate, I'm Simon Duffy, I'm the only one here.'

Her heart dropped. 'Damn, must have the wrong number. Sorry about that.'

'No worries. But I know where you can find her.'

'Huh?'

'Sal'. Isn't that who you're after?'

'Yes, yes! Is she a relative of yours?'

He laughed at this. 'Crikey no! I wish. Nope, Sally's a ring-in, rents a place sometimes on Chalmers Street.'

'You don't happen to have a number for her do you?'

'No such luck.'

Roxy scowled. 'Oh well, thanks anyway.'

'But, you know, at this hour you'll probably catch her down at Jenny's, I think she hangs around there a bit when she's bored.'

'Where's Jenny live?'

He laughed again. 'Nah, mate, Jenny's Fashion Empori-something or other. On the main street.'

Roxy thanked him then hung up and dialed the local directory for Jenny's contact number. Before calling, she checked her watch. It was close to 10am and the buzz in the breakfast room that morning had made it perfectly clear that old Frank's murder was now common knowledge. She knew these old towns: gossip spread like wildfire. If Sally had not known about Frank at 9am, she would surely know by 9.05, and certainly by now. Roxy called the shop.

'Hello?' a woman answered, her voice soft and barely audible.

'Sally Duffy?'

'Yes?'

'Sally, my name is Roxy Parker, I'm a writer from Sydney. I'm really sorry about your friend Frank O'Brien.'

'Oh?' There was a sudden sob at the other end.

'Look, I realize the timing is terrible, but I need to speak with you most urgently about him. It's the reason I'm here, can we meet?'

There was an intake of breath, a pause and then another loud sob from the woman at the other end and Roxy gave her a moment to compose herself.

'He's…dead,' she said eventually.

'Yes, Sally, I know. I was the one who found the body. I had to speak to him about something and I got to him too late. Can we meet up? Now? It's imperative. I know you were a good friend of his and I think we can help each other.'

There was another pause before the woman said, 'Why are you calling me? How did you get my number? How do you know we were good friends?'

'I'm a journalist, Sally, it's my job to know.'

'Well, how do I know you didn't, um…'

'I didn't kill him, Sally, if that's what you mean. I needed to speak to him about a good friend of mine who was also murdered. I believe he knew the murderer and that's why he was killed. It's too much of a coincidence otherwise. Sally, the sooner we talk, the better, both our lives may depend on it.' It occurred to Roxy that if the murderer had spotted that postcard he would have deduced, as Roxy had, that Sally and Frank were good friends and may have shared their most intimate secrets with each other. In all likelihood, Sally Duffy was the next target. The woman was still hesitating so Roxy took a punt. 'Look, if you're not sure, call Chief Butler at the police station. He can vouch for me.' She was not at all sure whether the police chief would vouch for her, but it was worth a try.

'Alright,' she said abruptly. 'Meet me at the Speak Easy Cafe, corner of Flinders and Main Street. Give me ten minutes.'

As she hung up it occurred to Roxy that she did not know what Sally Duffy looked like. Fortunately, the cafe was empty when she arrived and, taking a seat near the back, she informed the manager, a middle-aged man with enormous ears and an inquisitive eye, that she was waiting for someone. Twenty minutes later a young woman, barely out of her teens, burst into the cafe and Roxy glanced at her and then away.

'Hello Sally, almost didn't recognize you, how you going?' The cafe manager called out and Roxy glanced back surprised. She had been expecting someone older, more Frank's age. Sally spotted Roxy and came directly over. Now it was the cafe manager's turn to be surprised and he followed her over, quickly pulling her seat out for her.

'Can I get you something?' he asked, darting quick, quizzical glances in Roxy's direction.

'A pot of tea, please,' she said, blinking back tears. Roxy ordered coffee and, once the manager had disappeared out the back, turned to the young woman with a reassuring smile.

'I'm Roxy Parker, obviously. Thanks for meeting me.'

The young woman simply nodded, clearly struggling to gain some composure. She was pretty in a plain, school-girlish way, and could not have been more than 20. Her ginger hair was tied into a ponytail down her back and her fair skin was splattered with freckles. Her dress was floral with a drop waist, and she wore a headband with the same matching print. She looked like a farmer's wife in the making, and a good 50 years younger than Frank O'Brien.

'I help Jenny out down at the shop from time to time,' she announced suddenly. 'If...if I hadn't been working, I might have been with him, with Frank...he might not have died.'

Or you might also be dead, Roxy thought but instead said, 'Sally, you need to pull yourself together, we need to talk about Frank, we need to work out who might have done this.'

'The police...'

'Have they questioned you at all?'

'No, no, they want me to come in later. I can't see why.'

'They're just trying to cover all the bases, don't worry about them. Sally, how did you know Frank? What was your relationship?'

The young woman peeled a handkerchief from her pocket and blew her nose loudly. 'He was a good friend. I met him when a group of us were cleaning up the old church earlier this year. He helped us out. The others thought he was weird. I just felt sorry for him.' She hid her face in the hankie and Roxy placed one hand gently on her shoulder. The owner arrived with their drinks then and eyed Roxy suspiciously as he placed them down.

'You okay, Sal'?' he asked dubiously.

'F...fine, thanks, Johnno...I'm fine.'

'I'm sorry about your old mate.'

'Yeah, thanks, Johnno,' she was pulling herself together again, madly wiping her eyes with the hankie. 'I'm okay, now, no worries.'

Reluctantly, he wandered away and, now more in control, Sally took several sips of her tea. 'Frank didn't have an enemy in the world. Who would do this to him?'

'I don't know, but I'm working on it.'

'How do you know him again?'

'I don't. I knew of him. He was a good friend of a woman I knew. I was writing her biography and, well, she suddenly turned up dead. I was hoping Frank might have some answers, that's all.'

'Beatrice Musgrave?'

The name caught Roxy by surprise. 'You *knew* her?'

'No, no, but Frank talked about her constantly. He was madly in love with her, you know?'

'I thought as much.' Roxy sipped her drink and grimaced. It was criminal what this town served up as 'coffee'. 'Had they been in contact recently, before she died, that is?'

Sally seemed surprised by the question. 'Yes, of course, they were going to get married. She didn't tell you?'

She sat back with a thud. 'No.'

'That's all Frank talked about, he was getting the old house ready for her.'

That explained the paint cans, and the expensive dinners in Sydney, and the jewelry bill. 'When? When were they planning to wed?'

'Early next year, I think. Frank said they had waited 50 years, another one wouldn't hurt.'

'Did he tell you anything about their daughter?'

She looked taken aback and her jaw dropped a little before she clamped it shut. She hesitated, as though wondering whether to trust the woman in front of her and Roxy didn't blame her. She didn't know her from Adam. She tried for her warmest smile. 'Beatrice told me about it.'

The young woman nodded and eventually said, 'He told me a little bit. He didn't know much himself. Just that they had given up a baby a long time ago, when Beattie was "weaker".' She spat out that last word and then glanced quickly at Roxy and softened her tone. 'That's how Frank put it, not me. He said if she'd been stronger things would have been different. Back then she had to do what her parents wanted her to do. Frank wanted to marry her, you know? And apparently she wanted to marry him. They both wanted to make a family together.'

'But Beattie married Terence Musgrave instead.'

'Yes,' the young woman sighed. 'What a fool! She chose money over love. I would never do that, never! It nearly killed him, you know? It was the reason he was so quiet, the reason everyone thought he was nuts. He wasn't, well, maybe he was nuts for her. He never really got over her.'

'So why didn't they marry five years ago when Terence died?'

Sally considered this for a while. 'I think Frank wanted to. But she said she needed to straighten out a few things first.'

'So that's why she was writing the biography?'

'Yes. Frank said she had to get it all out in the open before they could get married, before they could move ahead, you know?'

Roxy nodded sadly. *That was their mistake.* 'So what do you know about the daughter?'

'Nothing,' she said quickly. 'Just what Frank told me…they had given her up a long time ago and, well, he never quite said it, but I think they were going to try to make amends, to look her up, you know? But they never did.'

'Really?'

'Well, not that he told me.' She took a long sip of her tea. 'It's so sad. Frank seemed so happy for the first time, full of hope, you know?'

Roxy looked down at the murky brew before her. He had waited so long, and all for nothing. The fool.

'Who do you think did it?' Sally asked, anger clearly swelling up again. 'Who would do this to poor old Frank? Who?!'

'I don't know, Sally, but I have a feeling it has something to do with the daughter.'

'Why? Why would you think that? Maybe she's got nothing to do with anything.'

'Nah, I reckon she's the key to it all. I need to find out who she is. You have no idea at all?'

Sally squinted her eyes, trying to think. 'He never said, honestly, I don't reckon he knew. In fact I'm pretty damn sure he didn't know anything about her. He never even saw the baby.'

'So he was never told her name or the name of her adoptive parents?' It sounded inconceivable, but then those were very different times.

'I...I don't know. He never told me if he did.'

'What about *where* she was born? Surely he knew that?'

'Maybe Sydney. Or Adelaide. She was from South Australia you know? That would be my guess.'

Roxy shook her head. 'No, no, I doubt she could have kept it such a tight secret if she'd had it in a city where she knew a lot of people. No, my guess is she hid away and had the baby here.'

'Here?!' Sally looked incredulous then shrugged and finished off her tea. Suddenly her eyes were glazing over again. She looked like she was going to resume her sobbing, so Roxy quickly paid their bill and shuffled her out, unwilling to draw more accusatory stares from the cafe owner.

'What are you going to do now?' Sally asked, her tears back in control.

'I'm going to pay a visit to the local hospital. If Beattie had a child in Macksland, they should have it all on file.'

'Oh, wow, I never would have thought of that. You're really clever!'

Roxy waved her off. 'Nah, just been around the traps long enough.'

They walked down one street block towards Roxy's hire car when Sally grabbed her elbow. 'Can I ask you a huuuuge favor? Before you go to the hospital? Please?!'

'Sure, what?'

'I had to close the boutique to come and see you but I *really* need to get back there and open it or Jenny will chuck a spaz. The problem is I also need to see the coppers. You know, make my statement and all that. Do you think…that is if you don't mind…I mean…'

'What is it, Sally, spit it out.'

'Well, could you just keep an eye on the boutique while I run down to the copshop? I won't take long, I promise. Twenty minutes max.'

Roxy wasn't exactly in the mood to play shopkeeper but Sally seemed so desperate, so anxious, that she relented, and together they walked down main street past several blocks of shops, most with inscriptions pre-dating the 1900s. Jenny's Fashion Emporium was one of these, a brightly painted storefront wedged incongruously between a butchers and a bike shop. There was an elaborate sign out the front and two glassy eyed mannequins in the window, each donning hip trousers and glittering silver tops. Sally unlocked the door and waved Roxy through.

'Whenever I go to Sydney to visit the rellies, I always bring back some gear. Keeps it up-to-date, you know?'

'Good idea,' Roxy replied, 'although I think it would be dangerous work for me. I'd go a bit mad with the credit card.'

Sally laughed then. 'I know! I go *mental*. Anyway, have a look around, you might find something of interest. And if anyone comes in try to stall them. If not—'

'It's okay, I've done my stint of shop keeping. I can use a till, and I promise not to run off with the day's earnings.'

'Oh there's not much there. It's been a quiet week. I won't be long!' Once Sally had left, Roxy began looking around, sifting idly through the stock and pulling a variety of garments up in front of her to peruse in the mirror. She was surprised by the quality of the merchandise. There were only a few of the dowdy floral dresses that Sally clearly enjoyed wearing. This collection was mostly modern, the latest labels in the latest styles. Sally might be a country girl at heart but she clearly knew her designers. After sifting idly through the racks, Roxy perched up against the counter and began perusing the magazine collection, which was also contemporary. She scanned the pages of that month's *Vogue* and *Harper's Bazaar* before glancing at the clock. Almost an hour had passed. Frowning, she located her lipstick from deep inside her handbag and reapplied some to her lips, then scraped her fingers through her hair and wandered towards the door to peer down the street. That's when Sally came bursting through, red-faced and puffing.

'Are you okay, Sally? Come in, have a seat.'

'I…I'm fine. Sorry it took so long. They were so insinuating…they made out like I could have done it!'

Roxy shook her head angrily. She wanted to throttle young Dougie. He clearly didn't realize how upsetting his little game of Inspector Morse could be. 'Take no notice of them. They did that to me and I didn't even know Frank.'

'But I was his best friend, his only friend. Why would I do it?!'

'Honestly, don't give it another thought. I'm sorry they upset you. But I really need to get going now. Are you okay on your own? Is there someone I can call?'

'No. No, I'm fine.' She dabbed at her face with her hankie and tried for a smile. 'Are you going to the hospital now?' Roxy nodded. 'I'm sure you'll have no problem finding what you want. My neighbor Beryl Smith runs the records department and she's just lovely.'

'That's a relief. Hospitals can be pretty stuffy when it comes to handing over information.'

'No, no, Beryl is great, I'm sure she won't mind.'

As it turned out Beryl did mind. Very much. 'Those records are sealed,' she barked. 'We can't just have strangers wandering in off the street going through people's private business.'

'Oh, I completely understand.'

'Only the parties involved may access them,' she continued unabated. 'So, unless you are the adopter or the adopted, and I suspect that you are neither, then you can not have a look.'

Roxy had expected as much. After finding her way to the hospital, a crumbly brick structure with several large chimneys at one end and a modern extension which now served as the emergency ward on the other, she had inquired at reception and been directed down two flights of stairs to the basement. Beryl was sitting at a desk behind a glass petition, sorting through files and color coding them with fluorescent pens. The mere sight of her confirmed Roxy's fears. She had the look of a strict school mistress: starched helmet-style hairdo, spectacles hanging on a chain around her neck, and small eyes that squinted at you like she was trying to work out your game, like you might throw a punch her way at anytime.

Roxy tried another tack. 'Oh dear, I came so far,' she said, sighing heavily as she threw her hands in the air. 'All the way from Sydney, you know?' The woman didn't blink. 'And William Musgrave said I would have absolutely no problem.'

'William Musgrave?'

'You know, the owner of the Musgrave & Son department stores? I've been writing a biography on his recently deceased mother, you might have heard of her, Beatrice Musgrave?' The woman stared blankly so Roxy continued. 'Yes. Well, it's her file I'm after. Just to get some facts straight for the book, you understand? I'm wondering if I should just call Will up and get him to give his permission here and now.' She knew William would never consent but it was worth mentioning anyway.

'Well that's no use,' Beryl replied smugly. 'Only the adoptive parents or the adopted child can see those records. Other family members don't count.'

'Ahhh.'

'So it looks like you've wasted a trip, doesn't it?'

'It looks like it,' Roxy replied as civilly as she could muster. She looked past the woman to the rest of the office, spacious and jammed with several dozen filing cabinets. The answer lay in there, she knew that, she just had to work out a way to get in. 'Is there anyone else I can speak to?'

'No there isn't, I'm in charge here and I'm afraid I'm *all* there is.' There was a glimmer of delight in the woman's eyes now and it was clear she was thoroughly enjoying her little power trip, however mediocre.

'Okay, then,' Roxy shrugged, 'thank you so much for your time, I understand your position and I appreciate your time.'

'Oh, oh, well, thank you…' she was surprised by Roxy's change in tone, had clearly been expecting more of a battle, and tried for a smile. 'You have a nice visit.'

'Thank you, I'm sure I will. Good bye.'

As Roxy climbed the stairwell back up to the entrance she realized that there was another way to get to those files. She just wasn't sure if young Sally had it in her.

'You want me to do *what?*'

Sally had sounded excited to hear Roxy on the other end, as eager to solve old Frank's murder as she was. The local gossip was, police chief Butler thought the whole affair a wash out. 'Most likely a passing straggler looking for money,' he had told several of the locals. 'Maybe an old hobo or a young traveler desperate for cash, stumbled upon the church and old Frankie and got carried away. Maybe Frankie resisted, he was foolish enough to. Besides, I really can't see how anyone could benefit from killing the old coot.'

'That's why you have to help me,' Roxy said over the phone when Sally told her. 'I'm not asking *you* to do anything illegal. I just need you to distract Beryl long enough for me to slip in and check the files. Simple.'

The young woman hesitated. 'Oh I don't know. What if she suspects?'

'Why should she? She doesn't know we know each other and you can simply deny all involvement if I was to get caught. *Which I won't.*'

'Oh…um.'

'Look, Sally, when do you think she takes her lunch break?'

'12.30. That's about standard around here. Besides I've seen her at the milk bar about then once or twice. But that's no good.'

'Why?'

'Because she locks the office up then.'

'Oh.'

'No, no, I know what to do. Where are you now?' Sally's voice had lost its anxiety.

'I'm at the hospital, near the canteen.'

'Wait there. I'll be right up.' She hung up without saying goodbye and Roxy couldn't help a smile. 'We'll make a super-sleuth out of you yet,' she said to herself.

As Sally made her way to the hospital, Roxy bought a bottled water and took a seat by the window. It was just after midday. They would have to act fast if they wanted to distract Beryl before lunchtime. Ten minutes later Sally was seated beside Roxy, describing her plan in hushed, conspiratorial tones.

'It sounds good to me,' she replied and then, with a laugh, added, 'If you pull this one off, Sally, you might want to consider a career on stage.'

'Oh I don't know about that! Besides it won't be hard to cry for old Frankie. Give me a ten-minute start and then come on down.'

'Sure thing.' Roxy did as instructed, imagining the younger woman appearing out of the blue in front of old Beryl.

'I can't handle it,' she would cry, 'Frankie's been murdered and I don't know what to do!'

Beryl would be flabbergasted, of course, unused to open displays of emotion and yet oddly proud that her young neighbor had come to her for comfort. Of all people, Sally had chosen her.

'Now, now, dear,' she would soothe, 'it's all going to be alright. There's nothing to be afraid of.'

'But I miss him so much! And what if the murderer comes after me next?!' And then Sally would bawl so loudly, Beryl would be forced to take her outside, to comfort her in the serenity of the gardens beyond. *'Let me just lock up,'* she would say but this would only lead to further hysteria from the young woman and so Beryl would be forced to take her outside, away from the building and any listening ears who might suspect she didn't have the scene under control. If there was one thing Beryl liked, Sally had told Roxy, it was being in control.

Roxy checked her watch and then began slowly climb back down to the basement, hoping that Sally had been right about her neighbor.

'There's an exit out the back way from her office, so we'd most likely use that one. Just come in the front door, get what you need and leave the same way.'

Roxy hesitated at the bottom of the stairwell and, hearing nothing, edged herself slowly around, ready to leap back should she see signs of life. But both the corridor and the office were empty. Roxy dashed up to the door and turned the knob. It was locked! She looked around frantically. What was she supposed to do now? Then she noticed the reception window had been left ajar. It seemed Sally had been able to pull Beryl away before she got to that lock. Roxy checked the corridor again and then pulled her body up to the window panel and, flinging her legs around, leapt inside. At just that moment a flurry of footsteps could be heard coming from an office down the hall, followed by voices, which were getting increasingly louder. Roxy guessed they were workers taking their lunch break and estimated that they would turn when they got to the stairwell, that she would be safe in just a few seconds.

'I'll just grab Bezza,' someone called out and a separate set of footsteps began closing in fast. Roxy ducked under the counter, curling her legs tight to her stomach. She could not tell if her feet were poking out but it did seem like her heart was thumping loudly. Too loudly. An unfamiliar voice called out, 'Beryl?! Beryl, you there?' Deathly silence. After several excruciating seconds the footsteps started back towards the stairwell.

'Must've already gone for lunch,' the voice announced matter-of-factly and then the chatter continued as the workers climbed the stairs and faded out. Roxy sighed with relief and waited one second more. Hearing nothing but her own frantic heartbeat, she uncurled her legs and climbed out from under the counter.

The filing cabinets were like a maze behind her but it didn't take long to track down the cabinet for Alexander (Beattie's maiden name). Roxy had been banking on Beryl being as organized as she looked, and she did not let her down. On the side of each aisle was a sheet plastered with reference guides. 'Birth Parents, 1960-70' was, according to Beryl's directions, down in the red section, under the code: 'BP 2'.

Roxy flung the relevant drawer open and located the file within seconds. She was expecting a lot of dust, maybe a few tiny critters, as it was unlikely to have been opened in a very long time. Instead, it was fresh manila folder with the words Frank O'Brien & Beatrice Alexander scribbled in black marker across the top. The marker did not match the others in the drawer and Roxy's stomach turned. She opened the folder and stifled a scream. It was empty. A brand-new, empty folder. Somebody—the murderer?—had beaten her to this evidence. There was no other explanation.

'Damn it!' she hissed. *What was she to do now?*

She glanced at her watch. If Sally was keeping up the charade, she still had a few minutes to look around. Roxy flicked through the other files surrounding Mrs Musgrave's. If she could find someone with a similar situation to

Beattie's perhaps then she could find a common link, the attending doctor's name, perhaps, or the midwife's—someone who may have been party to the birth and could tell her what was missing from the file. This was a small country town and must have been even smaller 50 years ago. How many doctors could there have been? Within minutes she had located another couple who had given birth around the same time as Beattie. The mother's name was Milly Smith and no doctor was listed but the midwife was: Agnetha Frickensburg. Roxy continued her search. She found two more women who had used Agnetha during their births that year and four who had used someone called Zoe Callahan. She could not be sure that Zoe and Agnetha would even be alive today, but it was worth a try.

Committing the midwives' names to her memory, she quickly shut the cabinet and departed the office as she had come, checking that she hadn't left any footprints on the desk as she went and that she left the window ajar. Then she sprinted along the corridor and back up the stairs. When she reached the top, she slowed her pace down and, covering her face with one hand, as though coughing, she calmly left the hospital. She didn't spot Sally or Beryl on her way out and she didn't try to. She just needed to get out of there as fast as possible. She was in deep enough trouble as it was.

19 THE ANGRY YOUNG MAN

When Roxy returned to her hotel room she discovered a note that had been slipped underneath her door. It was from Police Chief Butler. He had a few more questions, could she please drop by the station, ASAP? She fetched her Filofax and a pen and jotted down the names: Agnetha Frickensburg and Zoe Callahan, then grabbed her handbag and jacket again, and let herself out. In the hotel foyer, Roxy came across the young barman from the morning before. He wasn't smiling, just gave her the once over and skulked into the side bar.

'Hello to you too,' she thought gloomily and made her way back to the police station, past the empty check-in desk and towards Chief Butler's office.

'You wanted to see me?' she said, leaning in through the open door. His head was down, reading some papers and he looked up, more than a little startled, and then out towards reception.

'It's empty,' Roxy announced, helping herself to a seat. 'Good thing I'm not a crim', eh?'

Chief Butler was not amused. 'I hear you've been snooping around where you're not welcome.'

'What do you mean?'

'I mean Sally Duffy. What were you doing talking with her this morning?'

'Where? Who saw me?'

'The Speak Easy Cafe, Miss Parker. Jonathan Brownie tells me you were down there with Sally asking her all sorts of questions.'

'And there's a law against that is there?'

'Don't come the raw prawn with me young lady,' he boomed. 'You could be in a lot of trouble here you know? Frank O'Brien didn't have an enemy in the world and then suddenly you show up and he's dead.'

'Are you now saying you think I did it?'

He sighed heavily, then got up and leant out his office door.

'Boomer!' A meek voice called something out from another office and a young policewoman rushed in, red faced. 'Where the hell have you been?'

'Just going to the loo, sir.'

'Yeah well wait until someone comes along to relieve you. You don't leave reception unmanned. *Never*. Got it? I don't care if you wet ya bloody pants. You stay at the desk until relief arrives.'

'O…Okay Sir, sorry.'

He 'hmphed' and then, slamming the door behind him, returned to his seat to glare at Roxy while stroking the scar on his nose. She didn't dare smile.

'Look, lady, I don't think you did it any more than I bloody did, but I can't have you wandering all over town interrogating the witnesses.'

'Sally Duffy is a *witness*?'

'Well, no, but she's the only one who seemed to like old Frankie and I don't need her upset, alright?'

'You're one to talk.'

'Huh?'

'Sally said you gave her a right working over earlier today.'

The police chief looked taken aback. 'I thought I was very gentle with her. Short and sweet I was.'

'Never mind,' Roxy said, brushing her fringe impatiently off her face. 'Look, I'm not trying to be annoying. I'm simply trying to investigate another murder—'

'Yes, well I made a few calls about that, to the guys at the Mosman branch and they tell me there was definitely no murder. It was suicide.'

'That's what they say. I suspect otherwise.'

'Oh, Jesus!' He was really getting riled now. 'You bloody journalists are all the same. Looking for a story where there isn't one.' He was stroking his cancer scar so hard now Roxy feared he would dig his way right through. She took a deep breath.

'Beatrice Musgrave was a friend of mine, Chief Butler.' Her voice was calm, almost mechanical. She had explained this so many times before. 'I'm just trying to get some honest answers about her death, whatever the cause. In the meantime, I'm also a journalist. You can't stop me from making some inquiries. Ask your wife, she'll tell you as much.'

The police chief was not impressed by this comment but he did not challenge it, either. He let up on his nose and relaxed back into chair. 'All I'm saying is, go easy, okay? I'm tryin' to run a respectable murder investigation here and I don't need little smart-asses from the big smoke coming in and twisting the facts. You've got no proof that this has anything to do with that Sydney society woman and twisting people's minds is not gonna help.'

'And if I do find proof?'

'You're not gonna find proof because I want you out of here. As far as the investigation is concerned, you're free to leave and that's exactly what I expect you to do. Pronto.'

'What if I choose to stay in Macksland? Lap up the sights a little?'

'Well, obviously I can't stop you now can I? But I don't want you interfering. I don't want you talking to Sally or to anyone about the case. At all. You want Frank's murderer apprehended? Leave it to the professionals.'

Roxy jumped to her feet and, unable to help herself, did a mock salute. Chief Butler restrained a smile. 'I promise to stop seeing Sally,' she said, 'if you promise me two things.'

He looked ready to hit her so she quickly said, 'Just keep a close eye on Sally, that's all. If I'm right about the motive, then she may be next. She knew Frank's private business and the killer might want to shut her up, too.' He nodded slightly not daring to acknowledge her remark but she could tell he understood and she doubted he'd ignore any possibility of another murder in his district. Frank O'Brien's brutal slaying was probably the first in a long time and, unlike his suspicious deputy, Roxy knew that Chief Butler was not looking forward to another one.

'And what's the second thing?' he asked.

'It's just a suggestion, you can ignore it if you like.'

'Yeees?'

'Check out the birth files at the old hospital. Frank O'Brien and Beatrice Alexander—that was her maiden name—they should be recorded as birth parents of a baby girl about 50 years ago. But I have a feeling you'll find the evidence has been, shall we say, tampered with?'

'How do you know that?'

'Just a hunch.'

'You get an awful lot of hunches, don't ya?'

Roxy bat her green eyes innocently. She was on her way out when he called for her to stop.

'Just one more thing.' Now she was the one to groan. 'If I was you, I'd keep your head down and out of trouble.'

'Oh?'

'It seems a few of the locals think you were somehow involved.'

'Why? Because I found the body?'

'Because you were asking about Frank just before he died.'

'But he'd clearly been killed long before I—'

'I know, I know. But the locals can be a bit bloody paranoid about outsiders. Just keep out of mischief and clear out as soon as ya can. Got it?'

She indicated that she did, and made her way back to the hotel. She had promised not to see Sally Duffy but that didn't mean she couldn't speak to her. She would return to her room and call her from there, and was just heading up the wide, wooden hotel staircase when the young barman called out.

'You still here?' he said, his lips twisted into a snarl.

'Yes I am. Got a problem?'

'As a matter of fact I do.'

She stopped walking and turned to face him full on. This threw him off for a second but he heaved his chest up and said, 'Me and the boys wanna know what your business was with old Frankie.'

'Old Frankie? You mean the guy you didn't even know existed yesterday?'

'Yeah, well I didn't recognize him in the suit. But I knew of him. Everybody did. He was a bit odd, but…well, he wouldn't hurt anyone. How did you know 'im? Why were ya askin' about him?'

Roxy sighed and came back down the staircase to the ground level. 'I don't think it's any of your business, but the truth is I didn't know him either. He was good friends with a woman I knew who was recently murdered. I wanted to speak to him about her. But I got there too late.'

'Or so you say.'

'The body had been dead two, maybe three days by the time I got to it. I, on the other hand only arrived in town yesterday. Just ask Chief Butler, and your manager.'

This surprised the young man and he stood staring at her for several dumbfounded seconds. She waved towards the stairs, indicating that she had places to be, people to call.

'Oh…Okay then, fine. Just checkin',' he said. 'So you and the other one gonna head off now?'

'Other one?'

'Yeah, the skinny bloke.'

This stopped Roxy in her tracks again. 'What skinny guy?'

The young barman looked perplexed once more and then backed away. 'The one also lookin' for Frank. Oh, never mind. Thought youse were together.'

'There was someone else here? Looking for Frank O'Brien? Did he give his name?'

'Nah, just came in, askin' for Frank just like you.'

'When was this?'

'About noon. Figured he was with you.'

Roxy squished her lips up to one side thoughtfully wondering who it might be. 'Was he staying at the hotel?'

'Not that I know of, just passin' through he said. Look, sorry if I came on a bit hard. It's just real odd, you know? First you, then him, then poor old Frankie shows up dead. We're all just wonderin' what's going on, you know?'

Roxy waved him off. 'Fair enough, too. I don't blame you, but you have to believe me, I had nothing to do with it. I am trying to sort it all out, though. Can you give me a quick description of this other guy? Was he young, old? Well-spoken—'

'Look he was skinny like I said. Olive skin.'

'Old? Young? What was the color of his hair?'

'Dunno, he had a hat on.' Suddenly there was a clash of glasses from inside the front bar followed by a smashing sound and several loud roars.

'Oh shit, I better go.'

'Can you tell me anything else? Anything at all?'

The young man scratched his head. 'Look, speak to Macey behind the front desk, she might've taken more notice. I really gotta go.' He raced off into the bar and Roxy stood staring after him, wondering who this new player in the game might be. Who else was on Frank O'Brien's trail? And what, if anything, did they have to do with his death, or Mrs Musgrave's for that matter? Roxy shook herself together, sat down on one of the steps, pulled out her phone and dialed Sally Duffy's home number. It rang for some time without answering so she placed the phone down and went in search of Macey. The receptionist also wasn't in and, eager for a shower, Roxy went up to her room. She still felt like she hadn't washed away the previous day's grizzly discovery. *It will take a lot of soap*, she thought absentmindedly.

As she reached the top of the landing a ghostly figure emerged from the shadows and Roxy jumped back with a fright.

'Roxy?' It was Sally Duffy and she looked like a mess. Her normally neat hair was flying loosely around her face and she was clutching her arms around herself as though cold.

'Sally? Are you okay? God, you nearly gave me a heart attack! What are you doing here? Do you realize I'm not allowed to see you? I promised Chief Butler.'

'Please! I have to speak to you.' The tremor in her voice sent a chill down Roxy's spine and she fumbled for her room key.

'Okay, come with me, quickly.'

They slipped into Roxy's room and she locked the door firmly behind them, then checked that the verandah door and windows were also locked and the curtains drawn. She pulled Sally to the bed and forced her to sit.

'What's happened, Sally? You look distraught.'

'I am, oh God, I…I…'

'Sally, take a few deep breaths, I'll get you some water.' Roxy jumped up and filled a glass from the small jug by the bed. As the young woman gulped it down, Roxy said, 'Is it Beryl? Does she suspect something? Did you get caught?'

'No, no, not Beryl.'

'Who then, Sally? What's happened?'

The young woman drained her glass dry and then wiped her mouth with the back of her hand slowly, as if trying to put something into perspective. Finally she said, 'There was someone at home when I got there.'

'Someone? You mean like a burglar?'

'I don't know. I could see him there, through the door.'

'Was he tall and skinny?'

'Tall and skinny?'

'Yes, the barman tells me there's been some skinny guy lurking about.'

'Oh my God! Yes he was! Do you know him?'

'Not sure,' said Roxy. 'So what did you do?'

'I…I just turned around and ran. I came here. I don't know where else to turn.' She started to weep then and Roxy moved closer, placing her arm around her shoulder, trying to sooth her.

'You don't live with anyone?'

'No.'

'And you're sure there was someone there? That it wasn't possibly a shadow? Your mind playing tricks with you?'

'No, no!' Sally turned towards Roxy and her eyes were dancing excitedly. 'Jenny threw a surprise birthday party for me last time I was in town and, well, when I walked up to unlock the door after work, I noticed someone through the bubbled glass to the left of the door. I never knew you could see through it, but, well if you pull the fern back, you can. I was just checking the fern, to see if it needed watering and I spotted Jenny standing there and I knew something was up. As soon as I opened the door, there she was, to the left of the door ready to shout 'surprise!'. For some silly reason I've been checking that side ever since, you know, to check she isn't about to spring me again.'

Roxy smiled. 'So you checked it tonight and spotted someone?'

'Yes. I thought, at first it was Jenny again, but the shape was all wrong. And you know, skinny like you said. Jenny's a fatty, you can't miss her. In any case I could tell it was a guy.'

'So what happened?'

'Well, I stopped. I was right near the door, I was hesitating because I remembered what you said about the murderer maybe coming after us, you know?' Roxy nodded her head. 'So I kinda waited a second. I was gonna call out. But then the figure kinda grew even taller.'

'Taller?' Roxy wondered suddenly if the young girl's mind was simply playing tricks on her but remained quiet and let her continue.

'It was like he was leaning over and then straightened up because suddenly he was quite tall. I just turned around and bolted.'

'Do you think he saw you?'

'I…oh, God, I don't know! What if he's still there? What if it's the murderer?! What are we going to do?'

Roxy considered her words for several minutes and then grabbed her bag. 'Only one thing to do,' she said. 'We're going back.'

20 STRANGERS IN THE NIGHT

Sally's house looked deserted from the road but the two women approached it slowly, carefully, Roxy's heart beating wildly through her shirt.

'Shouldn't we call Chief Butler?' Sally whispered.

'By the time he gets here the intruder'll be gone,' Roxy whispered back, stopping by the front gate and pulling Sally down to crouch behind the thick fencing that encircled the house. 'And if he's not, their flashing police cars will scare him off.'

'Sounds okay to me!'

'Shhh! This might be our only chance to get a glimpse of him. Now, where's the part of the door you can see through?'

Through the gaps in the fence they had a clear enough view of Sally's front door, and she pointed to a thin strip of bubble glass to the left of the door almost obscured by a palm tree planted just in front.

'You can only see through it when the sun's going down,' she whispered. 'It's too dark now.'

'Oh great,' Roxy sighed. She had hoped the culprit was still hunched there, waiting for Sally's return, and that she would somehow recognize the shape. Tall and skinny sounded like one of many possibilities, and already faces were flashing through her mind: Fabian Musgrave and his wife, Sofia, both fitted that description, as did William Musgrave and even Beattie's lawyer, Ronald Featherby. Now that the glass was no longer transparent, she wasn't quite sure what to do. If they entered, they might both be killed. She tried to think, to work out what to do.

'Look,' Sally was saying beside her, 'let's just—'

'Shhh! What was that?' They both listened for several seconds and Sally was about to speak again when Roxy threw her hand up to her mouth. There was a definite rustling sound coming from the side of the house, somewhere near the boundary bushes, and getting closer. Roxy reached for the small alarm in her handbag and pulled it out, ready to let it off if need be. They waited another few seconds and then Roxy's heart did a triple somersault as she spotted someone clambering out of the bushes and onto the road, not more that six meters away. She heard Sally gasp beside her.

'Who the bloody hell is that?' the young woman asked, her voice more angry now than terrified.

'I can't tell!' Roxy whispered. The man was clearly wearing some sort of hood and it was obscuring his face. 'Just lay low.'

They watched as the figure stood up and began walking briskly in the opposite direction. From where they were hunched neither woman recognized the shape, although Roxy felt there was a trace of familiarity in that walk. In any case, Sally had been right. It was definitely a man, and he was tall and slim.

Roxy turned to Sally and put both arms on her shoulders. 'Listen Sally, you run straight to the police station and tell them in which direction he went and give them a description. For now, do not mention me. Got it?'

The young woman gulped loudly and nodded her head. 'But what are you going to do?'

'I'm following him.'

'You can't! You could be killed!'

'Listen, Sally, it's the only way. Otherwise we'll lose him. Now quickly, go!' She gave the girl a forceful shove and watched as she ran off back down the footpath in the opposite direction. Then breathing deeply, Roxy turned, stepped out on to the footpath and followed the intruder.

It was a dark night but Roxy could still see the man's thin figure several blocks up. He was walking briskly and she had to jog a little to keep up. At the end of the street he turned around, as though suspecting something and Roxy threw herself behind a tree, hoping he had not seen her. He hesitated, then, looking both right and left, crossed the street and headed back towards town. She waited several seconds before following after him.

Macksland was almost a ghost town when they approached it, only a few restaurants still open, the shops and other services closed long before. Roxy checked her watch. It was nearly 8pm. The man, still unrecognizable from such a distance, was walking in a definite direction towards Roxy's hotel. She watched as he strode swiftly along the street and then gasped with surprise when, pausing briefly to look around him, he pulled open the door to the main reception and strode confidently in.

Chief Butler was just sitting down to a bowl of hot apple pie and ice-cream when his Deputy called and, reluctantly, he took the phone from his inquisitive wife and boomed, 'This better be bloody good!'

'It is sir,' the young policeman stuttered back. 'It's Sally Duffy. She says there's a prowler at her place.'

Butler sat up straight. 'Did you check the place out?'

'Yes sir. No-one sir, but the place was done over pretty good. It's a right mess.'

'Anything stolen?'

'Not that we could see but Sal' will check it out later. She did spot the crim', sir.'

'She did!?'

'Yep but not a good description, I'm afraid. He headed into town so I'm on my way with her now.'

'Right, good. Look, be alert, okay? Cruise the main streets, see if anyone looks suspicious. I'll see you down in front of the station in 10 minutes, got it?'

'Got it, sir.' They hung up and the police chief frowned. It looked like the city chick might have been right after all. He pushed his dessert aside and grabbed his coat. 'Sorry, love,' he called out to his wife, raising one solid hand to stifle her inevitable questioning. 'If there's anything to report you'll be the first to know, I promise. I'll be home later.'

By the time Chief Butler reached the police station, his deputy and Sally were both inside warming themselves up with a cup of hot chocolate. They were laughing about something but quickly straightened up when the Chief walked in.

'Good evening Sally,' the police Chief said as he took a seat beside her. 'So tell me what you saw.'

Confidently, Sally related her story, careful to omit any mention of Roxy Parker.

'So let me get this straight,' Butler said, peeling his coat off and perching up against a desk. 'You got home at about 6pm, found someone prowling in your house and you're only just telling us about it now?'

Sally's throat drained dry. 'Well, I waited and watched, you see. To see who he was, what he was doing.'

'You watched for an hour and a half?'

'Um…well.'

'Come on, Sally, what's the story? I want the real version this time.'

Sally's eyes flickered across both policemen. Dougie looked worried for her but she could tell Butler meant business. Reluctantly, she said, 'Well, I went and got Roxy Parker.'

'Roxy Parker?' Dougie cried, clearly offended. 'The Sydney chick?'

'Yes. I didn't know where to turn.'

'Why didn't you come straight to us?' Sally blinked quickly. She realized now that she should have, she told them, but there was something capable about the ghostwriter, something that made her seem so trustworthy. She tried to explain this to the police chief but he waved her off.

'Okay, okay, so you both went back and checked out the house?'

'Yes.'

'And that's when you spotted someone in the brush? So where is Miss Parker now?'

Again Sally hesitated. Roxy would clearly not be pleased with her. 'She followed him.'

'She what!?' The deputy was almost beside himself. 'Who does she think she is?!'

Chief Butler raised a sturdy hand to silence him. 'You didn't see either of them anywhere? No sign at all?'

'No sir.'

He grunted and then reached for his coat again. 'Come on then, we'd better go and find her.'

He lead the way back outside and the three of them piled into his police car. They drove directly to the Shearer's Hotel and, motioning for Sally to stay in the lobby, the police Chief began ascending the staircase to Roxy's room with his deputy following fast behind. He located her room and knocked loudly on it. There was no answer and so he knocked again. Again no answer and he was turning to leave when the lock unclicked and the door swung open to reveal Roxy smiling brightly on the other side.

'Where is he?' Chief Butler boomed, stepping into the room. 'Did you see where he went?'

'Who?' she asked as innocently as she could muster and then noticed Sally cowering near the top of the stairs shaking her head apologetically.

'Don't even try to give me your lip young woman—'

'Oh, you mean the prowler?'

'More than a bloody prowler,' Butler roared. 'He broke into Sally's house and turned the place over!'

'Really? It's been messed up?' Roxy's face flooded with confusion.

'Damn straight it has. Now where did he go?'

'I don't know, honestly.' She sat down on the bed and looked up at the policemen as calmly as she could muster. 'I followed him as far as town and then lost him.'

'Lost him?'

'Yes. I think he might have dashed into one of the restaurants up the road a bit. He just vanished.'

Chief Butler eyed the woman for some time, trying to decide what to do. He turned back to his deputy. 'Okay, let's go. I'll check out the bowlo and the Chinese Restaurant, you check the Speak Easy if it's still open. We'll meet back in front of the post office in ten.' He turned back to Roxy who was sitting cross-legged, inspecting her nails as though disinterested. 'As for you young lady: I can't believe I'm bloody saying this but I want you back at the station first thing in the morning. Crikey, I thought we were rid of you! Sally's place has been trashed and it's clear we're dealing with a very dangerous criminal You're a blasted fool to be chasing after him like that. That's our job, got it?!'

She indicated that she did and watched them leave, dragging Sally reluctantly behind them. Roxy then jumped back inside her room and relocked the door.

'You can come out now,' she said softly and watched as the tall, skinny man uncurled himself from underneath the bed where he had hidden.

21 AN OLD FRIEND

Max Farrell brushed his fringe back off his face and sat down on the bed beside Roxy. 'Jesus, Parker, you'd think I was the bloody murderer the way you're behaving.'

'Well they could have locked you up for break and entry. What were you doing in Sally Duffy's house anyway?'

'I waited for ages outside your room and then the woman on reception, Macey I think was her name, said you might be at some girl's place. Said she'd seen you together a coupla times, so she gave me directions.'

'Jesus this really is a small town. So, fine, you go to Sally's place, but why did you break in? What were you thinking?'

'I didn't! The door was ajar so I went in. I called her name out a coupla times and there was no-one there. I was about to go back out when I noticed there was something odd about the place. It was a mess.'

'So it was trashed before you got there?'

'Well, yeah, I guess. God you don't think I did it?'

He was looking at her like he thought she was insane and Roxy shook her black hair quickly.

'No, of course not. Go on.'

'Well I noticed lots of shit everywhere and I figured either this Sally woman is one hell of a slob or someone had been there before me.'

'Then you heard Sally come up the path?'

'Well I heard several footsteps coming up the street, but I was already outside by then, so I hid in the bushes and then when I couldn't hear anymore I took off.'

'Hang on, let me get this straight. About what time did you turn up?'

'About half an hour ago.'

'So how long were you in the house?'

'About a minute. I saw that it had been vandalized and figured I should get the hell out of there.'

'That's when you heard us come up?'

'I guess so, yeah. I waited a minute or so in the bush and then came straight back here. To find you. What's going on, Parker? Is everything okay?'

Roxy stood up and began pacing the floor. 'Actually, no, everything's a bloody mess. Someone killed the old guy, Frank, before I got to talk to him.'

'Jesus! No wonder everyone was acting funny when I asked about him earlier today.'

'Now it seems the murderer might still be around.'

'You think he's the one who trashed Sally's place?'

'I have no doubt of it. He'd obviously just left before you got there. You may even have scared him off but it makes me fear that Sally is next on the hit list. I've got to act fast.'

Max grabbed Roxy's hand and forced her to stop pacing, forced her to look at him. He tried to give her his all-consuming smile, but this time it didn't quite reach his eyes. 'You don't have to do anything, Roxy. You're a writer not a cop. Leave the dangerous stuff to them and come back to Sydney with me first thing in the morning.'

Roxy wrestled her arm from her friend's grip. 'Don't patronize me, Max, that's what my mum's for.'

'I'm not—'

'I'm so close now, Max,' she said, her tone gentler. 'I know I can solve this thing. But I have to stay around at least another day. There are two people I need to see.'

Max sighed and reached into his carry bag. 'I come bearing gifts,' he said, producing a bottle of her favorite plonk. As he unscrewed the bottle, she fetched two water glasses and then they moved out to the verandah to enjoy their drinks. They stayed well back from the edge, far enough to be out of sight of inquisitive cops but close enough to soak up the view. From there, you could see the town, now just a few glistening lights left in the cold country sky. They sat drinking their wine side-by-side staring down at the street below without talking for several minutes. Roxy knew Max should be hiding but she didn't have the energy to drag him back inside.

'Why did you come?' she said eventually.

'To see if you're okay. There was something a little crazy about that old country guy at the funeral.'

'Frank. His name was Frank O'Brien.'

'Yeah, well, I kept thinking, what if he's the murderer? What if I never see you again?'

'So you came to rescue me?' Her voice was like a thin, taut wire, ready to snap at any moment.

'Of course not!' he snapped instead, angrier at himself than her. He should have known better than to try to help Roxy Parker. If there was one thing she would *never* admit to it was needing to be rescued. 'I'm your mate, Rox, I'm allowed to worry about you. Besides, I wanted to apologize. For what I said.' She remained silent beside him and he turned to watch her silhouette against the night sky. 'I'm a bloody idiot, I know that now. I…I shouldn't have said what I said. It wasn't fair on you.' He paused, but again she remained still. 'So I'm hoping I haven't botched our friendship completely…but I want to stay friends. I don't want to scare you off.'

Roxy was overwhelmed by a sudden, groggy sense of exhaustion and despair. Every limb felt weighed down and she could barely keep her eyes focused on the lights beyond. It had been a frantic two days. A frantic fortnight, in fact. She didn't have any energy left over for this man standing so forlornly beside her, waiting for her soothing words of comfort. But she wasn't up to another argument either, so she just pulled him close and hugged him to her chest. 'It's all going to be okay,' she told him softly, not believing it for a moment.

Chief Butler was in a very bad mood. After returning from town the night before, he had not enjoyed his dried out pie and his wife's probing questions, and had spent a restless night wondering about Sally's intruder. She had stayed over in his spare bedroom, despite her insistence to the contrary, and was sitting looking bored in his office now, nibbling on a muffin. She had managed to change her clothes, though, and was wearing blue jeans and a black jumper, her ginger hair scooped back behind oversized, dark sunglasses, and now looked a lot more like the young woman she was than the matronly shopkeeper of before.

Beside her, Roxy sat stony-faced and quiet. She too was wearing blue jeans, this time teamed with her red cardigan again. She had wanted to wash it first, to scrub the memory of dead Frank off its delicate sleeves, but she hadn't the time and her wardrobe was fast wearing thin.

'That's all either of you can tell me,' he was saying. 'Tall and skinny. That's all you saw.'

Roxy nodded cautiously. She had already deduced that the person Sally saw cowering behind her door at 6pm was not her friend Max, but the burglar, and most likely Frank's murderer. By the time Max got to Sally's house, a good hour later, the intruder had cleared out, leaving a mess behind. In any case, Sally had described the first intruder as tall and skinny and Roxy saw no reason to mention Max at all. It would only confuse matters and probably land them both in deeper waters than they could handle. Chief Butler had been happy enough to accept her presence at one crime scene, but now Max? It was too coincidental. Bustling him back on the plane that morning was a welcome relief. In more ways than one.

'No hair color?' Butler continued. 'No nationality? No sex?'

'Oh it was *definitely* a man,' Sally said and then looked across at Roxy for confirmation.

'But we can't be sure,' Roxy said. 'It was too dark.'

The police chief grunted. 'Okay, Sally you can go. I want to speak to Miss Parker here for a few minutes more.'

Sally shot an apologetic glance across at the other woman and then, slipping her shades firmly over her eyes, exited the office. Chief Butler turned to Roxy and she prepared herself for an angry outburst. But his tone was soft and conspiratorial when he said, 'We're very worried about Sally. We've checked out her digs and have reason to believe that the person who went through her stuff last night was the same person who killed Frankie O'Brien.'

Roxy nodded. It was just as she suspected.

'Now, we've arranged for her to go and visit a relative in Sydney for a while until we sort this mess out. In the meantime, I've passed the hospital's forged adoption files regarding Beatrice Musgrave on to the police in Mosman.'

Roxy couldn't help raising her eyebrows and Butler smirked back. 'Yes, yes, you were right. The guys in Sydney have suspected foul play from the start, but it's all being kept under tight wraps. The official word is, she killed herself. Period. That's off the record and I don't want a word of this going anywhere.'

'I knew it!' Roxy said. 'I knew I wasn't crazy. But why all the secrecy?'

'Something about not wanting to alert the murderer to their suspicions. I guess complacency can make you slip up. But it's all top secret and I don't want to hear one word about your blasted journalistic ethics and the public's right to blah, blah, blah.'

'It won't go past this room, I promise you,' she said. 'Who do they suspect?'

'I gather one of the family members, they said something about a big family secret about to be aired, but of course you know all about that.'

Roxy smiled back without saying a word. Deep down she felt vindicated. This was not a wild goose chase after all. And finally someone agreed with her.

'In any case,' he continued, 'the Mosman detective in charge of the case, Detective Superintendent Maltin, wants to see you the second you return to Sydney. I think you've got a hell of a lot of explaining to do young lady.'

And I'll have a hell of a lot more by the time I get back there, she thought to herself smugly as she exited the office. Before heading to the police station that morning, Roxy had looked up the names of the two midwives she had taken from the hospital files, believing in her heart that one of them could provide the missing link, the identity of Beatrice Musgrave's illegitimate daughter. The first name, Agnetha Frickensburg was nowhere to be found but Zoe Callahan was still residing in Macksland and was more than happy to see her. As Roxy made her way back to town, she felt closer than ever to finally solving this baffling mystery.

22 INTERVIEWING GHOSTS

Zoe Callahan was a short, pudgy woman with thinning gray hair and an enormous, warm smile that lit her wrinkled face up like a well-worn Christmas tree when she opened her door. She would have been well into her 80s, her spirit clearly not diminished with age.

'I was hoping you'd arrive soon!' she exclaimed as she ushered Roxy through the doorway and into her fern-filled living room. Even her wallpaper was decorated in ferns, fading green fronds that gave a cluttered, jungle-like effect. 'I've just put a pot of tea on and the scones are still warm.'

Roxy took a seat by the window and looked around at the lively room, pot plants and picture frames battling for space between bright pillows and ornaments and dozens and dozens of Thank You cards, most adorned with pictures of stunned babies and storks.

'I've kept every one,' the midwife boasted as she placed the tea things on a spare bench to one side. 'They're from my mums and dads. I like to think of them as satisfied customers.'

'You delivered their children?'

'Every single one successfully. Well, if truth be told, there was Margie Dawson's twins, but they were doomed long before I got involved. And young Ginny. Well, she never called me 'til too late, see? Can't be helped. But other than them, my strike rate is perfect,' and she knocked loudly on the table below her.

'You still practice?'

'Ahhh, not really, dear, just look in on a few from time to time is all. Offer my ten pence worth. Now, how do you have your tea?'

When they had their fill and swapped more than enough small talk for Roxy's liking, she steered the conversation to Beattie Musgrave, formerly Beatrice Alexander. The older woman's smile slumped a little.

'Yes, well, it seems I've lead you on a bit of a wild goose chase. I knew her name rang a bell but now that I've had some time to look through my files, I realize that Agnetha worked with her, not me.'

Roxy couldn't disguise the disappointment in her voice. 'I was afraid of that. You don't know where I can find Agnetha do you?'

Zoe shook her head uncertainly. 'She hasn't been around for years. Last time I saw her was back in the '90s…looking the worse for wear I might say. Alcohol, I believe.'

'Oh?'

'Yes, she had a pretty bad accident, can't recall now what happened, but never quite got over it. Last I heard, she'd moved down south.'

'Could you be mistaken? Could any other midwives have worked with Beattie at the time?'

'Oh no dear, we were the only two back then. Now, of course, every hippie calls herself a midwife. But back then it was just Aggie and me. 'Course there was a steady stream of young doctors, most of them just out of school and pretty wide eyed, not much use when it came to the crunch if truth be told. One of them even fainted on me if you can believe that!' She hooted with laughter. 'So Aggie and I did most of the hard work. And then, after Aggie shot off, it was just me for the next 10 years. Oh those were good years.'

'Can you tell me anything about Beattie then? Did you know her at all?'

Zoe shook her head again. 'No, it was Frankie we all knew. If my memory serves me correctly, Beatrice was a toffee-nosed young lassie who thought she was too good for the likes of us, and Frankie for that matter. I wondered why he was with her. Then, of course, when I heard about the baby, well, that explained everything.'

'Why didn't they get married, do you know?'

'I suspect he wasn't good enough for her. She cleared out just as soon as the baby was born. Broke his heart.'

'And any idea what happened to the baby?' It was a crucial question but Zoe was already shaking her head. Then she paused.

'Oh dear, I wonder…oh, yes, you never know.'

'What?'

'Well, Aggie might have kept her own records, like I done.'

'Yes, but if she's disappeared….'

'Yeah but her daughter still lives in the old house. Perhaps you can ask her?'

Roxy's eyes lit up.

'Not a great relationship I believe,' Zoe was saying, 'and, as far as gossip goes, lost touch with each other a long time ago. That's why, if she's still hoarding the old woman's things, I bet she won't mind you going through them.'

Not only did Agnetha Frickensburg's daughter not mind the intrusion, she even helped Roxy sort through her mother's boxes for the relevant files. They were piled on top of each other in one half of an unused garage and had clearly not been touched in years, thick dust, cockroach droppings and spider webs shrouding the lot, like time's own seal.

'I've been meaning to get rid of these forever,' Lana said softly, shaking dust off several boxes and opening them carefully, as if terrified of what she might discover. Lana was in her mid to late 40s, overweight and mumsy looking with an apron over a floral dress and floury handprints across the lot, proof that she'd recently been baking. She worked part-time as a childcare teacher, she told Roxy, and had a brood of her own. Throughout her house were oversized photos of that brood, all crowding happily around their Mother Hen. 'I guess I always secretly hoped she'd come back,' Lana was saying and she stopped suddenly, tears springing to her eyes. Roxy could almost see the giant lump forming in her throat.

'When did you last see your mum?'

'About 16 years ago. Christmas. She was drunk...was drunk all the time back then.' Lana laughed a dry chortle that belied her saddened heart. 'I'd just had my third.' She indicated one of the photos of beaming children, as though her whole life was measured in births.

'And you haven't heard from your mum since?'

'Oh, a postcard on the odd birthday. That's about it. We... we never really got on too, well, you know? She had me quite late, and was always more interested in everyone else's kids than her own. Or mine for that matter.' She reached a hand up to still the tears that were now flowing from her eyes. 'The worst thing is not knowing if she's alive or dead. If only I knew she was okay.'

Roxy shot her a warm smile and looked away as Lana reached for a tissue and blew her nose. It seemed like bad luck had befallen everyone who ever came in contact with Beatrice Musgrave, from Frank O'Brien to her grandson Fabian, and now the woman who had brought Beattie's elusive daughter into the world, the midwife. They continued searching through the boxes for almost an hour when Lana let out a modest squeal of delight.

'I think I may have found it!'

She handed Roxy a folder marked with the relevant date and the writer took it excitedly. Inside, the midwife had penned the names of 11 clients for that year including a 'Beatrice Alexander' listed as 'birth mother'. There was no birth father named but there were details of the adoptive parents. Roxy could have leapt for joy. She copied down the words, 'Johnson, Limrock Lane'.

'You are an absolute champion, Lana! Now, tell me, where can I find Limrock Lane?'

The large block of land mocked Roxy with its emptiness. Not even the foundations of the old Johnson house remained, just a bleak patch of grass struggling to grow, with an old camphor laurel on one side and a ramshackle fence on the other. Roxy stood on the pavement and sighed. Nothing had been easy in this search and it wasn't about to start now.

'Ya lookin' for sometin?' came a scratchy voice behind her and Roxy swiveled around to find an elderly man standing there, staring expectantly towards her. He looked straight out of the 1950s in a bowling shirt, cream trousers and a small cane hat. Olie would be green with envy.

'Yes. I was looking for the Johnson house,' she said.

'It's gone.'

'I can see that. Any idea where they moved to?'

'Yep. Six feet under.'

'I'm sorry?'

The old man let out a weary sigh. 'They died love, bad car accident 'bout 20 years back. What'd ya want with 'em?'

'Just looking them up for an old friend. My name's Roxy Parker.'

'Urrr,' he grunted and then produced a skinny hand for her to shake. 'I'm Cyril from next door. Wanna cuppa?'

Coffee was the last thing Roxy needed, her brain so wired by yet another near miss, but she nodded her head anyway and followed him into the house next door. It was as old-fashioned as its owner, with barely a mod-con in sight. Roxy sat down in a brown vinyl sofa while the old man made their coffee, filtering freshly ground beans through a vintage steel Atomic coffee maker. It smelled divine and her spirits picked up. Perhaps someone in Macksland *could* make a decent cuppa.

'They were real quiet types, you know,' he was saying, calling out from above the hissing on the stove. 'Kept to themselves a lot. Angus was a mechanic, owned a car yard down off Main. She did quite a bit for the local charities, you know. We used to get along well, Joyce and me. She had trouble sleepin', too, so we'd sit out the back and yak for a while. I kinda liked them in their own way. 'Cept for that horrible daughter of course.'

Roxy's stomach fluttered a little but it was a casual voice that said, 'Oh?'

'Yeah, Marian. A right little brat. Always gettin' into trouble, shopliftin' and stealin' cars.'

Marian Johnson, Roxy thought excitedly, *I finally have a name.* As the old man handed her a cup of the strong, delicious brew, she said, 'Perhaps Marian had some issues to deal with,' and, noticing the look of confusion on his face, quickly added, 'You know, being adopted and all.'

'Oh, yeah, I see.' He sat down across from her and studied his coffee. 'Not an excuse if you aks me.'

She took a long, joyous sip. 'That is wonderful, thank you! Tell me, you don't happen to know where Marian is now, do you?'

'Wouldn't wanna know. My guess is jail. Why?' He shifted in his chair and eyed her strangely. 'What ya really up to? What ya want with them? You're not really lookin' them up for an old family friend are ya?'

Roxy hesitated before saying, 'I'm a journalist.' The man smiled smugly at himself. He thought as much. He clucked his false teeth noisily and indicated for her to continue. 'I'm doing a piece on a wealthy Sydney woman called Beatrice Musgrave who recently died. I believe she may have been the birth mother of Marian Johnson.'

He cackled to himself. 'Manic Marian Johnson come from good stock you say? Now that's one for the books!'

'Well, I'm not 100 percent sure. You don't happen to have a photo of Marian do you?'

The man rubbed one leathery hand slowly over his chin thoughtfully for a few seconds and then, placing his cup on the kidney-shaped coffee table in front of him, struggled to his feet and wandered over to a side cabinet in which at least 10 photo albums were stored. 'You know, I probably do,' he said, grabbing five and handing two of them to Roxy. ''Ave a look through them and see if you can't spot 'em.'

'Well, I don't really know what I'm looking for—'

'Family shot, two kids, one in a wheelchair. Can't miss it.'

'Wheelchair?' Roxy's eyebrows shot up.

'Yeah, the oldest daughter was a cripple. You didn't know that?'

Roxy shook her head, opened the album and began scanning the pages. Midway through the second album she spotted the shot he had mentioned and felt a pang of excitement. She held it up to the light. It was in black and white, badly exposed and tattered around the corners where time had played its hand. The snapshot had been taken on a stretch of lawn in front of an old wooden house and, judging from the small camphor laurel on one side, Roxy guessed it had been taken right next door before the house had been torn down. There were four people in the photo including a middle-aged couple who must have been Marian's adoptive parents, Joyce and Angus Johnson. They were both smiling meekly into the camera, dressed in what looked like their Sunday-best: he in long socks, shorts and a short-sleeved business shirt, she in a formless spotted frock with a small hat over curly short hair. Beside them, a young girl of perhaps 15 or 16, was hunched over in a wheelchair. She had straight lightly colored hair and was not looking at the camera, but towards her parents with what seemed like a smile of delight. Behind her stood another girl. She looked about the same age as the disabled girl but she was standing with her hands on her hips, half concealed by the wheelchair, and she wasn't smiling so much as scowling towards the camera, mocking the photographer. Her hair was darker than her sibling and curly and she had thick, bushy eyebrows across a plane, angular shaped face. Roxy had seen that face before but it was the girl in the wheelchair who sparked her attention.

'What's her name?' Roxy asked the old man and he thought for a few minutes. 'Can't quite remember, love. It was a long time ago. Sounded like a flower, I think. Suited her, I thought. She was a sweetie.'

'Lotus?'

'Nah, that's not it…'

'Lilly?'

'Lilly! That's right. Lillian!'

Roxy beamed. The jigsaw was starting to come together. 'If I promise to return this photo to you in one piece, can I borrow it for a bit?'

He shrugged. 'Can't see why not. Ya gonna put it in ya story?'

'Most likely, yes.'

'Gonna mention me?'

Roxy laughed. 'I'll see what I can do!'

He was already jotting down his name and details for her. 'It'd be good to see my name in print. I've never made it in print before. Once I got interviewed by the RSL Club's newsletter but they never used it. Would love to see me name in print.'

Roxy took the paper he was handing her and, along with the photo, slipped it into her handbag. 'Well I'll try my best,' she told him, shaking his hand warmly. 'You've been an enormous help.'

'Ya welcome, love.'

'Just one thing?'

'Yeah?'

'Was it definitely Marian, the abled one who was adopted?' He looked at her strangely so she added, 'It couldn't have been Lillian, could it?'

'God no. Who'd wanta adopt a retarded kid?'

Roxy cringed at his extraordinary insensitivity but said nothing, just shot him a quick frown. When she got back to her car she took the picture out again and stared at it for some time in the broad daylight. She trusted her memory implicitly and knew she had seen the face of the disabled girl before.

She had a fairly good idea who the other girl was, too.

Back at the hotel Roxy made three final calls. The first was to book a flight back to Sydney on the last plane out that afternoon, and the second went through to Agnetha Frickensburg's daughter, Lana.

'I forgot to ask you something when I stopped over,' she said when Lana answered. 'And this may sound strange, but it's very important. Did your mum happen to be missing any fingers?'

Lana seemed unconcerned by the question. 'Oh yes. That was the whole problem. She lost three of the fingers from her right hand in a car accident a few years before she disappeared. She could still work okay—she was left-handed—but it seemed to scare a lot of young mothers away. They didn't want her bad luck to rub off on to them, I suppose.'

Roxy felt a brief moment of triumph before her heart dropped. Lana deserved to know what had happened to her mother, but she wasn't the right person to tell her. After she hung up she dialed Police Chief Butler.

'You still around?' he asked jovially enough.

'Hey, I'm on the 6 o'clock flight,' she promised. 'But I think I might know what happened to Lana Miles' mum, Agnetha Frickensburg.'

Chief Butler paused trying to connect the names for some seconds. 'Oh, the missing midwife?' he said at last. 'I remember now. She took off a long time ago. Had her daughter worried sick. Still drops in here every now and then, asks us if we've heard anything.'

'Well I think she went to Sydney. If you call the police chief at Rushcutters Bay, I think you'll find they have a Jane Doe who fits her description.'

The lights of Sydney's CBD sparkled on the horizon as the plane began its descent and Roxy let out a long sigh of relief. The country might be slower and cleaner, she thought as she fastened her seatbelt happily, but Sydney was the place where she felt most at home. She could get lost in Sydney, that's why she loved it.

When she got home, she checked all her messages and was surprised to find there wasn't one from Max. 'Fine,' she said aloud. 'We both need some distance.' Yet she couldn't help feeling a stab of disappointment. It was Thursday night after all. Roxy replayed her messages. Maria had called with an update on some work she had on offer and there were two panicked messages from her agent, Oliver. 'Where the hell are you?' he demanded. 'I'm worried sick! Call me!'

She stepped out of her clothes and slipped into her bathroom for a long soak in some bath salts. She was exhilarated now, feeling closer than ever to solving Beattie's baffling murder, but she needed to get her head together first, and a long, hot bath just might help. As the tap gently streamed with warm water and the salts worked their magic on her weary limbs, Roxy slipped into a sense of calm. She felt her mind go blank and went with it, not trying to steer her thoughts in any specific direction.

It was only later, once she had eaten something and poured herself a generous glass of Merlot, that she allowed herself to return to the case. With the file of Heather Jackson in hand, she sat on the sofa and began flicking through for recent pictures of the famous artist. Once located, she couldn't help smiling. Heather Jackson was now older, blonder and definitely more sculptured, but there was no mistaking those ice-cold eyes. They were the same eyes that scowled out at her from a tattered family snapshot taken on Limrock Lane all those years ago.

They were the eyes of Marian Johnson.

23 MEETING GILDA MALTIN

The Mosman Police Department was bustling with life when Roxy strolled in and it took some time for an attendant to see to her. But no sooner had she mentioned her name, she was being ushered through to a back office with the words Detective Superintendent Maltin inscribed in silver lettering on the front.

'Come in! Come in!' came a woman's voice and Roxy opened the door to reveal a very pretty, petite blonde beaming back at her behind a cluttered desk. She leapt up and stretched one hand out to shake Roxy's hand while motioning her to a seat with the other. Her hair was cut in a shaggy pixie style and she was wearing a long string of beads over a black bodysuit that accentuated a small cleavage. 'Brave woman,' Roxy thought, glancing back out the office window to the station bustling with men.

'Thanks for coming in,' Gilda Maltin said. 'Did you bring the transcript?'

Roxy produced a disc from her bag labeled 'Beatrice Musgrave Interviews' and handed it across the desk. 'No luck getting the tapes from Ronald Featherby?'

'Oh I thought I'd give him a miss for now,' Gilda replied with a wink. 'Everyone's a suspect, you know how it is?'

Roxy nodded, wondering if that included her.

'I'm just glad you kept a copy,' Gilda was saying as she popped the disc into her computer and waited for it to whir into action. 'For a journalist, you're quite cluey!'

'Oh I do try,' Roxy said with a smile. 'To be honest, I thought you were going to reprimand me for getting involved, like Chief Butler did in Macksland.'

Gilda laughed. 'Old Butler's okay. I've had to deal with him before, a couple of years ago. Just old-fashioned that's all. No, I'm happy for all the help I can get.' She turned her attention to her screen. 'Okay…yep, it all appears to be here. Now,' she turned back. 'I'd like hear what you've found, if that's okay.'

Roxy hesitated. It was not that she didn't trust the well-spoken detective sitting smiling so sweetly before her. She just didn't like handing over all her hard-found research. As if reading her mind, Gilda said quickly, 'Hey, I'm not out to kill your story. I'd just like to put poor Beatrice Musgrave's soul to rest.'

'So you definitely suspect foul play?'

Gilda snorted. 'If Beatrice Musgrave killed herself, I'm a 16-year-old virgin! Absolutely I suspect foul play! I just can't seem to make anything stick. Everyone here's got a different idea about whodunit, so to speak. The boss thinks it was the son or the grandson.'

'And you?'

'I'm not convinced.' She reached for a large jar of moisturizer underneath some papers on her desk and scooped a generous amount out with two fingers. 'I don't think either men have it in them, to be honest.' She began rubbing the cream thickly into her hands watching as the liquid soaked in, and then held it towards Roxy, who quickly shook her head no. 'Actually, I think Willie and Fabs would have a hard enough time tackling a spider in the bathroom. No, I definitely think it was an outsider of some sort.

Probably this missing daughter. I finally got Fabian to spill the beans on that one, not that he had much to tell. Would you like a cup of tea? A softdrink? Water?'

Roxy shook her head no and then proceeded to tell the policewoman everything she knew, from Fabian's drug addiction and the threatening emails, to Beattie's final phone call and her experiences in Macksland. As Gilda listened, she scribbled the occasional note, her blond eyebrows knotted together intently. Roxy decided she liked her. There was an easy sense of self-confidence about her. She was the sort of person you could imagine enjoying a girlie gossip with over coffee and cake. Perhaps that's why she was so good at her job: she charmed confessions—or in this case, hard-fought, minute details—right out of you. Roxy guessed Gilda was close to 40 but couldn't really tell, she had a youthful energy about her. When she had finished speaking, Gilda sat back in her chair and began knuckling the edge of the desk with one hand.

'Velly, velly interesting. You ought to consider signing up for the force. You're quite a detective.'

Roxy laughed. 'Oh I don't think you guys could afford me.'

'So you've seen my pay packet, then? Pitiful! Tell me, who do you think done it?'

Roxy scrunched her lips together thoughtfully and pushed her glasses into place on her nose. 'I'm not quite sure yet but I'm determined to find out.' She caught herself then and shut her mouth firmly, but the policewoman seemed unperturbed.

'Just be careful, right?' Roxy couldn't hide her surprise and, noticing it, Gilda sat upright and clasped her fingers before her. 'Look, I probably should be telling you to lay off. I know that's what the boss would say. But I like you. You do good work and, as far as I can tell, you aren't hindering anything or writing salacious stories. Yet. I'm happy for you to continue with your inquiries if you like. Just keep everything confidential. And report back to me the second you find anything new. And whatever you bloody do, don't print a word of any of this until you've checked it all with me. Sound fair?'

'As fair as Snow White,' Roxy said. 'Is that it?'

'Absolutely. Have a good one!'

As Roxy strolled out of the police station she felt a flicker of guilt. She had not been completely honest with the personable detective. She had made no mention of that final interview with the Johnson neighbor and the photo that had, she now knew, revealed the real identity of Beatrice Musgrave's daughter. She told herself it was because she needed to check her facts first before pointing the finger. But the truth was probably baser than that. Deep down, she relished the idea of confronting snotty Heather Jackson all by herself.

As Roxy steered her car towards home, her phone rang. 'Roxy speaking.'

'Roxy? It's Loghlen here, how are ya?'

'Lockie! Fine, fine. You?'

'Good, yeah,' he said, his Scottish accent even stronger over the phone. 'You been away? I've bin trying to get you for days.'

'Yeah, Lockie, I've been out of town.'

'And yer not in the middle o' sometin' now?'

'No, no. I've just been rubbing shoulder pads with the Mosman Police department but I'm free now. What's up?'

'Well I thought I should let you know that I finally thought of that name.'

'Name? What name?'

'The maid. You know, Heather Jackson's lackey. The one who was gonna write the tell-all.'

Roxy slowed her car down and pulled it to a stop by the side of the road, then leant across to retrieve the Filofax and pen from her handbag. 'Okay, Lockie, go ahead.'

'Look, I'm no' sure about the spellin' but it's sometin' like Margarita Mosalas. I found it in one of me note books from Art school days,' and then as though embarrassed quickly added, 'Don't ask!'

'I won't even go there,' Roxy said with a laugh. 'She sounds Spanish.'

'Aye, very Californian of Heather to have Latino help. Quite pretty I believe, was pursuing a modeling career after she got the boot from Heather's. But then she just disappeared, or so they say.'

'What do you think happened?'

'Ah, look, she could be just livin' the quiet life in the sticks somewhere or gone back to Mexico or wherever she's from. I really wouldn't know. Why don't ya call your new police friends, get them to look her up?'

'Yeah, I could,' Roxy agreed, 'but I want to keep them out of it for now.'

'Well, good luck with it all, eh?'

'Thanks Lockie, you're a dream!'

Roxy pressed the 'end' button on her phone and then pressed the speed dial for Oliver Horowitz.

'She lives!' he said. 'Where the hell have you been? Don't you answer text messages anymore?'

'Sorry, I've been "out the back of Bourke" so to speak; crap reception.'

'What on earth were you doing out *there*?'

'Just chasing some leads. Sorry, I should've let you know.'

'Duh! After our last conversation you had me terrified! Jesus, Roxy, you're a handful. Where were you, exactly? What were you doing?'

'I'll explain it all later, I promise. For now I need a favor.'

There was a brief pause and when Oliver spoke again he sounded resigned to his ghostwriter's antics. 'What is it?'

'I need to find out about an unauthorized biography on Heather Jackson that was set to be published about 15 years ago. The author was her ex-maid, Margarita Mosalis or Moralis, something like that, but I don't have the name of the publishing house.'

'Hmmm.'

'I could probably look it up myself, Olie, but I know you have links in that area and it'd take you about a minute. Come on, you know you still owe me...'

Another pause and then the agent relented. 'Okay, I'll ask around. Be in my office by midday tomorrow, I should have the answers by then. I need to see you anyway.'

'Oh?'

'Check you don't have anymore suspicious scratches across your face.'

'Hi Shazza,' Roxy chirped as she pushed the door open to Oliver Horowitz's office just after 12 o'clock the next day. 'His Highness got you working on a Saturday, eh? That's a bit rich.'

Sharon looked up from behind her computer and smiled broadly, her cigarette managing to stay firmly in place between her lips as she did so. 'Blood oath. He gets rich, I get to do all the work. Slave driver.' She shrugged her head towards Oliver's office. 'He's in a foul one, darl', so take care.'

'He doesn't scare me,' Roxy laughed and tapped lightly on his closed office door before entering.

Oliver was staring at some sheets in front of him as she entered and simply waved her to a seat before returning to his work. Roxy sat down and waited, noting as she glanced around the room, that her agent had some new toys. There was a miniature basketball hoop with the Nike logo slashed across it and a giant teddy bear with a pink ribbon for breast cancer.

'Getting a conscience in your old age,' Roxy said but the agent ignored her and kept right on reading. So she waited some more.

'Oi!' hissed Sharon behind her. 'You want some coffee?'

'You read my mind, yes, thanks. Milk, two sugars.'

'Me too,' Oliver muttered.

'Good Lord! He speaks!' Sharon said, winking at Roxy before disappearing again.

'You okay?' Roxy asked Oliver as soon as she caught his eye.

'Huh? Oh, yeah, yeah…just a bit of grief from our mutual mate Miss Passion.'

'Oh? Anything to do with her ex-thug boyfriend Angelo?'

He glanced up and then away again. 'No, nothing at all. That's ancient history.' He shuffled the papers on his desk and then dropped them into a drawer to his right. 'Okay, forget about that. How the hell are you?'

'Good.'

'Jesus, Roxy, you gave me an almighty scare.' He squinted his eyes and scanned her face. 'No little pushes lately?'

'No, no. What's the problem?'

He leaned back in his chair and shook his head slowly.

'What is it? What have you found?'

'I spoke to my mate at Flatter Publishing.'

'And?'

'And….Christ, Roxy, how do you manage to land yourself in a pile of shit *every single time*? I send you to do an innocent story and the next thing I know, you're surrounded in bloody mayhem!'

Roxy shifted to the end of the scratchy sofa and glared at her agent. 'Come on. What did he tell you?'

'Here you go,' Sharon sang behind her and, reluctantly, Roxy waited for the assistant to place their coffees down before saying, 'Olie?!'

'Okay, easy does it. I don't know who gave you the tip but as soon as I started asking questions about one Margarita Moralis, Pete—my mate at Flatter—got real edgy. Said she was this close'—he indicated with two fingers held an inch apart—'to handing over her juicy book when she just vanished. This was pre-digital age, so they didn't have a dozen email copies they could turn to.'

'Oh I know all that,' Roxy replied impatiently. 'But was it foul play?'

'Does the Pope shit in the friggin' woods? It *had* to be, Roxy. The day before Margarita's due to reveal all to the publishing house, she disappears. The publishers go over there to find out what's going on and find she's just evaporated. Not a trace of her or her manuscript. They haven't seen either since.'

'And she didn't just take off? Maybe she thought better of it all? Maybe she was making it all up and decided to clear out before the truth came out?'

'Her clothes were all there, apparently, like she'd just stepped out for a fag. No way, babe, she took off, alright, but to a higher plane, I reckon.'

'And they never found the body?'

'Not that Pete knew. He said the publishing house made a damn good effort to try to find her, but they came up empty handed. Apart from them, I gather she was all alone in the world. So no-one else really bothered.'

'Hmmm.' Roxy sat back in her chair sipping her coffee.

'Another missing woman, I'd say.' Oliver stared at his own drink for some time. 'What are you going to do now? Had enough murder and mayhem for one month?'

'Not at all.'

'Oh come on Roxy, I think we both know you gave it your best shot, and my God it would have made a good story, but the way bodies are piling up, I'd say it was time to step out of it. No story's worth all this.'

'You've got to be kidding! The story's only getting better. Besides, if I was a bloke you'd be spurring me on.'

Oliver seemed offended by this but ignored her comment and asked, 'So, what else you been up to?'

'Nuh-uh. No time now, I'm afraid.' Roxy took a final gulp of her coffee and sprang to her feet. 'I've got a little confronting to do first!'

24 CONFRONTATIONS

The tall white walls that barricaded Heather Jackson's house from the rest of the world shone like snow under the harsh sun of the encroaching Sydney summer and Roxy pulled her car to a stop before the gate and pressed the intercom. Within seconds, the maid had answered.

'It's Roxy Parker again,' the young woman said and then, as confidently as she could, added, 'and I'd like to see Miss Jackson.'

'She no here,' the maid replied with what Roxy realized was her standard reply.

'Perhaps, then, you can ask her if Marian is there instead.'

'Who?'

'Marian Johnson from Macksland.'

There was a long pause before the intercom went dead and the gate began to swing open. Roxy repressed a smile as she drove up the driveway and parked outside the front, this time armed with a lot more than an old umbrella. When she rang the doorbell, however, it was not the anxious maid who answered her call, but a tall, middle-aged man with neatly trimmed brown hair and an expensive jacket over a chambray shirt and pleated trousers. He smelled of aftershave, and the hand that he extended to her was cluttered with gold rings, a thick gold bracelet hanging down from beneath his sleeve. *This must be his casual look*, she thought, grimacing at the overpowering perfume.

'At last we meet Ms Parker,' he purred before settling his lips into a wry smile. He waved one hand inside. 'Come in, please.'

'Jamie Owen, I assume?'

'You assume correctly. Please follow me.'

Heather's manager lead Roxy through the marbled entrance and right, along a wide corridor to a set of double doors through which he disappeared. Following him, Roxy found herself in the plush environs of an office, with a large, paper-strewn desk at one end and a maroon leather couch at the other. There were various computers, scanners and photocopiers lined up on a long table by the wall and a set of glass sliding doors, which lead out towards a garden and a pool beyond. Another wall was covered in glass louvers, now wedged shut against the cold. And on every wall there were portraits, bright, lurid Heather Jackson classics in all shapes and sizes. She admired them as he closed the doors behind her.

'Your office?' Roxy asked.

'My office away from the office. No rest for the wicked, Ms Parker.'

'Well, you'd know all about that.'

He ignored the comment and patted the space beside him on the couch where he had already taken a seat.

'My apologies I never got that information to you.'

'Oh?'

'The detailed biography you asked for. I will get onto that but I must say, Heather's past is not exactly relevant, it's her painting that we focus on.'

'You don't think the two are related?'

He shrugged, clearly not interested in opening this can of worms. He said simply, 'So what can I do for you?'

'Actually, I was hoping to speak to Heather directly.'

'That's not possible. You can speak to me.'

'It's a private matter.'

'We have no secrets here.'

Roxy chewed over this for a few seconds and then reached into her handbag and retrieved the photo she had taken from Heather's old neighbor in Macksland.

'Not even this little secret?' she asked, placing the picture in front of him.

Jamie barely glanced at the shot before he shrugged. 'So you've been doing a little snooping. Good for you,' he said and then smiled wryly again. 'As I said, we have no secrets here. This does not perturb us.'

'But it's not exactly public knowledge is it?'

'And not exactly a secret. I can't help the fact that not one journalist in 20 years has had the foresight to look into Heather's past.'

'And no-one ever asked?'

'Not a one.' Jamie shifted in his seat impatiently. 'Look, Ms Parker, what is all this about? You haven't come all this way to share happy snaps, surely?'

Roxy swept her fringe from her face and nibbled her lower lip contemplatively. She hoped she knew what she was doing. She took a deep breath. 'No, you're right. I came to tell you that I not only know who Heather is,' she said slowly, watching his face for signs. 'But I know who her mother is. Or should I say, was?'

Jamie shrugged again. 'Yes, Joyce Johnson, a fine woman.'

'No, Mr Owen. Her real mother. Her *birth* mother.'

His eyes squinted very slightly and he waited for her to continue. He was giving nothing away.

'Beatrice Musgrave,' Roxy said.

He didn't flinch. 'So?'

'So, you're telling me you knew?'

'Of course. As I've already said, we have no secrets here.'

'So you won't mind me making it public knowledge?'

'Not at all, although I don't see who it would serve. Heather has known about her birth mother for some time now. She has nothing to hide.'

'Then why all the secrecy?'

Jamie stood up and, wandering over to his desk, perched on the end so that he was now looming over her where she still remained, seated on the couch.

'There's no secrecy, Ms Parker. But there's also no need for revelations either. Heather has made a success of herself on her own merits. On her own terms.' His nose crinkled up distastefully. 'She doesn't feel the need to cloud everything with this bit of gossip.'

'Beatrice seemed to think it was a good idea.'

'And look where it got her.'

Roxy's eyebrows shot up. 'Are you saying she was killed over it?'

Jamie laughed in a kind of mocking way. 'I'm not saying any such thing! It was suicide remember? You journalists really are experts at twisting the truth, aren't you?'

'Well how about this for the truth, Mr Owen: Beatrice was about to reveal Heather's true identity in her autobiography but before she got a chance to she turns up dead. It all looks a tad incriminating to me.'

The manager laughed again, this time more heartily. He appeared to be enjoying himself. 'Why on earth would Heather want to kill her birth mother, especially *before* the book came out? Heather had everything to gain from the revelation, including a swag of the old woman's money. I hardly think she has motive to kill.'

'Yet she didn't want the book to come out, you said so yourself.'

'Oh we are going in circles, Ms Parker!' He was irritable again. 'Heather doesn't *need* the money. I know you might find that hard to believe. But, well, Heather's an old fashioned gal from way back. She's built up a name all on her own. She doesn't want or need to be associated with anyone else, least of all traditionalists like the Musgrave clan.'

Roxy chewed over this for a few seconds and then asked, 'Whatever happened to Margarita Moralis?'

Jamie stared blankly back. 'Who?'

'Heather's maid for a few years, until she got the sack.'

'I vaguely remember her.'

'*Vaguely*? Surely she was your worst nightmare? She threatened to write a revealing book about your client.'

'Oh Miss Parker, if you knew how many fruit loops we have to deal with you wouldn't be asking such asinine questions.' He was already flicking through the papers on his desk as if preoccupied or plain disinterested. It irked the young woman and she could feel her temper returning. This guy was an arrogant jerk and she'd had just about enough of him.

'Cut the crap, Jamie,' she spat back. 'The book was written, about to be handed over when, according to the publishers, the author suddenly vanished from the face of the earth. It seems mighty convenient to me, and I'm sure my friends at the Mosman Police Department will have no trouble finding out what happened if you're not willing to talk.'

The lawyer glanced up from his papers and feigned a smile. 'Ahh, now I remember. Margarita Moralis. A slutty Spanish woman. Fancied herself the next J. Lo. It was all a publicity stunt for her singing career. That's why she disappeared. She couldn't go through with the book because it was a pack of lies and she knew she'd get hit with a lawsuit. Did her publishers happen to mention that when she disappeared, so did their hefty advance? No, forgot to mention that did they? Well why don't you go back and ask them about that? Sounds like a mighty scam to me. Go ahead and look Miss Moralis up. I'm sure her publishers will be most grateful. The police, too.'

Roxy considered this for a few seconds and then replied sullenly, 'I will.' She was unsure whether to believe him. Why hadn't Oliver mentioned the advance? That shone a whole new light on things. The look of amusement that swept across his face was more than she could bear and, realizing that there would be no more revelations here today, stood up abruptly.

'I'll leave now, Mr Owen,' she said as politely as she could muster, 'but it's not the last you've heard of me.'

He shrugged indifferently as she swept out of the room and back down the hallway to the marbled lobby. The housekeeper appeared from nowhere and escorted her to the door. 'To make sure I really do leave,' Roxy thought angrily. She took a quick glance towards the door that had opened so mysteriously the last time she visited and noticed that it was slightly ajar, only a dense darkness visible beyond.

'What's in there?' Roxy asked.

'You go now,' the maid hissed, as though her very life depended on it and swung the front door open for her.

Roxy relented and let the woman lead her out into the darkening driveway. But she was no longer feeling defeated. Thanks to her little foray into Jamie Owen's inner sanctum, she now knew for certain the identity of the woman in Heather Jackson's winning portrait *Not Drowning, Waving*'. It was hanging in the office, had pride of place behind Jamie's desk, and it was the spitting image of Marian's older sister, the light-haired girl in the wheelchair.

It was Lillian Johnson.

Murder. Mayhem. Death and destruction. It all screamed out at Roxy as she slowly flipped through her old scrapbooks hoping to find some news of the missing maid, Margarita Moralis. Oliver called these her Books of Death, but Roxy had turned to them for information in the past and hoped they would help her now. She could not recall cutting out any such article but then how would she? There had been so many murders since then, so many missing faces and mutilated corpses, most of them forgotten by the indifferent hands of time. Roxy began her search in the scrapbook titled the same year that Margarita had disappeared. But she knew that she would likely have to keep looking through later scrapbooks for someone fitting her description. Indeed it often took many years for bodies to be recovered, if at all.

As it turned out, it had taken almost two years for the then-decomposed body of Margarita Moralis to show up, still wedged behind the wheel of the car she had been driving when, according to the almost nondescript news article, she had 'crashed through thick forest one dark night to die alone, unnoticed for years'. The article, which was headlined 'Forgotten Crash Victim Found', did identify the victim as 'aspiring singer' Margarita Moralis, but made no mention of Heather Jackson or her tell-all book. Nor did it mention any money found with the body. It simply stated the cause of death as 'accidental'.

'Why then did I even cut it out?' Roxy wondered before reading on. When she saw the words 'Police have not ruled out foul play', the penny dropped. She had expected a follow-up article confirming that it was, indeed murder, but after scanning the next few pages she realized no such article was forthcoming. She wanted to know why. Surely the police had twigged when they learned the driver's identity? Surely they, or the publisher, had connected her to the Heather Jackson tell-all? There was only one way of finding out, it was time to pay her new friend another visit. She grabbed her jacket again and headed back out.

Standing beside the snack dispenser, kicking the side with one heeled shoe, Gilda Maltin looked even smaller than she had behind her desk and, as Roxy strode towards her, she wondered, yet again, how the police detective managed to remain so self-assured in such a macho world.

'Does nobody get Saturdays off anymore?' Roxy said and Gilda swung around to face her, her thin eyebrows raised with a mixture of surprise and delight.

'Roxy Parker,' she said, scooping up a chocolate bar from the tray below her. 'I didn't expect to see you back here so soon. Can I offer you a piece?'

'No, thanks, I'm more of a savory girl myself. Can we have a quick word?'

'Absolutely!' She lead the way back to her office and, slipping into the seat behind her desk, began munching on her bar. Roxy sat down in front of her.

'I've got a favor to ask.'

'Go ahead.'

'Have you heard of the name Margarita Moralis?'

Gilda stopped chewing long enough to give the name some considered thought and then said, 'Oh, yes, you know it's *kinda* familiar, but nothing's quite connecting. Why?'

'I'm just doing some research on a story about the artist Heather Jackson.'

'Yeah, I know her. Abstracts. Not my kinda stuff but there you go.'

'Yes, well, Margarita was her maid and—'

'And she disappeared suddenly! Now I remember her. A guy I was seeing at the time was working on the case. Real asshole—the guy, not the case.'

Roxy couldn't help laughing. 'Well I know her body was recovered from a car wreck about two years later but I don't know if they ruled the crash as accidental or foul play.'

'And you're just checking your facts, right?'

'Right.'

'For your story?'

'Yes.'

'So what does Heather Jackson have to do with Beatrice?'

Roxy bit her lip. She had revealed more than she intended. 'Oh you're a smart detective, you'll be running the force one day.'

'That's my intention,' she said, then placed her half-eaten chocolate bar aside and began tapping away at her computer anyway. 'Well, if as you say, they found her, it'll all be in here.' She worked away for some time and Roxy kept her fingers crossed. This could be the missing link.

'Now, let's see.' Gilda pulled the screen around so Roxy could also get a glimpse. 'Yep, here it is and you're right, we did find her. Eventually. It's strange that I don't remember it, though. It must have been very low-key.'

'It was,' Roxy replied. 'Just one small news story.'

'That probably means the police weren't giving out a lot of details. Let's see why.' She turned back to the screen and began reading: *Margarita Angela Moralis, aged 27, found deceased at the bottom of Piers Hill.* Let's see…*Cause of death: blunt force trauma to the head and spine, consistent with a car accident. Cause of car accident: faulty brakes.*' She glanced up at Roxy with a rueful shrug. 'Not real hopeful I'm afraid.'

'So there were no suspicious circumstances at all?'

Gilda began pushing the cursor down the screen reading as she went. 'Hmm, hang on a minute, this sounds a bit odd. It says here that she had *substantial damage to her elbows and upper torso.*' Roxy sat up. 'Oh, no, no, it says they *could have been consistent with a violent car crash.* See, it's hard to say for sure when the body is so badly decomposed. Strange she wasn't discovered for so long. Must have been a pretty quiet part of the world.'

'Yes I think it was thick forest. And no mention of major amounts of cash found on her?'

Gilda glanced up at her suspiciously. 'Not that I can see. What's all this about, Roxy?'

Roxy shifted in her seat. 'Right now, I'm working on a bit of a hunch and to be honest I'd rather not say. Not until I sort a few things out.' Gilda did not look impressed so she quickly added, 'But you'll be the first person I call if there's anything to report. I promise.'

The detective placed the last bit of chocolate in her mouth before curling the wrapper into a ball and flinging it neatly into the paper basket by the door. 'I'm gonna let this one go, Roxy,' she said, wiping her mouth with one hand. 'But I've got my eye on you, and I like you, so do me right and I won't do you wrong. Got it?' Roxy nodded her head vigorously and made a quick exit.

25 CYRIL COMES THROUGH

It was Sunday morning and Roxy needed to stop prancing about as Hercule Poirot long enough to get her own life back in order. As mundane as it was, there was laundry to do, floors to be vacuumed and a wine rack that desperately needed re-stocking, if only for her sanity.

There was also the small matter of her mother. After a strained conversation the night before, they had agreed to meet up at a café on Lorraine's side of town for lunch, and while Roxy grumbled about it, she realized it was for the best. There was only so much of her Mother's biting commentary about her 'grotty inner-city lifestyle' that she could stomach.

After her chores were done and when the time was right, she slipped into her most demure dress, thick tights, 1920s-style pumps and a black beret, and drove her VW across the Sydney Harbor Bridge to the gleaming café in Lane Cove.

Lorraine gave her the once-over and a slight smile passed across her lips. Roxy took that as a compliment and dropped a quick peck on her mother's cheek, then sat down in the chair across from her. She glanced around. The café was bursting with well-dressed types, mostly soccer mums and restless kids stuffed into stiffly ironed white clothes that just begged to be ruined. She watched a small boy tackling a large piece of chocolate cake and gave him about two seconds before mummy dear started fretting.

'So you're not going to tell me where you've been?' Lorraine was saying and Roxy shook her head.

'Nothing worth mentioning. Got a menu?'

'I've already ordered for you.'

'Huh? Want to burp me afterwards as well?'

Lorraine snorted. 'You always get the same thing, darling, let's face it.'

'I do not!'

'A latte, two sugars, and a vegie focaccia. Sound about right?'

Actually, it sounded great but Roxy was not about to tell her mother that. 'Not at all what I would have ordered today,' she spat back.

'Then I apologize. What did you want?'

'I want a giant piece of chocolate cake.' She knew only too well that she was behaving like the little boy to her left but it was her mother's fault she decided. If Lorraine was going to treat her like a child, she might as well enjoy the fringe benefits. Her mother's eyebrows shot up but she called the waitress over and reordered.

'And I'll have an espresso not a latte, thank you,' Roxy added. Then she sighed. *Why did her mother bring out the worst in her?*

'So how are things?' Lorraine asked.

They settled into idle chatter after that and it suited Roxy just fine. While she was eager to get back home and get her thoughts in order, she knew she had to give a little of herself and her time to her mother, too. Their relationship was a lot like a bad marriage. If they didn't keep putting in the work, making the effort, they would eventually drift apart. There were just too many differences between them now. Yet Beattie's death, and her sad relationship with her own son—the way he barely tolerated her!—gave Roxy pause for thought. She knew she didn't want to become that person, the intolerant child. So she ignored her mother's politically incorrect comments and kept the conversation light and breezy. And by the end of the hour, they both departed in better moods than they had started, and she smiled as she got back to her apartment in one piece. *Perhaps they were both finally growing up?*

By Monday morning, Roxy was ready to get back to the case at hand. The problem was, being a freelance writer, you never can tell when work will suddenly strike, and first thing that day she logged online to find a barrage of emails in her inbox. They were mostly from enthusiastic editors keen to snap up many of her story ideas. Fortunately, most of the deadlines were some way off, so Roxy answered them accordingly and scheduled the work in for the following few weeks. She was going to be busy and at least her bank manager would be happy. Itching to get back to Beattie's death, she forced herself to do a little preliminary work on her freelance features first. If she didn't set up some interviews and do a few hours of research now, she would be behind the eight ball pretty soon.

Finally, with that done, she switched from work mode back to sleuth, and opened the file on Heather Jackson again. She scanned slowly through it and when she reached the end, Roxy quickly jotted down the details of her recent meeting with Heather's manager, Jamie Owen, including his insistence that Heather Jackson (aka Marian Johnson) had absolutely no motive for murdering Beatrice Musgrave. Roxy grabbed a pencil from a small, silver cup to the side of the computer and began chomping on the end as her brain went into overdrive. She hated to admit it, but Jamie was right. Surely the artist could only profit from the revelation that Beattie was her real mum. Not only was it a step up in the world for the classic snob—the Musgraves were Sydney 'bluebloods' after all—but, even if she wasn't interested in the publicity, surely the financial rewards wouldn't hurt?

Judging by Heather's decadent lifestyle, Roxy had to accept that the financial incentives of the revelation would be a major reason for keeping old Beattie alive, at least long enough for her identity to be confirmed.

Roxy placed the chewed up pencil to one side and began typing again, this time recording her recent meeting with Gilda and the information she had provided about Margarita's death which, she was sure, had to involve foul play. This was equally baffling. If Margarita had been killed to secure her silence, was Heather behind it or was it the work of her over-zealous manager? And did either of them have it in them? Her immediate response was an unequivocal yes! But then there was the matter of the missing publisher's advance. Perhaps a third party, a greedy agent or boyfriend, was behind the whole thing?

Roxy pushed her seat back from the screen with exasperation. What a can of worms this had turned out to be! She stared out at the view for some time. She could feel something niggling at the back of her head. There was something she had missed, something really obvious. But she couldn't for the life of her work out what. It was time for a little mental retreat. Roxy jumped up, ditched her jeans for a tracksuit and joggers and then headed out onto the street for a power walk.

It was late afternoon and the park down at nearby Rushcutters Bay stretched like a large green blanket, empty and waiting for the 5pm knock-off. Then, it would be crawling with weary suits cutting through on their way home from work, joggers anxious to enjoy the last rays of sun and couples catching up on a little quality time with their kids and/or assorted pets. For now, it was eerily quiet and, checking her watch, Roxy began to circle around it, picking up speed as her body heated up. At one point, her path lead her past a small side street and she spotted two drivers politely exchanging numbers after what appeared to be a clash of bumper bars. Roxy's brain began to whir but she shook her head and kept walking. Now was not the time to think. Now was the time to rest her mind and work her body instead.

An hour later, as she tossed her sweaty tracksuit into the washing basket and prepared to step into the shower, her brain finally broke through. Car accidents! There were an awful lot of car accidents in Heather Jackson's life. Not her, of course, but people closely associated with her. Heather's parents were both killed in a car accident, Heather's midwife was maimed in one. Heather's worst nightmare, Margarita Moralis, conveniently turned up dead in one. Roxy lathered her body in soap and then washed it off quickly, dried, dressed back into her jeans and a fresh, long-sleeved T-shirt, swirled a striped scarf around her neck and returned to her computer. That's when the doorbell rang.

'Still talking to me?' Max said with a shy smile as Roxy let him in.

'Of course I am, how are you?' Roxy planted a fat kiss on his cheek before leading the way upstairs. She was keen to concentrate on the case tonight but was also eager to smooth things over with her good friend before their relationship was beyond repair.

'Have you had dinner yet?' he asked and, when she shook her head he produced a bag full of steaming Chinese food. 'Ta-da!'

'You're a hero,' Roxy said with a laugh. 'I couldn't even think about cooking tonight. Merlot?'

'Actually, have you got a softdrink?'

She cocked her head to one side, surprised. 'Sure.'

As they ate and drank, Roxy and Max caught up on each other's lives just like old times, but Roxy knew it was only a matter of time before the whole messy ordeal would be dredged up again.

When Max didn't mention it she put her chopsticks down and said, 'Are we okay now? Do you think?'

He brushed one large, tanned hand through his unruly hair and looked up at her through soft brown eyes. When he finally smiled it was breathtaking. 'I'm a hardy bugger. I'll be fine.' He cleared his throat and said, 'You'll never believe who called and wants to give it another go.'

'Not the elusive Sandra?'

'The very one.' She smiled as warmly as she could muster and told him that was wonderful. 'I think so. And I'm really going to give her a chance this time, now that you and I aren't...' He let that dangle and downed a few good gulps of his softdrink. 'Anyway, enough of all that crap. How's the Beatrice Musgrave story going?'

Roxy cocked her head again. 'You really want to know?'

'Really.'

'Well, it's livening up, that's for sure.' Roxy proceeded to fill him in on everything he had missed since they'd separated in Macksland. She told him about the Heather Jackson connection, too, as well as her newfound friendship with the police detective Gilda Maltin.

'She sounds pretty cool. For a cop.'

'Yeah, I like her. And not just because she's a good contact. She's kinda got her shit together, you know?'

'Well, no, but I'm getting there, Parker. So, tell me, what do you think about Beattie's murder? From what you've learned, who do you think did the dirty deed?'

Roxy shrugged, tossing her black hair away from her face and relaxed back into the lounge, her long legs tucked up underneath her. 'I'm veering towards three possible candidates.'

'Oh?'

'The first is the grandson and/or his overly zealous brother-in-law, Angelo, with or without Sophia. I don't think any of them are as innocent as they make out. But if they did do it, I think it was more of a spontaneous thing—sort of like a threat that went wrong.'

'Like your little push on Elizabeth Street?'

'Yes, but obviously more deadly. My guess is, they went over there to beg Beattie to drop the book and, somehow, things turned ugly. Angelo may have struck her too hard and then had to throw her over the balcony to hide the evidence.'

'And the next candidate?'

'Either Heather's manager Jamie Owen or Beattie's old lawyer friend Ronald Featherby. Both men are tall and skinny.'

'So? Tall, skinny blokes are evil, suddenly? If that's the case I'm in deep shit.'

'Very funny. No, if you'll recall, Sally Owens said she saw a tall, skinny guy hiding inside her house the night it was trashed and after Frank O'Brien was killed. Maybe it was one of these two men and they were most likely protecting the interests of a well-paying client.'

'So you think whoever killed Beatrice also killed Frank?'

'Absolutely. And probably the midwife before that.'

Max picked up the plates and took them into the kitchen. When he returned he said, 'But what about this Margarita Moralis then? Is she related to the whole thing or not?'

'I don't know. Maybe her book was more than a tell-all, maybe she had also discovered Heather's real identity and was going to spill that in the book. If you think about it, that could have scared almost anyone—even Beattie herself. Remember, Margarita's book was due for release 15 years ago. Beattie mightn't have been ready to air her dirty laundry back then. Her high-powered husband was still alive, after all. Then again, Margarita's book might have nothing to do with any of it. Not one little bit.'

'Arrgghh!' Max groaned, dropping into the sofa chair opposite her. 'So who's your third suspect then? Is there a butler lurking about somewhere?'

'Actually, Heather Jackson's my third suspect. I can't understand why she's being so secretive about her past. She's an artist, not a moral crusader, surely no-one really cares that she was adopted or who her real mother was? But there's one other thing about Heather that points towards her.'

'Mmmm?'

'Car accidents.'

'Huh?'

'A lot of the people from Heather's past have been wiped away in car accidents. It just seems an odd coincidence.'

Max squirmed in his seat. 'You've lost me. What are you getting at?'

'I honestly don't know. But here's the thing: Heather hates publicity, right? Well, why? Surely it can only work to her advantage. My guess is she's hiding from her past, she doesn't want anyone to know she was a scrawny little loser who grew up in small-town Australia and got in scraps with the police. Think about it, why else would she recreate herself like she has? She's changed her name, her face, her entire life. And the key people who could have been around to reveal her past are all dead: her midwife, her adoptive parents, her real parents. And probably the maid. And God knows were her poor sister is.'

He looked confused.

'Lillian, the one in the wheelchair. I wonder where she ended up? There are far too many missing people and strange coincidences.'

'So tell me about these car accidents. Were they all recorded as foul play?'

'No, that's the problem. But Heather's adoptive dad used to run a car yard. Maybe she picked up a few tricks along the way, like how to make brakes muck-up at just the right moment?'

'But it doesn't make any sense.' Max sighed. 'I mean, I'm not particularly keen on my old school photos ever seeing the light of day, either. Jesus, you should have seen me when I was 14. It's frightening! But do people kill to hide bad photos? What could possibly have happened in her past to make her so desperate?'

'I don't know!' Roxy cried and then pushed herself up off the sofa. 'Want a tea?'

'Sure.' Max followed her into the kitchen. 'So if she is bumping them off, why?'

'That I still don't know. There has to be some secret in her past, worse than the truth about her parents. I just need to work out what. Herbal or the real-deal?' She held up two tea boxes.

'Huh? Oh, give me herbal, I'm strung-out enough as it is. This is all kinda spooky stuff, Parker. I hope you know what you're getting into.'

'Too late now, Maxy,' she said with a faltering smile. 'Too bloody late.'

'So what happens now?'

'Well, I guess the first thing is to find out if she was handy under the bonnet.'

They returned to the lounge room and Roxy put a blues CD on while they sipped their teas. They sat quietly for several minutes when Roxy suddenly jumped up.

'I've got it! Her neighbor, the one I told you about, the one who gave me the family picture?'

'Yes!?'

'Well, why don't I ring and ask him? He seemed to know a lot about her.'

Max glanced at his watch. 'Because it's almost 11 o'clock. Bit late for home calls isn't it?'

Roxy dashed into the bedroom to retrieve the neighbor's details from her Filofax. 'I don't think so, he sounded like an insomniac.' She began to dial. 'Cyril? Hello, it's Roxy Parker from Sydney, I was there the other day looking for the Johnson fam—'

'Yes, yes,' he crackled at the other end. 'I was wonderin' whether you'd call.'

'It's not too late?'

'Nah darl, sleep's never been big on me agenda. You written yar story yet? Am I in it?'

'Still writing it, Cyril, but I think you will make the copy, yes. I just wanted to ask you a couple more questions about Heather—I mean, Marian Johnson.'

'Fire away, I ain't goin' nowhere.'

'Did Marian ever get involved in her dad's mechanics business?'

'Now let me see... yeah, you know I think she did. Actually if I recall correctly, she had quite a way with cars. I always thought she'd settle down eventually and take it over. Guess I thought wrong. You found her yet?'

'Um, no,' Roxy lied. 'Did you ever hear of her getting into trouble with cars?'

'How do ya mean?'

'Well, did she ever play with people's engines or brakes— just to stuff them up a bit?'

'Oh, not that I heard about. Although I wouldn't a put it past her, that's for sure. Apart from the car shop, the only thing she ever showed interest in was mischief.'

'And her painting, of course.'

'Painting?'

'Yes, didn't Marian do a bit of painting, you know, art work?'

There was a brief pause on the other end before Cyril croaked, 'No love, you got it all wrong. There was a lotta paintin' goin' on but it was never by Marian.'

'Oh?'

'No, no, it was Lilly that done all the paintin'. You know, the one in the wheelchair? She was alright, too. I even bought one of hers from the local fete. A picture of Mother Theresa. Can't imagine where it is now, out in the old shed I reckon.'

Roxy was speechless for several seconds, but when she found her tongue she quickly asked, 'It's not abstract is it?'

'Oh I don't know anything about art, love, but she sure don't know her colors. She had blue skin and gold eyes. Still, it seemed to work, ya know. Kinda pretty in a funny way.'

'I'd find that painting and hold on to it, Cyril,' Roxy told him. 'You just might have a masterpiece on your hands.'

As she hung up, Roxy's heart was pumping double time. She glanced across at Max who was watching her, intrigued.

'What?!' he asked.

'You got a spare hour?'

'Huh?'

'Come on, grab your camera.' She raced into her sunroom. 'We've got some snooping to do. But first, I've got to make a stop in cyberspace.'

26 BREAKING IN

Tall casuarinas cast eerie shadows across the street and Roxy hoped Max couldn't hear her heart pounding beneath her thick sweater as they sat cocooned in her blue VW two houses down from Heather Jackson's. In one hand she held a small Magnalite flashlight, and in the other a map of Heather's sprawling mansion.

'Now let me see if I've got this straight,' Max said in a hushed tone. 'You think Heather's disabled sister is the one who's got all the painting talent, and that Heather is passing her work off as her own?'

'Absolutely. Don't you see it makes perfect sense? It explains everything: why Heather's so desperate to hide her past. If anyone finds out that it was Lilly who was the artist in the family, not her, than she's sprung. There goes her credibility, her raison d'être.'

'But maybe Heather was also into painting; maybe the disabled sister copied her stuff and the busy-body neighbor never noticed. I don't mean to sound disparaging but she is well, you know, disabled.'

'Doesn't mean she can't paint! Besides, the work is pretty crude, perhaps she has some use of at least one hand. It's beautiful but it's not fine brush strokes. Look, I know there are still questions which is exactly why we have to get in there and see for ourselves.'

'But why do you think she's in there? If she is being held, she could be almost anywhere.'

'It's just a hunch, but I sensed her when I was here earlier. I caught sight of what could be her wheelchair in one of the rooms. Trust me on this.'

'Okay, but you seriously want to break into Heather Jackson's house? Now? Why don't you just call the cops?'

'Oh, and tell them what? That I think Heather's got her poor sister tied up in a dungeon and is forcing her to paint against her will?'

'How do you even know Lilly's doing it against her will? Maybe she's all for it. Lilly paints, Heather's the front woman.'

'Fine, then why all the dead bodies? Somebody's been killing people to shut them up and my guess is, it's Heather.'

He sighed. 'So, what's your plan then?'

Roxy shone the flashlight on the map and pointed to a corner of the house where a greenhouse stood. 'We have to make our way to the west wall of the house. There's a gardener's shed here.' She indicated it on the map. 'If we're lucky the security won't be as tight as the front or side gates.'

'But you don't know for sure?'

'Fraid not. But it's worth a try.'

'Where did you get the map anyway?'

'A fan's home page, but it seems to be correct.' She could almost feel him rolling his eyes in the darkness beside her.

Eventually he said, 'And what if you're wrong about all of this?'

'Then I'm wrong. Big deal. I'll look elsewhere for answers. Look, all I'm asking is that you stay handy with the car in case I need a quick getaway. I don't expect you to come in with me.'

Max glared at her for several seconds and then reached for his camera bag. 'No way, Parker. If you're going in, then I'm going in with you.'

The moon was just a thin, broken fingernail in the sky ensuring a welcome cover of darkness as the duo scurried quietly past the front gate to the west side of the property.

'It's a big place,' Max said in hushed tones beside her, but Roxy was deep in thought. She wasn't exactly sure what she was hoping to do once she got inside the place, but she hoped that instinct would lead her in the right direction, towards the wing of the house where the door had mysteriously opened and shut the first time she had visited.

Following a tall, rock wall, Roxy and Max walked for what seemed an eternity before they came across a side gate covered in vines.

'Is this the gate you were talking about?' Max asked.

'Hope not,' she replied, tugging at the chains that were holding it securely in place. 'We're not going to get through this.'

'What about scaling the wall?'

'With what? No, it's too tall.' Roxy peered through the darkness down the rock wall beyond. 'There's got to be another entrance. This one looks like it hasn't been used in ages.'

They continued walking until they reached the north-west corner of the property, and then tried the back wall but it, too, seemed rock solid.

'The map's obviously wrong, Parker.'

'There has to be another gate,' she insisted, turning back to retrace their steps along the west wall. 'I can't imagine the gardener fronting up to the main gate every day. It doesn't make sense.'

'Perhaps he uses the delivery gate on the other side?'

'There are no gardens that side. No, he has to have his own entrance. Keep looking.'

About a metre from the side gate, Roxy suddenly stopped. 'Hang on a minute.' She backtracked a few steps and reached into what appeared to be a mass of vines. Her hand was rewarded with a small brass knob. She turned it and gasped as the hidden gate swung inwards with a giant creak. 'I knew it!' she gushed.

'How the bloody hell did you spot that?'

'Women's intuition,' she replied with a wink. 'Come on.'

Reluctantly, Max followed her through, leaving the gate slightly ajar for a quick getaway. Once their eyes had adjusted to the darkness, Roxy could make out a mass of bushes in front of them and beyond that, small glimpses of the lights that shone on the garden immediately fronting the house.

'If we follow this wall around to the back of the house we won't be so conspicuous,' she suggested and began leading the way. Halfway along, she halted. 'What was that?!'

'I didn't hear anything.'

'Hmm, keep an eye out. There could be guards for all I know.'

'Brilliant.'

'Come on, we'll be okay.'

Heather's house loomed large, like a giant fortress in the dark and, apart from a few lights at the front, the back half was pitch-black and lifeless. Roxy shone her torch quickly on her watch. '1.05 am,' she hissed, 'they should be asleep now.'

'Either that or they're watching us on a monitor inside, evilly sniggering as they stroke a fluffy white cat.'

'Huh?'

'Never mind,' Max said. 'Too many James Bond movies.'

When they were directly behind the house, Roxy suggested they make their way to it through the bushes, rather than using the path and Max agreed. Anything to remain out of sight.

'Once we get to the house, keep your head down and just follow me. I think I know where I'm going.'

'Your confidence is comforting,' he replied drolly and did as instructed.

There were several doors along the back of the house and Roxy chose the one closest to the corner, it had several pipes leading out from it and the window beside it was not curtained. It turned out to be what she thought it would be, the laundry. Another door, which obviously lead into the main house, was closed. She checked her map. They were just a corridor away from what the online article called 'the secret wing'. She tried the handle and smiled when it turned easily. She opened the door and peered through. A low light at one end revealed a long corridor, just as the map had said, and Roxy could just make out the words 'No Entry' on a door along one side.

'That has to be where Lilly is. We've got to get in there,' she whispered to Max who was breathing short, nervous breaths behind her.

'What if it's locked?' he managed to say.

'Then we'll try the one to the right. But we've got to try.'

Timidly, they edged out of the laundry and down the corridor. A quarter of the way along they heard a door slam in another part of the house. They stood rock still, listening. Suddenly Max grabbed Roxy's hand, 'Quick!' he pulled her back down the hall and into the laundry again, closing the door as quietly as he could.

'What are you doing?' she whispered.

'Shh! Listen. I heard voices.'

They stood deadly still and waited. There was only silence. Roxy pulled the door forward just an inch and peeped through. Still nothing, and then out of the quiet they heard a muffled laugh. She jumped back, treading on Max's toe and causing him to moan.

'Shhh. Sorry, but you're right. Listen.'

They pricked their ears and could vaguely make out a conversation but it was too muffled, too far away. They heard a door open somewhere down the corridor and Roxy peeked out again. There was somebody down there but she couldn't make out who it was. In any case, they were standing directly in front of the prohibited door, the one near the front entrance where Roxy had seen a flash of silver inside. It could very well have been Lilly's wheelchair, which means it could also lead them to Heather's sister, and the answers to all of Roxy's questions.

She had to get in there and find out.

'Get some sleep, you need it!' a woman's voice said and still Roxy could not see who was speaking but the prickle that was now running like electricity down her spine told her she had heard that voice before, but not at this house. It was followed by the same laugh they had heard earlier. It was a strange, stifled laugh; more nervous than joyful. Then the figure shut the door and turned towards them.

Roxy nearly jumped out of her skin and fell back against the laundry wall, her eyes wide with shock.

'What?!' Max hissed. 'Who is it?'

'It's Sally!' she hissed back. 'Sally Duffy, from Macksland!'

27 THE STUDIO

Little Sally Duffy, Frank O'Brien's supposed best friend, was waltzing nonchalantly down the corridor like she owned the place. Roxy threw a finger up to her lips to implore Max to silence and waited for her to pass. Only when she had done so did Roxy allow herself to breathe.

'Sally? The one who had her place trashed?' Max asked, dumbfounded.

'Yes!'

'But—'

'Shh! This is weirder than I thought. We'll wait a few minutes then I want you to stay here while I go down and look in that door.'

'No way I'm coming with—'

'You have to stay here, Max. If anything happens, at least you can run away and get help. It's our only chance.'

He was not happy but nodded reluctantly anyway, eager to have the whole ordeal over with. 'But you still don't know if Lilly's through that door.'

'That's why I have to go and see. Let's just hope she's alone.'

They waited a good 10 minutes and then Roxy gave Max's hand a quick squeeze and slipped out into the hallway. This time, she reached the door marked 'No Entry' without interruption and quickly opened the door and slipped in. Max watched her from his station in the laundry and felt his heart lurch. He should never have let her talk him into this, if either one of them was caught, they could be in some serious trouble. *Deadly trouble.*

Another hallway greeted Roxy, but this one was smaller and there were just three doors leading off from it, towards the front wing of the house. Roxy guessed that if Lillian was being held in here, she was most likely not in the first room. That was too close to the exit out. With her heart galloping at a record speed, she tried the second door. It opened easily and she stepped inside, enveloped by darkness. She swung the door shut and stood listening intently for several seconds but only silence sang out. Then she noticed the smell.

Methylated spirits, she said to herself. *And paint.* This had to be the studio. She waited for her eyes to adjust to the darkness and gradually began to make out what were no doubt paint easels and canvasses piled up against every wall. She waited another second and then turned on her flashlight. The canvasses that danced beneath the light were truly magnificent. There were smiling faces, sad faces, purple faces and green. Some were almost finished, some barely begun, but each bore Heather Jackson's trademark style—garish, colored mouths twisted oddly with brightly painted eyes and nostrils. Picasso meets Ken Done. It was just as she expected but there was something unusual about this room. She continued flashing the torch, careful not to let it face the open window, lest someone be looking. Then she realized what it was. The easels, of which there were at least four, were all set at a very low level. Whoever was painting these portraits was either super short or seated in a chair. Or, she thought sadly as she spotted a paint-splattered steel contraption in the corner, a wheelchair.

Old Cyril at Limrock Lane was right.

Roxy noticed, too, that a wide doorway lead into what looked like a disabled bathroom and beyond that another wide door, which she guessed lead to Lillian's bedroom, the third room down. But Roxy had seen enough. She flicked her torch off and turned to leave.

That's when the door swung open with a loud thud and the room was suddenly bathed in bright fluorescent light.

'Roxy Parker!' came a surprised voice and she looked around to find Sally Duffy standing, wide-eyed in the doorway. 'What on earth are you doing here?'

'I could ask you the same question,' Roxy replied, squinting from the sudden brightness.

'I live here,' she spat back, her voice now missing its innocent, girlish tones. She looked older, too, her childish pig tail replaced by slick, straightened strands, her freckled face powdered over, and her floral drop-waistline dress substituted for a pair of black hipster pants and a bright pink, V-neck tight-T. 'What's your excuse?'

'Oh I just thought I'd drop in, say G'day,' Roxy said, feeling her stomach tighten as the reality of her situation sunk in. She straightened her glasses with a burst of renewed confidence. 'So, your cute country girl persona was all an act? I should nominate you for an Oscar.'

'Thank you, I even impressed myself. Of course I visited enough times to see how it was done. Mum showed me the rest.'

'Heather's your mother?'

She shrugged her assent and sauntered inside the room, stopping to press a nondescript white button by the door, before walking through the bathroom and testing the door on the other side. It was locked. She smiled with what looked like relief and then took a seat in the paint-splattered wheelchair, pulling a packet of cigarettes from her pants pocket. 'Ciggy before she gets here?'

'No thanks. I prefer my lungs carbon neutral.'

'Pity,' she said, lighting one up, 'we could've called it your last.' She sucked on the stick and breathed the smoke out through smiling lips.

'Oh, I see,' Roxy replied, edging her way towards the garden louvers. 'You're going to kill me the way you killed your grandfather Frank?'

'Don't call him that!' Sally spat. 'He deserted my mother at birth, he deserves no titles.' Then, appearing to lighten up she added. 'The fool never even suspected a thing, you know? Thought I was happily praying behind him. Praying! Moi?!' She sniggered. ''Course I should have made it look like suicide. I got a bit carried away, I'm afraid.' She sounded as though it were all a game; it sent a chill down Roxy's back. 'No, I guess Mum'll think of some way of getting rid of you.'

'Faulty brakes perhaps?'

Sally's eyebrows shot up impressed. 'We have been doing our homework, haven't we?'

'I know all about it,' Roxy replied. 'And so do the police. They have my full report. Anything happens to me, they'll know where to look.'

'You're bluffing.'

'Try me.'

Sally shrugged again and continued smoking. It didn't look like she cared one bit, and that was even more chilling.

'So *you* were the one who snuck in and ditched the hospital file? While I was conveniently minding the dress shop, right?'

Sally smiled proudly again. 'I know! And you didn't have a clue, right? Then—hilarious!—I had to help you break in all over again. You must have got a mega surprise when you found the folder was empty!'

'Yes, Sally, yes I did.'

'And you never suspected me? Really?' The look in her eyes was imploring. She genuinely needed to know she'd pulled it off. Roxy replied, 'You're sneakier than a rat, Sally. Your Mum would be proud. So that means you also trashed your own place to make it *look* like you were the next victim?'

'Yep, made up the whole story about the intruder. Although I can tell you I was *stunned* to find that guy loitering in my yard when we got there. God knows who that was! Bloody lucky break for me, though.'

Roxy was about to tell her it was Max when instinct shut her up. Sally didn't need to know she had allies who might just be lurking in a nearby laundry. It occurred to her, though, that she needed to buy some time, give Max a chance to get back out onto the street to find help. That could take him ages. She felt another flood of panic. What if they had caught him, too?

She quickly asked, 'But why'd you have to kill old Frankie?'

'Oh puh-lease, don't get all sentimental on me. The guy was a fruitcake, it's not like anyone was going to miss him. If you hadn't showed up he would've been rotting away for *months*. No-one gave a shit about him, you know? Better off dead.'

'Well if you hadn't killed Beatrice, she might have—'

'Beatrice?! Hilarious! The guy was delusional. As if that snotty Mosman matron would desert her luxurious mansion for a grotty old farm house out the back of nowhere!' She laughed at this. 'Did you see the way he was doing it up? Like he thought a lick of paint would change her mind?'

'How do you know it didn't?'

'Why else do you think Mum sent me to that Godforsaken dump for six months? To befriend that old fart and see what was going on. Nah, I've got the letters to prove it. Beattie felt sorry for the guy, hell she fucked his life over after all. He never got over her dumping his ass for some preppy Sydney guy. She felt bad, she kept in touch, but that's as far as it went.'

'So you were also the one that went through his house after the murder?'

'Ah, can we be careful with the language, please? I didn't murder him, I euthanized him. Honestly, you have to believe me, he's much better off dead. You know?' Again, that imploring look. 'Mum tells me he's with Beatrice now, so it's a win-win.' She took another long drag on her cigarette. 'But yes, I took the letters, a few incriminating photos. That's all.'

'But why bother with the letters? Why kill Frank? Heather never did write the autobiography so your secret was safe. You killed her before she had a chance to.'

'Ahh, there you go again. Careful with the language, lady!'

Roxy wanted to reach over and thump the young woman but she needed to hear the truth so she feigned a smile. 'Sorry, you *euthanized* them both. How very thoughtful of you. But tell me, why not just leave Frank be? He couldn't hurt you now, surely.'

'Duh! He had to go. The nutcase couldn't let it be. Decided it was her last wish. Was gonna finish her memoirs for her. Well, can't you see he had to be stop—'

'That's enough!' It was Heather Jackson, standing rigid at the entrance to the room, a long velvet dressing gown on, her manicured fingers clinging tightly to a small handgun. Roxy felt her heart stop. She glanced quickly around her, but there was no easy exit. Heather waved the gun at her daughter, an angry glare flickering in her eyes. When she spoke again, her voice was eerily calm.

'That'll be all thank you, Sally-Anne, I'll take it from here.'

'Pity,' she replied, springing to her feet. 'I was beginning to enjoy myself.'

As she sashayed out, Heather asked, 'Is the room secure?'

'Yep, still locked. She didn't go in.'

Heather nodded and waited for her daughter to disappear down the hallway before asking matter-of-factly, 'Why are you in my house?'

Roxy took a deep breath. 'I know all about you, I know what you've done.' She was trying to sound confident but came off wobbly and uncertain instead.

'Really? You break into my house in the middle of the night to tell me that?' Before she could answer Heather was waving the gun again. 'Put your hands on your head and start marching.'

Heather steered Roxy back down the corridor and into the main house, past a now brightly-lit entrance area, down the wider corridor and through the double doors to the office in which she had met with Jamie the day before.

'Sit,' she commanded as she grabbed a telephone and pressed speed dial. Roxy sat on the edge of the maroon sofa, her heart beating wildly. 'Get your butt over here,' Heather said into the phone, and then glancing towards Roxy, added, 'We've got an intruder that I might just end up shooting. Accidentally of course.'

She hung up and then sat down in the chair behind the desk, placing the gun in front of her. Roxy could feel sweat trickling down her brow and underneath her shirt. She didn't doubt for a minute that the older woman was serious.

'Everything Sally-Anne just told you was a lie,' Heather said. 'The poor child is delusional. A little, well, *challenged*, shall we say?'

'Just like your sister, Lillian?'

Heather's mouth twitched and she began to straighten down her hair where it was frizzing up in places.

'My sister Lillian is both mentally and physically challenged, Miss Parker.'

'But she can sure paint a great portrait, can't she?'

She stopped playing with her hair. 'What's that supposed to mean?'

Roxy tried to calm her heart beat down. If she could just keep the woman talking, she might have a chance.

'Heather, I know that it's your sister Lilly who's the artist. You've been passing her portraits off as your own ever since that first one, that award-winning self-portrait, remember?' She waved a hand in the direction of the portrait of Lilly, staring down at them now, mute yet oddly accusatory. 'What did you do? Promise to send it in for her and then switch her name to your new, fake one, so you could take the credit?'

Heather glanced quickly behind herself at the painting and then back at Roxy with what looked like genuine bemusement. For a split second Roxy had a sinking feeling she was on the wrong track, that she was accusing an innocent woman. *This woman was good*, she thought but plunged on regardless.

'I know you killed six people to keep your insipid little secret, starting with your parents—'

'My parents? You really are delusional. They were killed in a car accident. I was hundreds of miles away.'

'And what about Margarita Moralis? The midwife Agnetha Frickensburg? Beatrice Musgrave? Frank O'Brien?'

Heather laughed then, a low, gurgling laugh but for the life of her Roxy couldn't tell if it was nervous tension in her voice or disbelief. When she had gathered herself she replied coolly, 'So, you think I killed all of these people…um…why was it again? To hide the fact that my spastic sister is a genius?'

'Yes I do.'

'Let me give you a few tips on publicity, Roxanne Parker. It might help you if you ever actually break the big time,' she paused, raising her plucked eyebrows, 'and we both know *that's* never going to happen. If, as you say, Lillian was the great artist in the family, why would I hide that? Do you think the likes of Stevie Wonder would be half as popular if they were "normal"?' She used her fingers in that annoying way people did when indicating quotation marks. 'It's the greatest publicity stunt in the world.'

'Then why all the secrecy surrounding her? Why lock her away in a special wing that's out of bounds? Why is the studio designed and set up for a disabled person?'

'She's not locked up. She's free to leave, ask her yourself. And I didn't say she didn't paint, Miss Parker. She just isn't any good at it.'

'Then you won't mind me also asking her to paint my portrait?'

Heather's eyes narrowed slightly. 'You haven't a shred of evidence and if you think I'm going to let you wander off to start barking your accusations to the world, destroying me and everything I've worked for, all the hard years I put in, you've got another think coming.' She picked up the gun and pulled back the lock. 'Even if you were right—which you are not—let me tell you something, Miss Parker. Painting the blasted portraits is the easy bit. I'm the one who's had to do all the publicity tours, waste endless hours of my life pretending to be interested in the tediously dull questions of reporters like you. Do you think that your slag boss at *Glossy* would even be vaguely interested in interviewing me if I dribbled constantly and couldn't string a sentence together?' Her voice was rising now, she was losing some of her cool, and she was flinging the gun around like a toy. 'Ohhhh no. You people want pretty pictures in your pretty magazines. The more glamorous the better. Beattie didn't see that, the fool. She comes tearing in here bursting with her good news, "I'm your mummy! Isn't that *fabulous*, darlink!?"'

'You weren't happy to be reunited?'

'Happy? The woman dumps me at birth, not so much as a glance in my direction they tell me, and then I'm supposed to open my arms wide and welcome her back. Give me a break.'

'But surely the money—'

'I'd be ruined! They'd do what you did. Poke around, ask questions, do exposés on my shitty upbringing. And then they'd learn that little Lilly was the artist, not me—' She caught herself and shut her mouth with a thud. She straightened the gun up, aiming it straight for Roxy's temple.

Roxy hugged her hands tightly around herself and, as she did so, felt a hard lump in her jacket pocket.

Oh shit! The car keys.

She was still carrying the car keys. She had forgotten to give them to Max. A ball of lead developed inside her stomach and she felt instantly nauseas.If her friend had got out for help, there was no way he could walk anywhere in time. They were in the middle of the 'burbs, no police station close by. All the surrounding houses were McMansions like this one. He'd be lucky if he got anyone to open their door to him in the dead of night, let alone answer the doorbell. She had to hope he'd brought his mobile, and that a patrol car was just happening past.

But what were the chances?

Roxy swallowed hard and decided to grovel. It was time for a change of tack. 'Please don't shoot me, Heather,' she tried, 'I don't need to tell anyone. It can be our little secret.'

The older woman sniggered. 'My God you're all the same. You, Beatrice—' she spat that word out as though it were poisonous—'you think that I can somehow be bought with your pathetic pleads and promises. That woman broke her first and most important promise to me, she dumped me into the arms of a stranger and left me to fend for myself. At one hour old. *One hour*, Miss Parker, can you even imagine how that screws a person up?'

Roxy didn't have to imagine, she was witnessing it first-hand. Heather Jackson was a sociopath. But she decided to keep that little observation to herself. 'I *can* imagine,' she said instead. 'What Beattie did to you was unforgivable. You have every right to be angry.'

'Damn right I do.'

'I could write that! I could explain how it was, how empty and bereft that left you.' She was grasping for straws now but Heather had lowered the gun slightly so she continued on, trying to drag in gasps of air as she spoke, her pulse racing. 'I could write a really inspiring story about how you turned your life around, became the amazing person that you are, and… and the incredibly successful business woman you clearly are.' Roxy hated the words as she said them but she was fighting for her life now, and they both knew it. The only arsenal the ghostwriter had was words, and from what she could deduce of this woman, flattery and hyperbole were her best weapon. Heather was certainly listening, her eyes screwed into thin slits as she appeared to contemplate what Roxy was saying. She forged on. 'Even better, I could tell the whole world what Beatrice Musgrave did to you. Expose her for who she truly was.'

'No! No more publicity for *that woman*.'

'No, no, no, you're right, let's leave her out of it.'

Heather looked suddenly impatient, glancing at her watch. 'Where the hell is he?'

'Jamie? Your agent, he's coming? Is he a part of all this?'

'Yes he is, but I don't need to wait for him.' She pulled the gun back up and pointed it directly at Roxy again.

Suddenly a low tap sounded at the door and once again Roxy's heart beat triple time. Heather lowered the gun slightly and stood up.

'Jamie is that you?' No answer. 'Sally-Anne?'

The door swung open and a frail looking woman in a wheelchair buzzed slowly through. Her head was tilted awkwardly to one side and in one hand she was holding a small white buzzer, which she was using to steer the chair. She was wearing oversized spotty pyjamas and had a determined look on her pale face, her lips wedged into a thin line. Heather sprang from her chair, the gun still firmly in her hand and stepped out from behind the desk.

'Lillian! What are you doing out of bed? Come on, now, let's get you back. Sally-Anne? Sally!' She screamed down the hallway. 'Where the fuck are you!'

The next few moments were utter chaos. Lillian suddenly picked up speed and rammed her chair into her younger sister's shins bowling her over, the gun flinging in the opposite direction. Roxy pounced on it just as the doorbell began echoing through the house.

Heather let out a long, agonized, 'Nooooooo!' and made a dive for Roxy and the weapon. Roxy jumped out of the way, grappled for a louver, pushed it open, and then flung the gun out before it could do any harm. She turned back to find Heather bearing down upon her, a look of absolute hatred splotched across her face, her hair frizzing up in all directions. Before she could reach her, Lillian came to the rescue again, wedging her wheelchair between her sister and Roxy. She looked up at the writer with certitude and determination, and Roxy whispered, 'Thank you.'

Lilly then dragged her eyes back to her sister. 'Noooo,' she said slowly. 'No… more.'

Heather stopped moving and glared at Lilly. Then she turned the full voltage of her hatred onto Roxy. 'You fucking cow, what have you done to me?!'

Roxy stood her ground. 'You did all this to yourself, *Marian Johnson.*'

'Don't you call me that!' she roared. 'My name is Heather Jackson. Heather! Jackson!'

'Well then, Heather Jackson, you're under arrest,' came another woman's voice from the doorway, and all three women swept around to see Gilda Maltin standing at the door. Roxy's legs almost gave way as relief washed through her like a warm bath. Behind Gilda four uniformed police officers loomed, and within seconds two of them were placing handcuffs on Heather and leading the woman out, a look of outrage across her ruddy face.

'But… but *she* broke in here…' she was saying. 'I… I haven't done anything wrong!'

'Yeah, yeah, tell someone who cares,' Max declared, suddenly appearing beside Gilda, a wide smile creasing up his entire face. He held out his arms to Roxy and she ran into them then, just as quickly, pulled herself free and grappled for the car keys in her pocket.

'But how… how on earth did you get help? I was certain you'd never get back in time.'

'Oh you can blame me for that,' Gilda said. 'I've had my guys following you for a few days.'

Roxy took a few deep breaths and found her way back to the couch, falling into it before her legs really did drop from underneath her. Eventually she said, 'And there I was thinking you trusted me.'

'I did trust you, Roxy. I trusted you to lead us straight to the murderer.' Gilda winked. 'If it wasn't for my undercover cops, Max here might never have got help in time. They were just down the road wondering what the hell you were up to. They'd already called me and I was on my way.'

Max nodded. 'Yeah they spotted me bolting down the street and picked me up. It took me some time to explain it all… I'm just glad you're okay.' He joined her on the sofa and grabbed her back in a giant bear hug, ignoring her resistance. Slowly, Roxy let herself melt into him, the tension seeping out into his strong, warm arms.

Suddenly she had another thought and pulled herself free. 'What about Sally? Did she get away?'

'Tried to, we nabbed her doing a swifty out the back gate. She's on her way to the station now,' said Gilda. 'Also picked up the manager on his way over. Now he wasn't a happy camper I can tell you that. Both of them have already started pointing the finger firmly in Heather's direction. Such loyalty, it warms the cockles of your heart.' She turned back to several officers standing to attention at the door. 'Okay gang, let's seal the place off and start searching for evidence.'

'This might help.' Roxy reached into her pocket and produced a mini tape recorder which was still on 'Play/Record'.

Gilda shook her head laughing. 'See, I told you I could trust you.'

The rest of the night was a bit of a blur. Wearily, Roxy and Max gave a uniformed office an abridged version of the night's activities, promising to make their own way to the Mosman police station the next day for official statements. Then Max drove her home, parking the VW close to her apartment block and seeing her to the front door.

'You had me terrified tonight, Parker,' he said, his fringe dropping low over his eyes. 'Leaving you to run and get help has to be the hardest thing I've ever done.'

'Well I'm glad you did,' she said, smiling.

'Yeah, I guess leaving you seems to be all you what from me, hey?' There was no bitterness in his voice, just resignation, and before she could think of a reply he was hugging his jacket tighter and heading off down the stairwell.

Roxy watched him disappear, then stepped into her tiny unit and felt relief wash through her all over again. She loved her home, its serenity and coziness. It was a million miles from the chaos and corruption of the world outside, and she was so relieved to be back. For a few minutes there, she had not been sure she would ever see it again. Roxy locked the door securely and turned towards her bedroom, bone tired.

That's when she spotted the file on Beatrice Musgrave sitting open on the coffee table. Slowly, she picked it up and her throat suddenly constricted, tears welling up in her eyes. She wiped them away impatiently. She was too weary to cry tonight, too emotionally and physically drained. Death had come so close, had nipped at the edges of her smug little life, but she had survived, and she was not going to break down now. She was too bloody tired. Tomorrow could be meltdown day. She closed the file and placed it to her lips, giving it the gentlest of kisses.

'Good night, Beattie. Rest in peace.'

And then, without taking her clothes off or washing the day's grime from her face, Roxy fell into bed and into the deepest sleep she'd had in a very long time.

EPILOGUE

Lillian Johnson looked radiant as she buzzed her chair through the fashionable crowd that had gathered at a trendy inner-city gallery for the first legitimate showing of her abstract art. By now the story of Heather Jackson's elaborate fraud had hit all the headlines, quite sensationally so, with no mention of Beatrice Musgrave, Roxy noticed. The police had not released the information publicly, and she wasn't about to spill the beans, either. That was no longer important to the ghostwriter, and it would do Beattie's memory no service either. The socialite's daughter had turned out to be a sociopath, and if she knew Beattie the way she believed she did, that was not something the elderly matron would have wanted publicized. If only for the sake of William and Fabian. Whether they knew the full story, she did not know, but she did note that they weren't here tonight.

As for Lillian Johnson? She had become a celebrity in her own right and while her tale of being hidden away by an evil sister for years was fabulous media fodder, it was her artwork that really inspired people. Roxy was thrilled by the twitters of praise that were now emanating around her.

She was standing to one side, a glass of champagne in hand and beside her were Max, Oliver and the police detective Gilda. 'Heather Jackson was wrong,' Roxy told them with a sad smile, 'There's nothing off-putting about Lillian at all.'

'Oh she was just justifying her own greed,' Gilda said. 'But she certainly underestimated her sister's mind. She might not be able to talk very well but she's as switched on as the rest of us. And she definitely underestimated Lillian's strength. I gotta tell you, Roxy, if she hadn't come along when she did and started ramming that maniacal sister of hers, you mightn't be with us today.'

'I'm well aware of that and still working through it, thanks very much for reminding me,' Roxy replied with a shiver and a smile. 'I gather poor Lilly knew nothing about her sister and niece's murdering spree? Or the fact that she was even being duped?'

'Not a thing. They restricted her contact with the outside world and monitored what she watched on TV and read in the papers. You're just lucky Lillian was awake when you broke in. She says she heard the whole thing and that's why she came to your rescue. Actually I think she thought *you* were the maniac until Sally started talking. And then of course when she saw her sister with the gun… Deep down she knew they were bad eggs, but she had no idea of the extent of it.'

'So how did she get out? I gather the doors were locked?'

'The adjoining bathroom door was locked but not the main bedroom door. It seems they missed that one.'

'But didn't she wonder why they locked her away, why she wasn't allowed out?'

'Oh but she was! They took her on occasional excursions I believe. They just did it incognito, always using vans from the delivery entrance, and going to out of the way places. She thought nothing of it. As long as she was left alone with her paints, she was content. Apparently she was often asked to paint people she didn't know or like, as a "favor" to her sister, but she never really thought anything of it. Had no idea her sister was passing them off as her own. If you look at the artworks at the house, all the signatures have been removed. She was none the wiser. I gather, though, that Lilly didn't much like her sister and niece but it seems she trusted them both implicitly. That's why she moved in with them after her parents died. By the way, that was the only murder you got wrong.'

Roxy looked up from her glass. 'Oh?'

'Yeah. The Johnson's did die in a legitimate car crash, from a brand of brakes that were known to be faulty. That's where Heather got the idea for Margarita's death. She gave her the same model vehicle to use, took out the working brakes, put in the faulty brand and waited for the accident to happen.'

'Bloody lucky it happened on a lonely stretch of road!'

'Heather Jackson was one of the luckiest con artists I have ever met,' Gilda agreed. 'It's a miracle no-one twigged until now.'

'Until nosy Roxy Parker, you mean,' said Oliver and they all drank to that.

Roxy ignored them and asked, 'What about the midwife?'

'That was her first little test of the brakes. It didn't quite work, though. Agnetha was just maimed. Heather had to finish the job, of course. Agnetha was threatening to tell all. It seems she'd been blackmailing both Beatrice and Heather for years, and that's partly why Beattie decided to tell the truth once and for all. Better to make a clean breast of it.'

'So the designer clothes she was wearing?'

'A gift from Heather, I suspect, to shut her up. When that didn't work, we believe Heather killed her but not before slicing the extra fingers off in the hope of hiding the old midwife's identity.'

Max laughed then. 'Idiot! If only she'd known that would be the one thing that would catch Roxy Parker's attention.'

'Yeah,' Oliver said. 'If she'd just let old Agnetha drown no-one would have noticed. She would have been just another sad Sydney statistic. Silly woman.'

'So what about Beatrice?' Roxy continued, desperate to get the facts. It had been a few weeks since that dreadful night, but it was her first chance to properly catch up with the policewoman. Roxy had been preoccupied with ticking off a few freelance articles and licking her wounds, while Gilda had been tied up with the investigation.

She took a long sip of her champagne and then said, 'Well it seems your first interview with Heather for *Glossy* magazine sped that murder up a bit.'

'How do you mean?'

'Sally tells us—and thank God for her, Heather has been characteristically tight-lipped—that during your interview at Lockies Cafe, Heather overheard you say Beatrice Musgrave was about to reveal something big.'

'Aye!' chirped Lockie who had joined the group during the conversation. After quick introductions were made he said, 'Remember, Roxy? Heather was on the phone and I asked you to a shindig the following Monday.'

'And I said no because one of my clients was about to reveal something BIG. Damn it. If only I'd kept my big mouth shut.'

Max shook his head at her. 'Hey, come on, you weren't to know Heather had set the whole thing up to see what you knew.'

Roxy sighed. 'Yeah, I just thought she wanted to be interviewed by the great Roxy Parker.' She shook her head angrily. 'So Heather panics, realizing she's running out of time, and races over there to throw poor Beattie off her balcony.'

'Charming isn't she?' That was Oliver. 'Come on guys, enough of the gore, let's go and get some tucker, I'm starved.'

'Any chocolate?' Gilda chirped and Roxy allowed herself to laugh for the first time in a long while as they zigzagged through the crowd and past dozens of Lillian's wonderful, bright portraits, towards a table set up with a range of hors d'oeuvres. They each helped themselves and then returned to their quiet corner.

'So what about that dodgy grandson, Fabian?' Max wanted to know before stuffing an elaborate prosciutto and asparagus concoction into his mouth.

'Oh he's pretty harmless,' Gilda replied and then turning to Roxy, said, 'Of course you could still press assault charges on the thuggish brother-in-law.'

Roxy shook her head. 'No I don't think so. That lot have got problems of their own. Good riddance, I say. And what about the lawyer, Ronald Featherby?'

'He's pulled the client confidentiality card on us. Not saying very much at all.'

'Sneaky bastard.'

'Yeah well, in any case I figure he knew of Beattie's past but had zip to do with Agnetha's murder. Not really his style. We're pretty confident it was all Heather's doing, with a little help from Jamie and Sally-Anne.'

Suddenly the crowd began to part and Roxy spotted Lillian being wheeled towards them. An enormous smile enveloped her face and Roxy felt as if she was seeing the portrait, 'Not Drowning, Waving' in the flesh this time: happy, content, surprisingly self-assured. When she was directly in front of Roxy she stopped and flung one hand, her only working hand, towards her. Roxy took it warmly in her own. A woman stepped out from behind her and also held out her hand.

'I'm Petra, Lillian's new assistant and we'd both like to say a warm thank you for everything that you've done.'

'It was nothing at all,' Roxy insisted and then, turning to Lillian asked, 'Are you going to be okay?'

Lillian's eyes lit up and she bobbed her head several times. 'Y-ee-es,' she said happily.

The assistant added, 'Lilly would like me to tell you that, as a special thank you present, she would love to paint your portrait some time. That is if you're available.'

Roxy couldn't contain her delight. 'I would love to! Thank you!'

Later, when Lilly had left, Lockie grabbed Roxy's arm. 'You *have* to let me come and watch! You have to!'

'Whoa, down boy!' She smiled. 'Of course you can come. I couldn't think of a better person to keep me company.'

And then Roxy took a long, slow sip of her champagne. It wasn't her favorite, Merlot, but tonight it would do the job. She raised her glass into the air.

This one's for you, Beattie Musgrave,' she said softly as the crowd swelled around her again.

ABOUT THE AUTHOR

Christina (C.A.) Larmer lives with her husband and two sons in the hinterland of Byron Bay, Australia, where she writes, edits and teaches self-publishing. She'd love to hear from you. You can contact the author or sign up for her newsletter at:

www.calarmer.com
christina@calarmer.com
facebook/CALarmer
@CALarmer

Printed in Great Britain
by Amazon